girls of summer

Center Point
Large Print

Also by Nancy Thayer and available from Center Point Large Print:

The Guest Cottage
An Island Christmas
The Island House
Secrets in Summer
A Nantucket Wedding
Surfside Sisters
Let It Snow

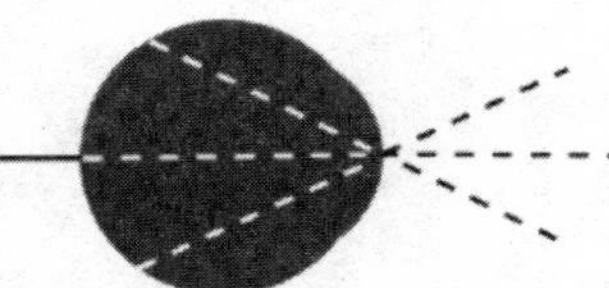

girls of summer

a novel

Nancy Thayer

Center Point Large Print
Thorndike, Maine

This Center Point Large Print edition
is published in the year 2020 by arrangement with
Ballantine Books, an imprint of Random House,
a division of Penguin Random House LLC.

The text of this Large Print edition is unabridged.
In other aspects, this book may vary
from the original edition.
Printed in the United States of America
on permanent paper.
Set in 16-point Times New Roman type.

ISBN: 978-1-64358-687-8

The Library of Congress has cataloged this record under
Library of Congress Control Number: 2020942066

For
Cassie, Nico, and Angelo of 44DS

acknowledgments

Did you know that Jason Momoa is *twelve years younger* than his wife Lisa Bonet? I know! Emmanuel Macron, the president of France, is twenty-five years younger than his wife, Brigitte. John Lennon was seven years younger than Yoko Ono.

I've always been fascinated by these couples. We're accustomed to older husband/younger wife teams, but recently age seems to matter less. One of my good friends is seven years older than her husband; another friend is sixteen years older than her husband.

This fascination was the starting point for *Girls of Summer*, and as Lisa (Lisa Hawley, not Lisa Bonet) says, it's good to know where you want to be, but sometimes you have to go in the opposite direction to get there.

I'm enormously grateful to my editor, Shauna Summers, for helping me get where I wanted to be with this book. Thank you, Shauna, for your perceptive and insightful editing.

Thanks to the superstars Gina Centrello, Kara Welsh, and Kim Hovey of Penguin Random House. Lexi Batsides, Allison Schuster, Karen

Fink, Jennifer Rodriguez, and Madeline Hopkins deserve bouquets of roses for all the great work they do. I'm so grateful to my agent, Meg Ruley, and her associate, Christina Hogrebe, at the Jane Rotrosen Literary Agency, and they know why!

Thank you, Sara Mallion, my brilliant virtual assistant, and Chris Mason of Novation Media, who make my website and newsletters and media posts colorful and fun. Susan McGinnis, I'm so grateful to you for your elegant help at the computer and everywhere else. Curlette Anglin and Tanieca Hosang, you know I couldn't do it without you!

I've lived on Nantucket for thirty-five years, and the realities of this island thirty miles out in the Atlantic are changing fast. Philanthropist and Nantucket resident Wendy Schmidt is president of the 11th Hour Project, an advocate for the wise use of our natural resources and a leader in ocean exploration. Wendy, thank you.

The annual and fabulous Nantucket Book Festival brought Sylvia A. Earle, oceanographer and National Geographic Explorer-in-Residence, to our island last year to speak about her book *The World Is Blue*. You can catch her gorgeous video *Mission Blue* on Netflix.

Ocearch, a data-based organization that collects information about ocean creatures, especially the great white sharks, often docks its research boat in Nantucket in the summer. Because of them, I have a shark-tracker app on my phone. Haven't needed it so far!

Nantucket's own Scott Leonard, of Marine Mammal Alliance Nantucket, is a hero, and if you don't believe me, try to take a web of plastic off a terrified and angry seal. Doctor Doolittle would faint. You can see some of Leonard's rescues on their Facebook page.

Independent bookstores are at the heart of connecting readers and writers. We're so fortunate to have Mitchell's Book Corner on Nantucket, and I'm grateful to Wendy Hudson, Christina Machiavelli, Dick Burns, and the multi-talented Tim Ehrenberg for being there. Thanks to Elizabeth Merritt and all the brilliant staff at Titcomb's Bookshop on the Cape.

And libraries! We are wildly fortunate to have free public libraries all over this country, and I send enormous thanks to librarians everywhere.

Every day I learn something significant from my Facebook and Instagram friends. My heart's capacity to love seems to be infinite, because I love these friends so infinitely.

The courage to love is what inspired me to write *Girls of Summer*. I think life is a lesson in building that courage, and I'm grateful for the friends and family who have taught me how to reach deep. Hugs and kisses to Ellias, Fabulous, Emmett, Annie, Sam, Tommy, Josh, and David. Godiva chocolate to Deborah, Tricia, Dinah,

Sofia, Martha, Antonia, and the multi-talented Sara Manela. My courageous and classy friend Jill Hunter Burrill is the grand master of how to love. Or should that be grand mistress? Whatever, she is remarkable.

And my husband, Charley Walters, is pretty amazing, too. We've been married for thirty-five years, and he's seven years younger than I am. He might just be the inspiration for this book.

Enjoy *Girls of Summer*!

girls of summer

one

Remember, Lisa's mother had often said, it's good to know where you want to be, but sometimes you have to go in the opposite direction to get there. Lisa knew her mother was right because her mother was, as was her father, a high school teacher full of knowledge and experience. She also knew that when they had married, her mother had wanted to have five children and her father had wanted to be a novelist. Instead, they taught in the Nantucket high school and had only one child, the fortunate Lisa, but they said they were extremely happy throughout their lives. So maybe they didn't get where they intended to go, but they ended up where they were meant to be.

Lisa thought about her mother's words a lot. Her teachers always told her that she could *make something* of herself. She could be an astronaut or a doctor or the governor of the Commonwealth of Massachusetts!

Lisa politely thanked them but secretly wondered why she should do anything other than what she loved doing most: swimming at Surfside Beach in the summer, biking around the island in the fall and spring, and creating entire wardrobes of clothes for her many dolls during the winter.

Actually, she knew why she should do something else: to please her parents. Even if it wasn't her fault—how could it possibly be her fault?—that they had no other children, that her father never wrote a novel, even so, she felt a powerful obligation to her parents, these people who had given her life, and that life had given her so much good fortune. They never *pushed* her, but she knew they expected and hoped for a lot from her. They gave her violin and piano lessons. Ice skating and swimming lessons. She mastered them, but she didn't excel at any of them. She never brought home a gold medal for her parents to put on their mantel.

Still, Lisa made mostly A's in her high school courses, and she volunteered for various island causes. She helped her mother clean house. She helped her father mow the lawn and rake the leaves and shovel the snow. She had lots of good friends, and two best friends, and she was never bored. Like her mother, she carried a book with her everywhere, in case she got stuck in a waiting room for the dentist or had to take the ferry to the mainland.

In high school, she had friends who were boys, but she never had a real *boyfriend,* which secretly worried her. Was she such a loser? It was true that she worked hard on her grades and spent a lot of time reading and sewing. After she graduated from high school, she learned that guys didn't ask her out because her parents, those brilliant high school teachers, terrified them.

When it came time to apply to college, Lisa wanted to attend the Fashion Institute of Technology, but her parents refused to send her there. So Lisa went to Middlebury College in Vermont to major in business administration and to learn how to ski, because who knew? Maybe she'd be a star at skiing.

In the summer, she returned to the island to work, because she needed the money but also because she loved working in retail, especially in the clothing shops. She helped hang, fold, smooth, and carry glamorous dresses for the posh summer women. She never wanted to be one of those posh women. She wanted to be the owner of the shop.

In college, she finally dated, although not very seriously. During her freshman year, the guys seemed all about partying. They got drunk, did stupid pranks, and laughed like donkeys. Over the next few years, it got a little better. The guys she went with tended to be on the jocky side, muscular, often incredibly handsome, always nice. But something was missing. They weren't, somehow, *enough.*

In late October of her senior year, Lisa went to a gathering with her girlfriends. The northern Vermont air was crisp, the mountains were blazing with crimson and gold, and she felt she was perched at the very edge of a new and exhilarating life. The party was held in an old Victorian house. The doors and windows were open, there was a bar in every room, and after downing a couple of beers with her friends, Lisa realized she hadn't eaten since breakfast and she was getting slightly dizzy.

She wandered into the long hall, squeezed between groups of people, and found herself in an extremely large, ancient kitchen with so many roosters on the tiles, plates, dishtowels, and implements that she wondered if she'd had more to drink than she'd thought.

"Hi," a man said.

"Oh," Lisa replied, and thought: *Wow.*

A British aristocrat stood before her, like a young Hugh Grant clone, complete with floppy hair, except this man's was dark. He was wearing a collared shirt and a blue blazer, and she squinted at this.

"I had to go to dinner with my parents," the man said, reading her mind.

"Oh, *dinner,*" Lisa moaned.

"Hungry? Come this way."

He put an arm around her shoulders and gently guided her to a table piled high with cheeses, crackers, a gigantic sliced ham, and other mouth-watering goodies.

But now that she was near food, she couldn't

eat. She was more self-conscious than she'd ever been in her life, and that was really not the way she'd ever been. This man was daunting.

"Who are you?" she asked.

He grinned. "Erich Hawley. Senior, majoring in economics. And skiing."

"I'm Lisa, a senior majoring in business administration." She smiled, tilting her head so that her glossy brown hair fell over her shoulder and down over her breast. Oh, wow, she thought. It had happened. She was flirting! "And I'm learning to ski, but I'm not a natural at it. I'm better at swimming. I live on Nantucket."

Much later Lisa would learn that those simple four last words would cause a giant misunderstanding. Erich assumed that living on Nantucket meant Lisa was wealthy. And wealth was what Erich was all about.

"Nice," Erich said.

"Very nice," Lisa responded. She felt bewitched, unable to think in words, overwhelmed with physical sensations. *This man!*

If Erich had enchanted Lisa, she had enchanted him right back. She knew she had a pretty face and a good figure, not to mention that glossy dark hair falling over her shoulder, but that couldn't explain why in that moment, in that crowded room in a rambling Victorian house at the northern reaches of the country, suave, cosmopolitan Erich Hawley chose *her.* Maybe it was her air of openness and naiveté, and she *was* naïve. Maybe it was sheer chemistry. Or maybe, and this was what she thought much later, it was fate, destiny, life's secret plan to get Juliet and Theo onto the earth.

Erich leaned close to her, his lips brushing her ear. "I can hardly hear you in this mob scene. Let me take you out to dinner."

"Thank you, but no. You just had dinner with your parents," Lisa reminded him, and she saw the quick flash in his eyes that she would later learn was a sign that she'd said something that interested him. That she hadn't jumped at the first opportunity to be with him. That she might possibly be a challenge.

"I didn't have dessert," Erich said, smiling wolfishly.

She went to dinner with him.

As she got to know him, she was even more charmed. Erich's parents were elegant multilingual Europeans with homes in Switzerland and Argentina. (Many of Erich's clothes were bespoke, tailored in London, although Lisa knew that shouldn't matter. But she did love his clothes.) Mr. Hawley worked for an important international Swiss bank with many initials. Erich was going to work there, too. This particular bank was an institution that helped fund improvement projects in less wealthy countries. In Lisa's mind, Erich became a kind of modern-day combination of King Arthur and Robin Hood. Very quickly she not only admired him, she *adored* him.

Erich had his own apartment, and for the rest of the year, Lisa more or less lived with him. She felt privileged to fix his dinner, clean his kitchen, do his laundry. Somehow she managed to keep her grades up, too, although she scarcely cared. For the first time in her life, she was happy to be Cinderella, and not until much later did she realize that Erich not only liked her in that role, but he had slowly, brilliantly, surreptitiously imposed that role upon her.

In April, Erich took her to New York to meet his parents, who had come up from their Washington, D.C., home on business. Lisa found them so terribly smooth and cultured that she became tongue-tied, probably because all three of the Hawleys would lapse into German or French when speaking with one another, and Lisa could hardly remember English in the glow of their brilliance.

But Erich's parents liked Lisa, and in May, just before graduation, Lisa brought Erich home to meet her parents. Erich thought that Lisa's family was the very model of old money, with their book-filled historic Greek Revival house and ancient Range Rover.

That weekend on the island made Lisa's adoration waver slightly. Erich was moving to

D.C. when he graduated, and every so often, he'd casually suggested that Lisa might like to live there with him. In Vermont, Lisa knew she wanted to go with Erich. On Nantucket, she wasn't so certain. It was as if she were one person on the island, and another person with Erich. She wasn't sure where she wanted to end up with her life, and she didn't know if Erich was the spot or a path in the opposite direction.

She intended to talk this over with her mother and with a couple of her best island friends. She wasn't clear about how she really felt. Did she love Erich or simply love the fact that he, cosmopolitan, elegant Erich, loved her? But Erich, who was a genius at marketing and presentation, surprised her the night before they left the island. He took her and her parents to Le Languedoc, one of the toniest restaurants on the island. They enjoyed a feast of oysters, lobster, and fresh baby greens. They were happily studying the dessert menu when the waiter arrived at their table carrying a standing ice bucket.

Lisa and her parents stared at the bottle of Dom Perignon in surprise.

Erich turned to the waiter. "Would you please bring the young lady's dessert now."

There was a moment of silence. The waiter reappeared, setting before Lisa a delicate white porcelain plate holding a small black velvet box.

"Erich?" Lisa asked.

"Open it," Erich told her, smiling.

Of course she guessed what it was. And she knew very well that she could make only one answer to the question the box held. She just didn't know if that was the right answer for *her*. She was in love with Erich—any woman would be. But she wasn't certain she could fit into his world, and she knew he would never consider living on Nantucket.

She opened the black velvet box. Inside was an emerald-cut diamond, at least two carats in size, set in a platinum band. She looked up at Erich.

"Lisa, will you marry me?" he asked.

Her breath caught in her throat and in that flash of silence she was aware that everyone in the dining room was watching them.

Trembling, she answered, "Yes, Erich. Yes, I will marry you."

Erich lifted the box off the plate, removed the ring from the velvet slot, took Lisa's hand, and gently slid the ring onto her finger. Leaning forward, he kissed her softly, chastely.

The dining room burst into applause. The waiter popped the champagne. As Lisa and Erich toasted each other, she decided she truly and wholeheartedly loved him. He was good, smart, handsome, and ambitious, and he had chosen *her*. She could sense how much this evening meant to him, how pleased he was that everything was so perfect, and she was thrilled to be a partner in the creation of the moment.

The next day, though, as she spent one last hour walking on the beach with her best friend Rachel, she admitted that she had doubts.

"You've met him, Rachel," Lisa said. "He's like a prince. Why would he choose me?"

Rachel laughed. "Um, maybe because you're beautiful and smart and kind?"

"But our worlds are so different. Can you see me in Washington, D.C., discussing foreign economies with people who know what they're talking about?"

"Sure I can," Rachel said. "I can see you doing anything. The question is, do you want to?"

"I do. I really do. I mean, I do want to marry him."

"But . . .?"

"But . . ." Lisa paused. "He doesn't laugh a lot. He never belly laughs."

"Maybe that's because he's not leaning on a bar drinking his thirteenth beer," Rachel suggested. "Come on, Lisa. Look at the man. He's important. His work is important."

"I know."

"Are you afraid?"

"Not afraid, no . . ."

"Do you believe he loves you?"

"I do."

"Do you love him?"

Lisa hesitated. "Yes, I guess I do."

"Then all the rest will work out," Rachel assured her.

Erich wanted the wedding to be held in Washington, where all his parents' friends could attend, where the ceremony could take place in the Washington National Cathedral and the reception at the Chevy Chase Club.

Lisa wanted to be married at home, on Nantucket, and friends of her parents had offered the yacht club for the reception, so that should be fancy enough for Erich's parents and his friends.

They argued. In less than a month, they would graduate from Middlebury, and that didn't leave them much time for a wedding before Erich began his duties with the Swiss bank. Most weddings on Nantucket were planned a year ahead, so most churches and wedding officials would be booked. She was her parents' only child. This was important for them.

"Maybe we should wait," Lisa suggested.

"Maybe we should elope," Erich countered. "We don't need all the fuss of a wedding, anyway. We've got more significant work to get on with."

The tiniest, almost unnoticeable chip of ice fell into Lisa's heart. Of course saving desperate communities was important, but couldn't a ceremony of their marriage be kind of important, too? Where was the romantic Erich who had so dramatically proposed to her in Le Languedoc?

They compromised. They were married in Lisa's living room by the local county clerk, with her parents and her best friend Rachel in attendance. Erich's parents were in Africa that month, and couldn't come. They sent flowers, champagne, and a silver ice bucket engraved with the couple's names and the date. After the brief ceremony, the small wedding party toasted with champagne, split the flowers among Lisa's mother, Rachel, and the county clerk, and the newlyweds headed back to Middlebury to pack up and prepare for graduation.

After graduation, the married couple moved to D.C. where Erich joined his father in the bank. Lisa and Erich rented a small apartment in Washington near the Mall, and Erich dove head-first into his work. Lisa cooked healthy meals and did laundry and spent the swampy hot summer visiting all the marvelous museums in the area. She missed Nantucket so very much—it was summer, after all. But she understood that this first year of marriage was crucial. She wanted to prove herself loyal, helpful. She couldn't leave Erich for two weeks or even one.

Besides, she was realizing that she had to change if she wanted to be the right wife for Erich. The more she saw of Erich's mother, Celeste, the more Lisa believed that Erich had chosen Lisa because she was warm, honest, receptive, a hugger, a toucher. Erich's mother was so very much not a toucher, not even with her son. Celeste was elegant, but cool, communicating her displeasure most often by simply lifting one cynical eyebrow.

Yet Celeste was kind to Lisa, even generous in her way. After Lisa's first huge Washington society party, Celeste asked if Lisa would mind if Celeste gave her a few pointers about, for example, appearance. She suggested that Lisa have her long, wavy hair cut into a neat chin-length bob, trim and tidy. She approved of the two expensive and simple dresses Lisa had bought for the numerous cocktail parties. Celeste suggested simple dark pumps with no more than a two-inch heel, anything higher was tacky. Accessorize with small earrings and perhaps, as Celeste did, with an Hermès scarf. Lisa didn't own an Hermès scarf, so Celeste told her to wear her pearls. When Lisa admitted she didn't own pearls, Celeste gave her a pearl necklace for Christmas. After that, Lisa received an Hermès scarf for every birthday and every Christmas. Lisa was grateful to Celeste for the pointers and the advice, even though Celeste seemed to give them out of a sense of duty rather than friendship or love.

It would be smart for Lisa to take part in some non-partisan organization, Celeste continued.

Lisa could make friends that way, and she could also be a representative for the bank. It was a good idea, Lisa thought, a great idea, actually. Washington was so enormous and complicated it made her feel lost, and when she took refuge in her apartment she was troubled by loneliness.

The National Museum of Women in the Arts was looking for an intern in their library and research center. It was a nice fit for Lisa. She was young, energetic, and knowledgeable about the arts. Once she started working there, she began doing research at night into women artists of past decades and centuries, and she loved it. Soon the cocktail parties where she'd once stood tongue-tied became fascinating, especially when she told some diplomat or correspondent where she was working. As the months passed, she became not the quiet, small-town Lisa, but an accomplished researcher and a minor expert on women's art.

Erich was delighted with the new and improved Lisa. Over the next few years, they took their vacations in foreign cities with great art museums—Paris, Amsterdam, Florence, London. They were really working vacations for Erich, who sandwiched meetings with diplomats, bankers, and scholars of economics. Lisa didn't mind going out alone; she preferred strolling through museums by herself, pausing when something caught her eye.

It was when she was twenty-eight, with the

dreaded year *thirty* looming over her, that she realized she was tired of traveling. She wanted to make a real home.

She wanted to have a baby.

One evening as they returned from a cocktail party and were getting ready for bed, Lisa said casually, "I've stopped taking the pill."

Erich sat in the overstuffed chair in their bedroom to take off his black patent leather shoes. "What pill?"

"My birth control pill."

Erich peeled off his black silk socks. "Are you sure that's wise?"

Lisa went to her husband and knelt before him, her hands on his knees, looking up into his face. "I want children with you, Erich."

His reaction was odd. He frowned, as if she'd spoken in an alien language he had to interpret. Then he said calmly, "Of course. Children would be good."

"I'll help you find a nanny," Celeste told Lisa the day Juliet was born.

Lisa looked at the sweet perfect face of her daughter, wrapped in a hospital blanket, wide eyes gazing at the bright new world. "I won't need a nanny."

"But your work with the women's museum!"

"I've resigned. I can always return to it. I don't want to miss a moment of Juliet's first few years."

"I think you'll find," Celeste said dryly, "that there will be many moments during your daughter's infancy that you'll wish to miss, especially those in the middle of the night."

"Oh, Celeste, you're so funny," Lisa said.

Erich was pleased to have a daughter, and he did share some of the work, walking a fretful baby in the middle of the night, carrying her in a backpack when they strolled along the Mall. Celeste and Erich's father—Lisa had never been asked to call him by his first name, so she always thought of him as Mr. Hawley—were helpful in their own very generous and controlling way. Erich's parents helped find a small house in Georgetown and, in celebration of Juliet's birth, they paid the down payment. Lisa's parents, thrilled at having a grandchild, came often to help Lisa with small, perfect, rosy-cheeked baby Juliet.

Erich rose quickly in the ranks of the Swiss bank. It helped that he was fluent in French, German, and Spanish. Lisa admired her husband, and understood completely all the time he spent traveling, especially because when he returned home, he was so happy to see her that she quickly got pregnant again.

When Theo was born, Lisa expected that her husband would spend more time at home, that he would be even more in love with her because she had given him a son, and yes, she knew that was an old-fashioned way to think, but she was quite sure that Erich and especially his parents thought that way. She was realizing, because of her babies, how she had coasted through her early adult years, letting life make her choices for her. Now the sweet, exhausting gifts life had given her—which she had chosen—forced her to pay attention to the choices she had to make to keep her children healthy and happy.

And maybe she paid less attention to Erich when he was home.

In fact, Erich spent even more time away from home, renting an apartment in Zurich. In their small charming townhouse, Lisa missed him as she changed diapers and mashed bananas and read stories, trying to keep her little ones entertained during the dreary winter and relentless summer heat.

And then: "Why not come home for the summer?" her mother asked.

The new, clear-sighted Lisa thought it through. In the summer, it would be as easy for Erich to fly to Nantucket as to Washington. Her mother would help with the babies, and best of all, they would be on the island, near the ocean, surrounded by her friends.

She packed up plenty of baby clothes and child paraphernalia and went.

• • •

She'd not forgotten the magic of Nantucket; she'd only banished it away to a corner of her heart. At Children's Beach, Theo shrieked with laughter as Lisa held him in the shallow waves. Juliet constructed sand castles and played on the jungle gym. They both were blissed out by the sight of the huge ferries coming and going, and they waved and jumped up and down, thrilled by the ship's horn. On rainy days, Lisa took them to the Whaling Museum and the library. And when her children were irritable from teething or a bad night from wetting the bed, her mother took them to the beach and Lisa took a nap. When Juliet and Theo were in bed for the night, her parents babysat while Lisa went to a movie or out to dinner with her friends.

Lisa talked with Erich at least twice a week, but of course he was busy with important business matters, so their calls were brief.

It was no surprise that they grew apart.

And, Lisa thought sadly, it was no surprise when the Hawleys more or less disappeared from her life, and her children's lives. The Hawleys and Erich were seldom even in the country, let alone on the minuscule island of Nantucket. To Lisa, Nantucket was the whole world, a perfect one for her children to grow up in, with its small town, friendly neighbors, golden beaches, and silver waves. She was glad she'd been able to travel to Amsterdam and Paris and Madrid, to taste foreign food and gaze upon foreign masterpieces, but with her two children in her life, she was more than content with delivery pizza and children's picture books.

In her heart, she realized she loved her children more than she loved her husband. Rachel and her other Nantucket friends told her this wasn't unusual, not in the early years. It took patience and perseverance for a couple to stay together at any stage. Lisa would love Erich again, Rachel promised.

The August Theo turned two, Erich flew into Nantucket for the grand birthday party Lisa had planned. Lisa invited several friends with children, and it was wonderful to have her husband with her for this occasion. She and her parents had set up a wading pool and all sorts of balls for the little ones and games for the four-year-olds. Erich helped carry the drinks and the ice out to the picnic table, and when the moment came, he brought out the enormous cake Lisa had made and sang "Happy Birthday" to his son along with all the friends. It was a rapturous moment for Lisa because it was simple normal life, a family celebration with her husband there.

That night, after the children were finally asleep, she and Erich made love, very quietly, because they were in her parents' home. Afterward, Lisa cried.

Erich cradled her against him. "Are you sad?"

"I am. I miss you so much. The children miss you so much."

"Are you lonely for our friends in Washington? For our home there? Is it hard living here with your parents? You know, we could fly home tomorrow. Well, not exactly tomorrow, but earlier than we'd planned."

Lisa lay silent, thinking.

"Although I couldn't help you pack and all that. I've got to be in Zurich on Wednesday."

With her head nestled against his chest, hiding her face, Lisa asked, "Erich, why did you marry me?"

She felt his chuckle deep in his chest. "What a silly question. Because I love you."

"But we're hardly ever together," she reminded him.

Erich pulled away from her, lying on his back, staring at the ceiling. "This again. Lisa, you knew it would be like this. I never deluded you."

She'd angered him with her clinginess. "I'm sorry," she said, pressing against his side. "I just miss you so much."

"I need to sleep." Erich closed his eyes, and quickly dropped off.

Lisa lay awake for a long time, scolding herself privately for being so needy.

• • •

The next day was better. Erich talked with Lisa's parents, played with his children, then swept Lisa off to dinner while the grandparents babysat.

He took her to Le Languedoc, where they hadn't been since Erich so romantically proposed to Lisa. They ordered lobster and a dry white wine, and Lisa listened to Erich discuss the financial state of South Africa. Well, she tried to listen to him. She couldn't interrupt his monologue about world affairs with her own bits and pieces of local news—the Hy-Line was adding fast ferries, the new library was opening this fall, Rachel was pregnant again. But when the waiter came to remove their plates, she gathered her courage to present him with the idea she'd been thinking of for days.

"Erich," Lisa said, "do you think we have enough money to buy a house here, on the island?"

Erich paused and frowned, gathering his thoughts. As Lisa looked at him, she saw how he had aged—and he was only thirty-three. He'd gained weight and he had bags under his eyes and his skin was the pasty white of someone who never got out in the sun.

Well, she thought, she must look much older to him. She hadn't lost the baby fat from Theo—ha! she hadn't lost the baby fat from Juliet. She couldn't remember when she'd last had a decent haircut and styling. She knew she had some serious renovations to do on herself before she returned to Washington.

"You want to buy a house here, on the island?" Erich asked. "Heated, with insulation?"

"Well, I hadn't thought about that, but if we could afford it, yes. Then we could come here for Christmas!" She liked the gleam in Erich's eye, as if he could envision more time on Nantucket for them all.

Erich leaned back in his chair and smiled. "What if we simply bought a house here to be our permanent residence. You'd like that, wouldn't you?"

Lisa blinked. She *would* like that, so why did this suggestion make her so nervous? "I think so." She talked it out. "The children could have a real yard to play in, and their grandparents—I know your parents love the children, but they travel as much if not more than you do. So Mom and Dad could help out, be there in an emergency. I'd have my friends around, nearby. Yes, for me and the children, it would be wonderful. But what about you? It's almost as easy to fly here as it is to Washington, right?"

"In the summer, yes. In the winter, not so easy. But I can see how much you'd like this."

"I would, yes. I'm lonely when you're traveling, and everything is just more difficult." Lisa leaned forward and took his hand. "But what about you? Do you like the idea?"

"It was my idea in the first place," Erich reminded her. "I want you to be happy, Lisa."

Lisa knew she *should* be happy. The house they bought was in town, a historic old Greek Revival not unlike her parents', with a large yard. The children were certainly happy, with plenty of friends and a wonderful school and doting grandparents who had them for overnights so Lisa could go out with her friends. Lisa worked part-time at the hospital thrift shop, keeping her vow to buy nothing, and occasionally weeding out the treasures she'd left in her room at home and donating them to the shop. At the end of the summer, wealthy women dropped off the clothes they hadn't had a chance to wear, and Lisa bought a few dresses and suits for herself. They would be perfect for going out with Erich.

Erich. Well, Erich certainly *seemed* happy. He came home at least twice a month, staying for no more than three or four days, and when he was there, he was kind but absentminded, both to the children and to Lisa. He'd had a vasectomy—he told Lisa after the fact, adding that there were enough children in this troubled world. He was there for the holidays, Christmas, Thanksgiving, Easter, and the Fourth of July, and he tried to make it home for the children's birthdays, and for Lisa's. After a night or two on Nantucket, his body's internal clock adjusted to EST, and he made love to Lisa, or something like love.

What she missed most, both when he was home as well as when he was gone, were the simple physical touches that made her heart melt, that made her feel like they belonged together. Of course she got plenty of hugs and kisses from Juliet and Theo, but none from Erich. He did not hold her hand when they went out. He didn't put a protective arm around her shoulders when they ran through a sudden shower. He didn't draw her close to him when they watched TV. He didn't sleep spooned against her, but lay on his side facing the wall. He did nothing physical that gave her the safe, warm sense of snuggling with a partner in a nest. When she tried touching him, he only smiled at her. And moved slightly away.

Why hadn't she noticed this before? Was she too blinded by his handsomeness, his kind but innate superiority, his sophistication?

She talked it over endlessly with Rachel.

"*He* hasn't changed," Rachel said. "Your expectations have changed. You thought you'd have a marriage like your parents have. Instead—oh, don't people say time and again that men won't change and women won't stop trying to change them? You have two children. The magic is gone. Be glad for what you have."

It wasn't until the children were nine and eleven that she had her brilliant idea. "Erich," she said one night on the phone when he was in

London and she was in bed, "I had the best idea! Let's take the children somewhere in Europe this summer! Somewhere you have to be, Zurich or Paris, it doesn't matter, but Zurich would be nice because you could show them where you work and they could know where you are when you're gone. You could work during the day, and I could see the sights with the kids."

After a long pause, Erich agreed. "That's a great idea. Let me look at my calendar. I'll get back to you."

"I'll get back to you?" Lisa laughed. "You sound like we're making a business deal."

"Well, what do you want me to say?" Erich snapped, exasperated.

He'd never taken that tone with her before, and it was the tone as much as the words that woke Lisa out of her trance, that made her realize the truth. "Erich, do you love me?"

"Of course I do," he told her, sighing. Before Lisa could respond, he added, "Look, we're older now. We shouldn't have made such big decisions when we were still in college. Even the most mature of us can make mistakes."

"Am I a mistake?" Lisa asked.

"Am *I?*" Erich countered. "Think about it seriously, Lisa. We had lots of chemistry when we met, and probably just about as much curiosity, because our lives are so different. At first I thought it was going to work out because we seemed compatible, and we had some good times traveling around Europe. But since the children came . . ."

"Go on. Finish the sentence."

"Fine. I will. Lisa, I thought you'd be able to live my life. You're beautiful, or at least you were. You're smart, but you're not ambitious. You're happily stuck in that hospital shop playing with other people's junk and holding bake sales for the school when you could have been helping me entertain truly important people. If you had, for example, tried to learn Arabic, or even German, we might have made a great team . . . but that is not what you did. I don't know if you're afraid, or if you have an inferiority complex, or if you simply like being a *hausfrau*. It's not your fault, but you and I are on completely different paths."

For a long moment, Lisa was quiet. "Wow," she said softly when she could get her breath.

"I'm glad we're having this discussion," Erich said. "I was dreading it. I don't want to be cruel, Lisa, and I did love you, but people change. You've changed the most. Be honest with me now. If I asked you to take the kids to your parents, toss your toothbrush in your bag, and fly to London tonight, would you do it?"

Stunned, she didn't answer. Couldn't.

"You see? You're just another overweight mom stuck in the sticks, living off my money and not earning it, frankly. I don't think you really even like sex. You were willing in college, I'll admit that, and you were such a novice, it was fun. But once you had your children, you were done. I want to be with someone sexy, uninhibited, enthusiastic, who's willing to let me do whatever I want."

"Erich, stop." Her heart sped up. Quietly, she said, "It sounds like you have a . . . a mistress."

"I think of her as a lover."

"I suppose she speaks several languages."

"As a matter of fact, she does. She's half Iranian, half Spanish." Erich sighed. "Look, Lisa, we had a good run. You can't help being the way you are. Let's be adults and move on."

Lisa held tight to her dignity so she could respond in a cool, rational, *sophisticated* way. "Yes, let's."

Juliet was eleven, Theo was nine. Lisa was forty.

two

In the divorce, Erich Hawley gave Lisa full custody and legal assurance of generous child support and college tuition. The wonderful old house with a large yard on a quiet street in the heart of Nantucket was already in her name.

Lisa gave Erich his freedom, and he took it, vanishing to Europe and Asia and who knew what other countries.

For a few years, she tried to pass on the news of their father's important life to her children, but when it became obvious that Erich had no time for any kind of relationship with his children, she stopped trying. She was hurt that Erich had no interest in his children, *their* children, but more than that, worst of all, it broke her heart for Juliet and Theo to have no father in their lives. In an emergency, of course, she could always call on her mother and father, but that wasn't really the same. She faithfully attended ballet recitals, swim meets, school plays, soccer games. She called every Saturday night "Movie Night," and ate pizza with them while they watched *Shrek* or *Stuart Little* or Harry Potter movies. She traveled off-island with them to Boston to see *The*

Nutcracker at Christmas, and several times she took them to New York to see a Broadway show and the Guggenheim (they'd loved the spiral ramp) and the Empire State Building. They spent Christmas and Thanksgiving and the children's birthdays with her parents, and Juliet and Theo seemed happy, or at least not emotionally ruined by the lack of an attentive father.

It was Lisa who was emotionally ruined. In the very beginning of the divorce, she was too busy to face the pain and humiliation that lay in her heart. As time passed, and the children seemed cheerful and stable, as she painted Juliet's bedroom lavender and papered Theo's room with Luke Skywalker and Chewbacca, her own feelings began to emerge, slowly, insistently, and then all in a rush, suddenly, like water bursting a dam.

She had not been *enough.* She hadn't been beautiful enough or exciting enough or cosmopolitan at all. She'd never thoroughly mastered French, she could never in a million years look like Audrey Hepburn, and after she had kids, she'd missed as many social events as she could, wanting simply to be at home.

What had she been thinking to marry Erich? What had possessed him to marry *her?* She'd been sure she'd loved him, and certain that he'd loved her. Brilliant Erich didn't make a mistake in choosing her . . . she'd simply been less than he thought she was.

Revelation after revelation bloomed from her heart like storm clouds, darkening her view. She was short—well, five foot five. She could pinch more than an inch of fat. She was smart, but not smart enough, not *driven*—when she resigned from the National Museum of Women in the Arts, Karen Weninger took her place and within a year published an entire book on Mary Cassatt.

And more, and worse, while she'd been married to Erich, some of her close hometown friends had moved away. Rachel, her best friend forever, was still on the island, and even though she worked with her husband in a local legal firm, she always had time to talk to Lisa. Often they went out for a girls-only drinks and dinner.

Her parents still loved her, and thank God for them. More important, they doted on their grandchildren and often asked one or both of them to come for the weekend, staying overnight. Lisa knew her parents expected her to *get out there,* to go to parties and really anywhere that single men might be.

She couldn't do it. Even the thought of flirting with a man was terrifying. She spent her free nights alone in her house with a romantic comedy on the television and a bowl of popcorn in her lap. And she knew very well that the salt on the popcorn would make her bloated, but she ate it anyway, defiantly.

"You're getting fat," Rachel said, one evening

when she forced Lisa to join her for dinner at a quiet restaurant.

"Thanks. Thanks very much." Lisa thought she'd hidden her weight beneath a loose summer dress, but Rachel had been her best friend forever. There was very little she could hide from Rachel.

"Stop it. I'm not trying to insult you. I'm worried about you, Lisa." The waiter approached. Lisa waved him away. "It's been what, two years now, and your social life is limited to your parents, your children, and me."

Lisa lifted her chin defiantly. "I'm content with that."

"No, you're not. I think you're afraid."

"Why shouldn't I be?" Lisa shot back. She concentrated on stirring her cocktail with its small ridiculous umbrella. "I've been dumped, completely. My ex-husband doesn't even want to see our children—as if they have no worth to him." Tears welled in Lisa's eyes, so she picked up her cocktail, removed the damn umbrella, and tossed the whole drink down her throat. "I know I don't."

"Oh, dear Lord, we've been over this a hundred thousand times. Erich's an asshole. He's a narcissist, he's not capable of loving."

"He was very—" Lisa began.

Rachel interrupted. "He was a con man. He thought he could make you his puppet, and when that didn't work, he dismissed you and went on to another act. But, Lisa, you are more than what Erich thought of you. So much more." Rachel reached over and took Lisa's hand. "Honey, so many of your friends want to see you. I know you've been invited to join book clubs, and you should, and you should also show up at parties. Summer's almost here. Think of the beach parties we'll have."

Sulkily, Lisa said, "I can't go to a party alone."

Rachel lost her patience. "Oh for God's sake." She dropped Lisa's hand. "Of course you can. Or go with Buddy and me. You've got to start dating again."

Lisa shook her head. "I'm not ready to date."

"It's been two years."

"I'm not ready."

"You should see a therapist. Even take anti-depressants. You're so gloomy, you're depressing *me*."

Lisa lost her temper. "Rachel, you're a good friend to put up with me. But you need to stop this. Please believe me, I have no interest in men. *None*." She didn't share her deepest thought, her greatest fear: that no one would be interested in her.

"All right, then," Rachel said. "At least get a job."

There are times in our lives when we would simply sink beneath the waves of our sorrows, the tides of our fears, and drown in our own misery, if it weren't for our friends. Later, Lisa would realize just how amazing Rachel had been, what a loyal, generous, loving friend, to stick with Lisa when she was in her most unattractive and pathetic moods, to coax her back out of the bleak cave of her darkness into the light.

Lisa owned her home free and clear, and Erich's child support paid for the necessities, so Lisa didn't *need* to work, and she knew that in this she was fortunate. But she also realized what Rachel had said was right: She needed to get a job.

Nantucket had several fine art galleries, and the Nantucket Whaling Museum and the Atheneum had some valuable paintings, but Lisa felt sad when she remembered her days at the women's museum in Washington. She'd been happy there, and optimistic, young and part of the world.

But now, forty-two years old, divorced and dumpy—because even if she didn't look totally dumpy, she certainly had been dumped—right now it often took courage for her to leave the house. During their last few meetings to discuss the divorce, Erich had told her he had come to realize she could never be *glamorous*. That she had fooled him in college, being pretty enough to seem like she could become beautiful and sophisticated. Instead, she became dowdy and provincial. Those words did not vanish from her mind or her heart. They were there when she looked in the mirror. They were there when she dried herself after a bath. They were there when she walked down Main Street, hiding her eyes behind sunglasses. She was terrified that she'd see pity in the eyes of the people she'd known as a child. A glance from a man made her heart flap with fright.

It took all of her courage to apply for a job. One evening in Lisa's living room, when Rachel had dropped by for a drink and the children were bonded to their one hour of watching TV, Rachel told her that Vestments, the year-round women's clothing store owned by Vesta Mahone, needed a new sales clerk.

"You'd love working there," Rachel insisted. "Playing with all those gorgeous clothes."

"They are gorgeous clothes," Lisa agreed. "I'm not sure I have the right . . . qualities . . . to work there."

"What are you talking about?" Rachel put her glass down on the table so hard it almost shattered. "Honest to God, Lisa, sometimes I get so angry with you! And you know what else, you make me tired. You are so *feeble,* so *pathetic,* and you were never that way before your divorce. Did Erich abuse you? Did he *hit* you?"

"Of course not." Lisa tried to laugh. "I'm sorry if I seem—"

"STOP IT!" Rachel yelled. "Don't you dare

say you're sorry. Stop *whining*. Lisa, you know what? You aren't the person you used to be. I miss you, the real you."

Lisa nodded. "I get that. I think the divorce pulled the rug out from under me, Rachel. It was the last thing I was expecting. It made me feel . . . inferior."

"Fine, but that divorce was two years ago. Look. I think you should see someone."

Lisa laughed, almost hysterically. "I am *so* not ready to date."

"I meant a therapist." Rachel was adamant. "I think you should take that job at Vestments and start seeing a therapist."

Lisa shook her head. "If I see a therapist, everyone on the island will know I've got emotional problems."

Rachel snapped, "For God's sake, Lisa, *everyone* on this island has emotional problems!"

"But I will apply for the Vestments job. I like Vesta, and I could use the extra money."

"Yeah, to get yourself a decent haircut," Rachel said.

Vesta Mahone was young and ambitious. With her great explosion of curly red hair and her tiny little body, she was unmistakable in any group. She'd grown up chic and savvy in Montclair, New Jersey, gone to the New York School of Design, and was intuitive and clever.

Vesta was frank when she hired Lisa. "You're perfect. You'll pull in the older shopper."

"I'm forty-two, Vesta," Lisa said.

"I know. That's what I meant. The older shopper."

Lisa privately doubted that anyone over thirty would want the clothes with fringes, sequins, ruffles, and chains that Vesta sold, and they probably wouldn't wear the skirts and dresses that stopped five inches above the knee and plunged deeply in the neckline. But Vesta sold a range of clothing, including silk dresses and cashmere sweaters that Lisa wished she could afford, and all ages of women flocked to her store. Vestments was a success.

Slowly, Lisa came back to life. The sensuous pleasure of fabrics reawakened her. Cashmere as light as a snowflake. Silk, cool and liquid. She'd forgotten how a color, say fuchsia, could make one woman look sallow but make another woman blaze.

Lisa watched. She learned. At night, instead of weeping at a romantic movie on TV while her children slept, she pored over fashion magazines. She studied pictures of the women at the Nantucket galas. She bought a small notebook and began making lists of who wore what and how old they were and how wealthy. Before long, she'd made a collection of information, this time about fashion and fabrics. In the evenings, after dinner, she sat at the dining room table with her children. They did their homework; she did hers. She liked making one-of-a-kind books by taking a thick loose-leaf notebook and covering it with fabric, then making a matching bookmark. She made an album of cuttings from magazines and newspapers, glue-sticking in photos of celebrities and writing her thoughts about their clothes in the margins. Juliet and Theo loved having her there at the table with them, all three of them with their heads bent over their work, murmuring to themselves about square roots or Revolutionary soldiers or sarongs.

Maybe those were her best years, when everyone in her house was busy and happy.

One November morning, a quiet time at Vestments, Lisa was straightening the clothing in the racks. Vesta was doing the window. Her mannequin wore low-slung camo pants, a cashmere sweater that stopped at the midriff, and cargo boots.

"That's insane," Lisa said.

"That's the look these days," Vesta told her.

"Women want to have their torsos exposed to the cold air?"

"Lisa, my target clientele aren't exactly hiking through the Arctic."

"Well, they aren't shopping here, either," Lisa

countered. Vesta was ten years younger than Lisa and hooking up with an ever-changing cast of almost-perfect men. When Lisa had started working at Vestments, she'd been impressed by the younger woman's confidence. Now, two years later, Lisa was confident herself. "Listen to me," she said to Vesta's firmly straightened back, "I've been doing the research. I know the people on the island and what they wear. I know the parties they'll have over the holidays. Women want to be sexy and gorgeous, but not . . . slutty. Slutty works fine for some of the summer people but winter is different."

"My clothes are not slutty." Vesta turned away from the front window and faced Lisa.

"Look." Lisa went behind the counter, picked up her large bag, and pulled one of her notebooks out. "Here's what I think you should sell."

Vesta looked. She made a humming noise. "Interesting, but, Lisa, we should have ordered them months ago. You know that."

"I do. And I did. Before you blow a gasket, I want you to know I used my own charge card. I have them at home. That's how certain I am. What can you lose by trying?"

"What are you trying to do? Take over the shop?"

Lisa smiled. "No. Just part of it."

Vesta put her hands on her hips. "You crazy bitch," she said. "Okay. Let's give it a try."

• • •

The next few years were so busy Lisa thought she lived on coffee. Her choices of clothing sold out as fast as the store could hang them on the rack. The shop filled all the hours of her day and most of her dreams, and several times a year she went into New York with Vesta on buying trips.

One day, Vesta announced that she had finally met the man of her dreams. She was going to get married and move to Arizona. She was closing her shop. Lisa was stunned. Now that both her children were teenagers, they were just plain more expensive. They required braces, Doc Martens shoes with a special tread, class trips to New York City, computers, and videogames. It was her paycheck that paid for these extras, and she was glad to do it. But now what?

She called Rachel, so possessed with anxiety that her teeth were chattering. "What am I going to do?"

"Start your own shop," Rachel said calmly.

"Don't be ridiculous!" She'd been divorced from Erich for years, and yet the insecurity he had somehow subtly slipped into her mind still ruled her thoughts, her heart, her very self. When she looked in the mirror or sat at her computer, she was afraid she didn't look right, couldn't think right.

"Lisa. You are raising two fine children who are almost off to college. They will have lives of their own. Your work in the shop has proven you know what women want. Vesta's customers and your customers will keep coming. They know you and they respect your taste. By now, you know all about the financial side of the business as well as the public side. You can do this. You really can."

"I really can," Lisa repeated like a mantra. Rachel believed in her, and that made Lisa believe she could do this.

And she discovered that she really could.

With huge helpings of encouragement from Rachel and her other friends, Lisa negotiated with the owner of the building to take over the rent, and changed the name of the shop to *Sail*, which was very Nantucket and had all the letters of Lisa's name plus a hint of the enticing word *sale.* She held a grand champagne opening right in the middle of July and started off with a whopping profit. She hired college girls to help her in the summer, and after a few months of driving herself insane, she hired an accountant to do the books, because she did know how to keep the books, but she couldn't be in two places at one time. She was at her best buying clothes and matching them to her customers, a talent that had started when she was a child, making outfits for her dolls.

Soon she was a successful businesswoman, just like all the whaling wives who had run Petticoat

Row back when Nantucket was a whaling town.

At the same time, Juliet and Theo were in high school, and their bodies developed, and their personalities changed. They were often sarcastic, secretive, and cranky. Juliet was tight with her clique of girlfriends and she was either with them or on the phone with them, but she still made good grades and was usually good-natured.

Theo was not so easy. His best friend from preschool, Atticus Barnes, had been a good, smart, levelheaded kid, and Lisa liked having him around the house. But when the boys started ninth grade, Atticus stopped coming around so often, and when he did, he was sullen and preoccupied. Rumors went around that Atticus was doing pot and maybe more. Lisa worried that he would be a bad influence on Theo, and in a way, she was right.

For years, even though he thought he was hiding it, Theo had a crush on Beth Whitney, a pretty girl whose mother had died when Beth was three. Of course—it was always the way of things, wasn't it?—Beth and *Atticus* started going together. *Damn,* Lisa thought at first, but later, after chatting with other mothers in the grocery store and during football games, she changed her mind. The other mothers thought it was wonderful that Atticus had a girlfriend. Now he would cheer up.

But Atticus didn't cheer up. The summer he

was seventeen, he committed suicide with an overdose of OxyContin. His parents found a letter on his desk at home, telling them he couldn't go on. Telling them where they could find him, at a lonely spot on the moors. Telling them he was always cold. Asking them to bury him in his down comforter.

It was a terrible time for Paula and Ed Barnes, for Theo, for Beth, and for the entire community. At the celebration of Atticus's life, Lisa had approached Mack Whitney, Beth's father. She didn't know him well. He was ten years younger than she was, a well-liked island man who had married his high school sweetheart, Marla. A carpenter who specialized in renovating older houses, he had a sterling reputation for honesty and excellent work. When they were only twenty-one, Marla gave birth to a daughter, the lovely Beth. Three years later, cancer took Marla's life and left Mack a widower.

Now this, the suicide of the boy Beth was going with.

Lisa wanted to say something to Mack, but words were so hollow. "Mack. I just wanted to say hello. This is so sad. I don't know if you know, but Theo was a good friend of Atticus and of Beth."

"Yes," Mack replied, staring straight ahead. "Yes, I knew that. The three were over at our house a lot. Atticus could be really funny."

"I know," Lisa agreed. She almost felt the sorrow steaming off the tall, broad-shouldered man beside her, and she wondered how much sadness he could carry. First his wife, and now his daughter's boyfriend. She had never gotten to know Mack, partly because she was busy with her shop, but also because she knew how many women his age, and younger, single and divorced, had tried to help him after Marla died. Lisa's friend Rachel, who knew everyone and everything, had laughed about the casserole brigade that had swarmed around Mack that first year. No woman had seemed to interest him, and as the years passed, Mack developed the reputation of a man who was obsessed with his work. He did show up for any function involving his daughter, and Beth got good grades in school, was always well dressed, and appeared to be a happy, normal girl.

Now and then a rumor would speed around the gossip circuit like an electrical flash that Mack had been sighted in a restaurant with some summer woman, but another sighting with the same woman never occurred. The few times Lisa had run into him, he had seemed content, but reserved.

"I just want you to know that Beth is welcome at our house, anytime."

"That would be great, Lisa," Mack said. "Beth likes Theo a lot, and she worships Juliet."

"She worships Juliet?" Lisa echoed.

Mack looked down at Lisa and grinned. When he smiled like that, he was so handsome he made every cell in her body perk up. When had she seen him smile, really smile, before?

"Yeah, she probably admires Juliet for all the things that drive you mad," Mack said. "The way she dresses, not quite Goth, not quite camo, but definitely cool. And attending MIT? She's a legend. And the three ear piercings, and the tattoo."

"You know about the tattoo?"

Mack was still smiling. "Sure. Lots of girls saw it when they showered in gym. All the boys want to see it, but as far as I can tell, no guys have."

"Good thing," Lisa said, rolling her eyes. "It's on her bum."

"Do you know what it says?" Mack asked.

"I do. Do you?"

"No. Beth wouldn't tell me. Is it a heart saying 'Luke Bryan'?"

"No. It's a heart saying, 'Stephen Hawking.' "

Mack threw back his head and laughed. Quickly, he quieted. "Well, that was unexpected. And totally inappropriate here."

Lisa gave him a guilty smile. "Sorry. But I'm sure the Barneses won't begrudge you a laugh, not even here."

Mack looked at Lisa, and she met his eyes, and for a few moments, no one said anything. *God,*

Lisa thought, *I'm crushing on a man ten years younger than I am.*

Forcing herself to drop her eyes, she said, "I should go."

Mack nodded. "It was nice talking to you."

Lisa walked away, toward the clutch of kids standing together, all of them sagging with misery. Theo was there, and Beth was by his side, and Theo's gaze was fixed on Beth as if afraid she'd disappear if he looked away.

From the moment he found out about Atticus's suicide, Theo mourned his friend and hated himself for not helping him, somehow. Lisa arranged for him to see a therapist—many of the students saw therapists that summer to learn how to deal with their shock and sorrow. One of their own, one of their best, had died. Theo learned to channel his grief and his natural excess of energy into body boarding and surfing. Lisa thought that while surfing Theo felt he had some small control over the incomprehensible world. He left at the end of the summer to attend the University of California at San Diego. Lisa knew he had chosen that college because it was near excellent surfing, and she both loved and hated that Theo surfed. It was dangerous. But plain old life was dangerous, too.

Her parents, only in their early seventies, were increasingly hampered with health problems. They moved to an assisted living facility on the

Cape. Lisa visited them as often as she could, but she saw with each visit how they were failing. Her mother had Alzheimer's and died a year to the day she left the island, and Lisa's father passed on only a few months later. Much of the money her parents got when they sold their Nantucket home had gone into a down payment at the assisted living facility, but Lisa inherited a healthy chunk of money, and never before had money made her so sad.

Juliet was attending MIT because she was such a natural with math and computers. Theo was in California. Lisa became obsessed with her work. She loved the camaraderie of the shop and the gorgeous college girls who worked in June, July, and August. She enjoyed her customers—most of them—and each day the shop was filled with gossip and laughter. If she suggested a dress or a sweater that someone bought, Lisa was as pleased as if she'd won a game. She started carrying jewelry and accessories.

When she turned fifty, a group of her women friends threw a party for her.

"You lucky duck," Helen North said. "You look fabulous and your children are off at college. Time for romance!"

Lisa laughed and shook her head. "Oh, Helen, it's too late for me. All the single men my age, if there *are* any single men my age, want to date thirty-year-olds."

"Try a dating site," Rachel suggested.

"I don't have the time," Lisa quickly countered. "Or the interest."

The weeks and months passed. Lisa discovered she was often exhausted from working all day, all week, for even though she was closed on Sundays except in the summer, she had paperwork to catch up on, stock to unpack or return. Finally, with trepidation, she hired another woman to help her year-round, Betsy Mason, new to the island and with a background in retail. Betsy had just turned thirty, and she was a crisp, practical, savvy young woman, and her cheerful presence brightened Lisa's life.

Juliet graduated from MIT and immediately took a job with a tech company in Cambridge. She came home for Thanksgiving, Christmas, and a week or two in the summer, but she always brought her computer with her. Theo loved San Diego, surfing as often as he could, only coming home once for a few days at Christmas.

Her life had changed again, like a car moving so smoothly onto a different path she'd hardly noticed it happening.

Early one evening she sat at the dining room table scrolling through her home computer, idly reading Facebook and Instagram posts, a glass of wine by her side. It was May, the beginning of the island's real spring. She was fifty-six years old. And alone.

She admitted to herself that she was lonely for the companionship of a man. She had plenty of women friends, some who were divorced or widowed. She often went out to dinner or to plays with them. She spoke to men at the Rotary or chamber of commerce events, but no one there interested her or showed interest in her.

Well, ha! Who would want her? Ever, or especially now?

"Stop it," she said to herself—she often spoke aloud to herself, and why not? "Don't be maudlin. You're healthy and well-off. You have two healthy happy children, and your life is good. You have nothing to complain about!"

Then the dining room ceiling fell on her head.

three

Not the entire ceiling, just a few fragments of plaster. But more was to come because the previous week Nantucket had experienced one of its gale force storms with whipping rain that went on for hours. Looking up, Lisa saw that rain had slithered from the upper edge of the fireplace chimney into her dining room, making wet spots and entire tunnels as if upside-down moles had burrowed all around the ceiling. It had to be fixed and she knew she couldn't do it herself.

During the almost thirty years she'd lived here, she'd taken the best care she could of her children. She'd spent time choosing organic vegetables and making "real" meals instead of pizza every day. She'd attended swim meets, school plays, and basketball games. She'd volunteered at the school library. She'd kept the house clean, comfortable, and welcoming. She'd placed flowers on the table and electric candles in the windows during the winter. The furniture was well-polished, she built glowing fires in the living room fireplace, and her beautiful garden was filled with herbs and flowers.

But she hadn't taken note of the casual,

extensive, sneaky deterioration of the house. When part of the ceiling fell on her head, exposing the wooden staves above, she knew she had to pay attention to the house or it would continue to fall apart.

She took up a pad and a pen and, feeling quite industrious, went through the house, looking at what needed doing. All of the "lights," the rectangular glass panes at the top of most of the ancient interior doors, rattled, not just when the door was opened or closed, but also when wild winds blew and drafts whistled through the house. They'd been that way for years. It was just part of the house. Many things rattled in an old house.

Now she knew they must be re-caulked, or something like that. She couldn't repair the dining room ceiling, but she *could* fix the lights. She googled a few sites and learned what to do. It seemed easy. The next day, she went to Marine Home Center and bought a tube of white caulking. She tied her dark hair back like Rosie the Riveter. She got out her stepladder—aluminum and light enough to carry, but strong enough to hold her—and climbed up to attempt to apply caulking in a nice straight smooth line along the base of the lights.

It was like trying to get a perfect stripe of toothpaste from the tube. Sometimes the caulk squirted and then exploded out. When she tried to spread it evenly with her fingernail, she smeared it onto the glass.

She was only making it worse.

She climbed down from the stepladder and sat on the floor and wept.

"I'm fifty-six years old," she said aloud. After all, there was no one there to hear her.

"I should sell this house. It's far too big for one person. I could buy a new house with crisp white paint on the woodwork." She was beginning to perk up. She usually did when she had a conversation with herself.

"I could sell my business, move off-island, buy a sweet charming place on the Cape, and have money left over for adventures. I could go on a cruise!" She nodded to herself approvingly.

Rising easily—yoga practice once a week—she stood and paced the room, thinking.

"Why would I want to go on a cruise? I get motion sick," she reminded herself.

"And I love this house. Someday I hope to have grandchildren running up and down the stairs. I love the island. I love my friends. I love my shop."

She looked out the window. It was May. Her tulips were in bloom and her daffodils were on the brink of blooming.

"I have the money to fix the place up," she reasoned. "I *should* fix this place up!" Her gloom evaporated. Ideas blossomed. She found her phone in the kitchen and called Rachel.

When Rachel answered, Lisa said, "I need the name of a carpenter, or a contractor, or a painter. I need major repairs on my ceiling."

"Good evening to you, too!" Rachel laughed. "What's brought this on?"

"The dining room ceiling fell on my head."

"What?"

"Well, just about a square foot, but the rest of it is bulging with water and I'm afraid it will collapse any moment. Plus, I've decided to have a lot of repairs done. Give this house a little love."

"Okay, let me think. You don't want just anyone. Plus, lots of guys won't even consider working for you because your place is so old. If you solve one problem, you'll find fifty others. You need someone responsible—what about Mack Whitney?"

"I think I know him."

"Of course you do," Rachel said. "His daughter, Beth, is Theo's age. She was the girl whose boyfriend committed suicide in high school seven years ago."

"Oh, of course. Gosh, how could I forget—Theo used to hang out with Beth because she was dating Atticus. For a while they were all so close, the three Musketeers, and then . . . Atticus died. Poor boy. Poor girl. The whole town was in mourning." Lisa hesitated. "I made Theo see a therapist."

"Yeah, lots of kids saw therapists after that."

"True. And we, well, Theo, sort of lost touch with Beth. She was in Theo's grade, but after Atticus, they didn't run with the same crowd. How is Beth? Have you seen her?"

"I have. She finished high school, went off to college, but she's back on-island now, I think. She's a smart girl, but she's had some rough times. She lost Atticus, plus you know her mother died when Beth was practically a baby."

"I remember that. What was her name?"

"Marla. Poor little Beth. Mack never remarried."

"That's right. He was always so nice. Gosh, now that it's all coming back to me, I remember wishing I could talk with him about being a single parent but I never suggested we have a drink or anything because he's so good-looking and I didn't want to seem to be flirting with him."

"You were the only woman in town who wasn't." Rachel laughed. "Friends would phone me in a romantic seizure if he so much as nodded at them."

"And he never remarried?"

"No. He concentrated on his work and his daughter. Never missed a recital or a soccer game. But I know he's a hard worker and a good guy. And he's a restoration carpenter so he won't want to tear your house down and build a new palace. He won't cheat you."

"You've sold me. I just hope he's got some time to take on a new client."

"If he doesn't, call me back. I'll put on my thinking cap."

"Great! Let's talk later, meet for lunch or a movie." Lisa clicked off, hurrying to find Mack Whitney's phone number in the short fat town directory. Last year the cover shot was of all the firemen together. This year, it was of all the post office employees. She spotted Robin and Vilma and Tita, and smiled at them. Warmth surged through her. This island was her home, and suddenly she was filled with excitement at the thought of restoring her beloved old house to its former glory, or at least to some semblance of sturdiness and beauty.

She found Mack Whitney's number and called, certain she'd get voicemail. When a low, pleasant voice said, "Hello," she was, for a moment, startled. People didn't often answer their phones these days.

"Oh, hi, um, I'm Lisa Hawley. My friend Rachel McEleny recommended you because my house is so old and the dining room ceiling just fell on my head."

"Are you all right?"

"What? Oh, yes, of course. It didn't *all* fall. But it will need to be replaced or repaired, and now that I'm really paying attention, I can see lots of big and small problems. The house was built in

1840, and I've tried to keep up with it, but I have a clothing shop on Main Street and that's taken all my time. I guess I've neglected the house."

"So you need a restoration carpenter."

"Yes. Please."

"Why don't I come take a look?"

"Great! When?"

"I've got free time tomorrow, around noon."

"That's wonderful."

"See you then."

"Wait—my address is—"

"I know your house."

"Oh, well, good. Fine. Thanks!"

Lisa tapped off and stood very still, thrilled and a bit frightened at what she'd started happening in her mild, safe life.

Mack Whitney arrived the next day at twelve-thirty.

When Lisa opened the door, she nearly passed out, shocked by the sensual gorgeousness of the man. How had she forgotten his . . . his . . . his *maleness?*

"Hi," he said. "I'm Mack." He extended his large rough hand for her to shake and held hers in his.

"I'm Lisa," she told him, "but of course you know that, you're here because I asked you to come, and I'm so grateful. This poor old house needs a lot of love." Oh, no! Could she say anything more embarrassing? It was all she could do not to slam her hand over her mouth and giggle like a tween. Two minutes with the man and she was talking about love and she never did that!

"I think I'm staring at you," Lisa admitted. "It's just, um, are you Dutch? You look like you are." Trying to make some kind of sense, she added, "I was in Amsterdam once." Could she sound any crazier?

"My mother was Dutch," Mack explained. "I was born here." He was still holding her hand.

"Oh, I see." Gently, she pulled away her hand.

"It's a beautiful house," Mack said.

"Oh! Yes, it is." Lisa stepped back. "Please. Come in. I'll show you the dining room. The house must have been stunning when it was first built. It's Greek Revival, you know, built in 1840, which is why the rooms are so small but still have fireplaces and the doors have those small rectangles of glass at the top so you could look in to see if something was on fire, but you probably know that."

She led him into the dining room. "Every room needed work when we bought the house. We did what we could, but the children were little—" She didn't say, *and my husband left me for another woman.*

She was caught in the past and at the same time in the present where Mack, tall and wide-shouldered, extremely *alive* here and now, stood waiting. She couldn't think what to do.

"So obviously you're concerned about the ceiling," Mack said, pointing to cracks in the plaster and ominous bulges.

"Yes, yes," she said, snapping back into her sensible self. "The water from that storm last week got in somehow. I don't understand. With the second floor and the attic above, how could water get to this level?"

Mack walked around, head back, studying the ceiling with its crystal chandelier hanging from the middle of the handsome plaster rosette that each of the downstairs rooms had.

"It hasn't damaged the rosette," Mack said. "My men could take down the ceiling—it will be a dusty mess, but if we don't replace it, it's all going to come down someday. We'll work around the rosette, put up fresh plaster and paint. And I'll need to get up on the roof and check the flashing around the chimney. If some of it's missing, that will be where the water got in. Water has its ways."

"Oh. Well, that's one major problem we need solved. Also, in the dining room, I don't know why I never got around to it, but part of the chimney is missing a brick or two, so I've never had a fire in here, haven't had the money to repair it—we've got four chimneys—and also there's no damper, so when the wind gusts above fifty-five miles an hour, it blows down the chimney and into the room. I—this is embarrassing, but it does work, kind of—I stuffed a crib mattress up inside there. It doesn't show and it's not perfect, but it's better than nothing."

"I imagine in a house this size, the heating bills are huge," Mack said. "I'll make you a damper."

"Oh, good. And my bathroom, I guess, we should look at next. It's old, and the sink was beautiful once, but the porcelain has worn away from the drain hole"—*Why,* Lisa thought frantically, was *hole* such an embarrassing word?—"so it's all black, metal, I suppose, and the faucets drip no matter what I do, so there are stains . . ."

" 'Lay on, MacDuff,' " Mack said.

Lisa realized she'd been talking to him and staring at him as if in a trance. As if while she talked she could keep him trapped so she could look at him. She knew he wanted her to take him to the bathroom, but first . . .

"Wow, you got the quote right," she said. "Most people say, 'Lead on, MacDuff,' but you said it correctly—'lay on'!" Lisa felt herself blush when she said "lay."

"Carpenters can read Shakespeare, too," Mack said, smiling.

"Oh, yes, I mean, no, I mean I didn't think you didn't read Shakespeare . . ."

"Well, I can't say I've read him lately. Mostly

I've watched baseball but I have seen the streaming plays at the Dreamland. And I bought the DVD of Branagh's *Hamlet*."

Lisa almost clapped her hands in surprise. "Wasn't that brilliant? The costumes were gorgeous."

Mack laughed. "Of course you would notice the costumes." Seeing Lisa hesitate, he added, "Because of your store, I mean. You know all about clothes."

"Well," Lisa said mildly, "maybe not *all* about them."

"Beth likes to shop there when she wants something special, and she's never disappointed."

"Oh, I'm glad. How is Beth?"

"She's great. Just finished getting her master's degree in museum studies at BU. She'd like to get a job involved with historic preservation. Eventually, she hopes to work with the Nantucket Historical Association."

"How wonderful," Lisa said. "Sounds like she's a smart girl. And one who knows what she wants to do."

"She is. You know her mother died when Beth was three—"

"I'm so sorry."

"Yes, it was terrible. Hard. We went through some rough years, but Beth's turned out just fine." Leaning forward, he showed Lisa his phone. "Here's Beth."

On the screen was a picture of a lovely young woman with long, lustrous blond hair and green eyes like her father.

"She's beautiful. She's got a marvelous smile."

"Thanks to the orthodontist," Mack joked. "You have two kids, right?"

"Right," Lisa said with a light groan. "You know about Theo. He was a darling child, but his teen years were crazy. And Juliet."

"Juliet was two years ahead, right? A nice girl."

"My first child. She was the smart one. She's in Boston now, working for some huge tech company. Theo's out on the West Coast. He went to college there, but mostly he surfed." Lisa paused, remembering. "My husband left us when Theo was nine, Juliet eleven. Thankfully, he set us up reasonably well financially. But he *really* left the kids. No phone calls, no visits, no Christmas cards, no birthday cards. We have no idea where he lives now."

"What a shit," Mack said. "Excuse my language."

"Oh, I've called him worse," Lisa said. "The thing is, I've always thought that Theo was such a wild kid because he had no father to show him how to be a man. And Juliet . . . it was hard on her, too." Lisa ran her hands through her hair. "I sound like I'm at a therapist's. Sorry."

"No need to apologize. Everyone has family problems. Look at poor Atticus Barnes. I knew

Paula and Ed. They were great people. They knew Atticus had depressive spells but never imagined he would commit suicide." Mack paused, then continued. "Beth didn't, and she was going with him."

"I know. Theo was best friends with Atticus. The three of them used to hang around here sometimes, especially if fresh cookies were on the counter. Beth was such a nice girl." Lisa looked down at her hands, as if she would find the right words there. "It was such a terrible time."

"I remember. Well, I can't forget."

"And Theo and Beth . . . after Atticus died, they seldom saw each other. I think it was too hard. Atticus had always been the center of their group. The magnet. Then he was gone, and they drifted apart . . ."

For a moment, Lisa found herself looking at Mack, seeing him both as a parent and as a handsome and interesting man. She also saw how thick his blond hair was, how green his eyes were, and how tall he stood, only two feet away from her.

He appeared to be equally interested in her. His smile was gentle, his eyes warm. The connection took her breath away.

But he was *ten* years younger than she was.

"Oh," she said, breaking the spell, "I need to show you the bathroom."

"Sure," Mack said.

She turned and led the way, hoping he hadn't noticed how her cheeks were burning.

A week later, Mack arrived in the morning with a pair of young men and all their ladders and toolboxes and electric power tools. Mack introduced her to the workers, who looked like weightlifters.

"This is Dave and this is Tom."

"Hello," Lisa said. "Thanks for coming to help."

Mack turned toward the men. "Okay. Here's the first project." He pointed to the ceiling.

Lisa hung around for a few moments, listening, as if she had any idea what they were talking about, until she realized she was really looking at Mack's body. He was a gorgeous man, and she didn't want to leave his presence. She was shocked. She hadn't felt this way in years. Had she ever?

Lisa pulled herself out of her reverie. "I'll be in the kitchen if you need me," she said.

But of course they didn't need her. They carefully lifted the paintings off the walls and carried them into the living room. They brought large rolls of plastic into the house and covered doors and walls to protect the rest of the house from plaster dust. Mack drove off to get something, and Dave and Tom set up staging and brought out their power tools.

Lisa was grateful for the narrow back stairs

leading down to the kitchen. She turned the kitchen into her everything room, which was fine, because the screened porch was off the kitchen, so she could wander out in the morning and listen to the birds waking up.

Her shop didn't open until ten—nine once summer started—so she spent an hour or so working on her financials on her laptop at the kitchen table, a cup of coffee at her side. But having the men in the house altered the routine of her days. It was difficult to add and subtract when Mack entered the house. She couldn't remember responding so physically to a man. She woke up happy, she was seldom hungry, problems were solved more easily, and it wasn't simply spring. Mack was gorgeous, tall, muscular, strong, and wide-shouldered, with long thick blond hair he held back in a low tail with a piece of string.

She wondered what color his chest hair was . . . and all his hair. He always wore jeans, an old T-shirt, and worker's boots. She fantasized about what he looked like in a suit.

Or in nothing.

Of course she knew she was being foolish, thinking of Mack that way. Nothing would happen between them . . . oh, but daydreams were so lovely.

Sunday morning, the workmen had the day off. So did Lisa, for one last luxurious Sunday before she geared up her shop for the summer crowd. Betsy Mason took charge of *Sail* this Sunday. Lisa lounged on her wicker sofa on the porch, sipping a glass of iced peach tea and reading a novel. It was her habit and her treat to slip over to the library on Saturday afternoons when Betsy was there to mind the shop. Lisa would go immediately to the new fiction section and browse, as content as a child in a candy store. This morning, she had four new books set out on the wicker table. For a few minutes, she studied each one, deciding which book to start with, and then she settled back in the sofa for a long, delicious read.

She was barefoot, in her kimono, when she heard the kitchen door open, and then Mack was there.

"Sorry," he said. "I don't mean to bother you, but I wanted to drop some equipment off so the boys can start plastering first thing tomorrow."

Lisa said, "That's fine—good Lord!"

They both looked at the plastering stilts in his hands. Made of steel and rubber, they looked like artificial limbs, and in a way they were, because, Mack explained, the guys would adjust them to the height they needed, fasten them to their feet and knees, and easily reach the ceiling. They had springs for flexibility and rubber soles to make them resistant to skids.

"Very space age," Lisa said.

"That coffee smells good," Mack said.

For a beat, Lisa didn't respond. He was here on Sunday when his crew wasn't around. He said the coffee smelled good.

"Would you like some?" she asked.

"I really would," Mack answered. "I don't know why, but I make crap coffee."

"Sit down," Lisa told him, gesturing to a chair. "I'll get you a cup. Cream, sugar?"

"Black works."

Her legs were curled up to the side, and when she swung them to the floor and rose, they were exposed. She pulled her kimono together, but the sash wasn't as all purpose as a zipper, and she knew Mack was looking at her legs. She glanced at him, and she was right.

She did have good legs.

Flushing, she slipped past him into the kitchen. When she brought back the mug, he was seated, just looking around.

"Thanks," he said. "Beautiful garden. And this is a wonderful space."

"It's waking up now," Lisa said. Mack smiled, she flushed. "I'm cleaning out the fallen leaves and sticks. Oh, and I've been spraying the tulips. If I don't, the rabbits eat all the flowers."

Mack nodded, not speaking, his eyes intent on her face.

What was happening? Was this the eye con-

tact thing people talked about? "Do you have a garden?" Lisa asked, a bit desperately.

"I guess you could say I have a yard. When Beth was a child, we used to plant flowers and stuff in the spring. Mostly I mow the lawn and water the old geraniums in the pots."

"I have some ten-year-old geraniums. I bring them in to over-winter in the house. I'll set them outside soon."

"Sounds like you're really good with plants."

Lisa shrugged. "They're easier to deal with than ceilings."

Again, the eye lock. Then, oh of course, here came the hot flash.

"What are you reading?" Mack asked.

"The new Charles Todd mystery. Do you like mysteries?"

"Very much, and thrillers, too. I'm reading a Lee Child book at the moment."

"Yes, Jack Reacher . . ."

"Who's your favorite mystery writer?" Mack asked. "I see you've got the new John le Carré here." He turned the book to face him.

"I don't consider John le Carré to be a mystery writer. He writes spy thrillers, don't you think?"

As they talked, the sun slowly moved in the sky, its light brightening the porch, and, Lisa thought sadly, exposing every line in her face. Why was Mack here, she wondered. Maybe her presence was comforting, like a favorite aunt's, or a teacher's.

"Would you like more coffee?" she asked.

"No, thanks," Mack said. "But what are you doing today? It's warm and sunny. Want to get sandwiches at Something Natural and go out to Great Point?"

Warmth flooded through Lisa, and an extreme joy . . . and an equally extreme fear. "Oh, I'm sure you don't want—"

Mack interrupted. "But I *do* want." His cheeks reddened. "I'd like your company. Hey, I could have brought the stilts over tomorrow. The reason I dropped in was to see if you wanted to do something today, outside. Away from the house. With me."

Lisa met Mack's gaze and gooseflesh broke out over her entire body. Did he *like* her? *That* way? "Well, then, so yes, I'd love to. I'll bring some cold beer and, um, cookies . . . but I need to get dressed. Just a moment . . ." She left the room. It was all she could do to keep herself from running up the stairs.

What should she wear? Jeans, sneakers, baggy cotton sweater—not *that* one with the V-neck, she didn't want to show even a hint of cleavage, this wasn't a date, this was . . . what? What *was* this? Could it possibly be in some weird way romantic? Oh, who was she kidding? She was ten years older than Mack. He was only a friend. She pulled on her sports bra so things wouldn't jiggle when they bumped over the soft sand. A loose cotton sweater, and her L.L.Bean quilted vest. Everything tucked tidily out of sight.

She hurried down the stairs. "Sorry to take so long."

"No problem." Mack held the door open for her, and they went out into the day.

They drove through the narrow roads out to the Milestone Rotary, turned left, and sped down 'Sconset road. They turned off toward Wauwinet, and soon were at the ranger station on the side of the road.

Mack had to let the air out of his tires at the ranger station so they could make the drive through the soft sand out to Great Point. It took them forty-five minutes to go about six miles, and the ride was so bumpy they couldn't really talk. But the views of the pristine beach with the glittering ocean lapping at it mesmerized Lisa. Orange-beaked oystercatchers, piping plovers, and gulls scurried back and forth over the sand and as they neared Great Point, they saw seals swimming or sunning themselves on the beach.

Great Point was a spit of land stretching between Nantucket Sound and the Atlantic. The currents from the two bodies of water met with a gorgeous rolling turbulence that attracted seals, fish, and people. The lighthouse, seventy-one feet of stone painted white, had been first built in 1784 to warn sailors of dangerous shoals. In 1986, it had been rebuilt with new lenses and solar-powered panels to fuel the light.

"Oh, wow," Lisa said when Mack brought his truck to a stop on the sound side of the point. "I haven't been out here in a long time. I had no idea about the seals."

For a while, they sat looking out the windshield at the dozens, if not hundreds, of seals wallowing on the sand. A trustees sign forbade people from walking toward the area where the seals were.

"Let's have lunch," Mack said.

"Good idea."

They left Mack's truck, carrying a basket, a cooler of iced drinks, and a plaid blanket down a slope of sand to the shore of the calm waters of Nantucket Sound. They spread the blanket on the beach, enjoying the late May sunshine, pleased that there was no breeze blowing to toss sand into their food. They sat on the blanket, with the basket between them, munching sandwiches and watching the aggressive horsehead seals bob up and down in the water, clearly trying to decide if the humans looked good enough to eat.

Mack told her, "Not long ago, seals were considered pests and killed. Their noses were brought into the town and the hunter got five dollars a nose. Then they were considered an endangered species and killing them became forbidden. Now we've come full circle. We've got too many seals, so the fishermen can't catch enough fish."

"I've read that the seals are attracting great white sharks," Lisa said, eyeing the rubbery pile of creatures rolling over one another, grunting and snorting.

"It's true. They've been spotted on the Cape and around the island. Funny how things change."

"Funny how time changes us all." The moment she spoke, Lisa wished she could swallow her words. She didn't want to talk about time. She was ten years older than Mack. She was in fifth grade when he was born! What was she even doing out here? She was so attracted to the man, and yet she needed to protect herself. He was only being friendly. "You know, Theo and Beth are the same age. I was thirty-one when he was born. I think you were much younger, weren't you?"

"I was twenty-one," Mack said. "And I was an idiot."

Lisa laughed. "Trust me, you can be an idiot at any age."

"True. I don't mean I was an idiot to marry Marla. I loved her. And if I hadn't married her, I wouldn't have Beth in my life."

"Tell me about Marla." Lisa gazed out into the water, giving him emotional space.

"I guess you didn't know her," Mack said.

"No. I was in Washington then." *And as I said, I was ten years older,* Lisa wanted to add.

"So. She was, well, she was my first love. She was pretty, sweet, and I suppose, in a way, she was maybe a little bit childish. I don't mean to criticize her. But she didn't like to face facts."

"Whereas everyone else *loves* to face facts," Lisa joked.

Mack chuckled. "She took things personally. I mean, like the electric bill. If it was high, she would burst into tears. She enjoyed cooking, and always tried to come up with something fancy for our dinner, but if it didn't come out just right, she was miserable. Even angry—at the casserole, or whatever."

"She sounds like a perfectionist."

"She was more of a dreamer. A romantic. She was crazy happy when she was pregnant, although the whole childbirth thing shocked her."

"Listen, the *whole childbirth thing* shocks every woman," Lisa said.

Mack was quiet for a moment, thinking. "She loved Beth. She was a great mother. I can't say our marriage would have lasted. We were too young and as it turned out, very different. But she was a great mother. Beth was her entire world."

"It's heartbreaking that she died," Lisa said softly.

"Yes." Mack cleared his throat. "But she was romantic even about that. She believed that she had achieved her destiny by bringing Beth to the world. She died at home. Hospice had been coming for a week. Marla knew she was getting weaker. She had me move Beth's little bed into our bedroom so she could be with her till the last minute. Beth sat on the end of Marla's bed and read stories to her mother. Of course, Beth couldn't read, so she made up the stories. Marla would lie there smiling, hearing Beth's sweet little voice . . ." Mack cleared his throat. "Sorry. I haven't talked about this for a long time."

Lisa wanted to hold his hand, touch him in consolation, but she remained still, not intruding on his sorrow.

"But Beth's all right, I think," Mack continued. "She was so young, and I guess she grew up thinking we were a normal family, the two of us."

"You've been widowed a long time. Did you never want to marry again?"

"Truthfully? No. I guess I never met the right woman. Plus, working full-time and being a single parent isn't easy."

"I've noticed."

"That's right." Mack looked at Lisa. "You were single with *two* children. How did that happen?"

Lisa smiled. "I guess I was an idiot, too. So was Erich. Maybe we all are around the age of twenty. We met at Middlebury, married before graduation, and moved to Washington, D.C. Erich and his father worked for a bank based in Switzerland that helped developing countries.

They traveled a lot, and spoke several languages."

"That sounds kind of glamorous."

"It was." Lisa picked up a stone and turned it in her hands, idly. "I wasn't. I never became what Erich thought I should." Quickly, because she didn't want to verge into self-pity, she said, "But I did have a wonderful few years traveling through Europe with him on our vacations. I saw Paris, Amsterdam, Rome, and I worked in the National Museum of Women in the Arts in Washington. I liked that a lot. Then we had the children, and I stopped working, and Erich traveled more for the bank, and I missed Nantucket . . . what do they say? We grew apart. We divorced, and I'm not sorry about that at all."

"Did he marry again?"

"I don't think so. I google him every so often." She laughed. "I don't mean to sound like a stalker."

"You're hardly a stalker. Erich sounds like a sociopath if he doesn't care about his kids. No wonder you've never married again."

"I've hardly had time to even think about that. When the children were in middle school, I started working at Vestments, and eventually I bought the shop and turned it into *Sail*. I enjoy it, and it helped our lives financially—" Lisa interrupted her train of thought. "And I have plenty of money to have repairs done on the house."

"It's a big house," Mack said. "Especially for one person."

"True. But Juliet comes home for holidays and for a week or two in the summer. Theo's in California, so he doesn't come that often."

"They're not married?"

"No. They've both dated, of course, but they're old enough now, twenty-seven and twenty-five, so I assume they haven't met the right person."

"You think there is a right person for everyone?"

Lisa cocked her head, looking at Mack. "I do."

"So do I," Mack said, and he held her gaze until they both blushed.

She had to break the spell or he'd think that she thought he wanted to kiss her, and that couldn't be right, not when he was looking at her with the sun on her imperfect and ten-years-older face. "Would you like some grapes?" she asked, holding out a stem.

"Um, sure," he said.

They ate grapes and gazed at the sea. After a while, they walked down the empty beach, away from the seals and Great Point. They trudged through deep sand up to the Great Point Lighthouse, the high stone tower casting an arrow of shadow over the marsh grass and wild roses. They half-slid down a sand dune to the ocean and watched the light change over the water.

"We should get back," Lisa said.

As they lifted and carried the basket, the blanket, and the cooler back to Mack's Jeep, Lisa was almost breathlessly aware of Mack's masculinity. His strong legs. His muscular arms. His hands, so much bigger and rougher than her own. His hair, slightly brown, slightly blond, was thick and slightly shaggy, which made him look even younger.

She needed to have her hair styled. She needed a manicure—and a pedicure, because summer was coming. She needed to lose ten pounds.

She needed to get real.

They made the bumpy ride back over the soft sand to the hard sand road and finally out to the blacktop. They didn't talk, but that was only natural. It was difficult to have a conversation while bumping over the sandy ruts. Lisa was grateful for the silence. She felt they were returning to normal, to just friends.

Mack stopped at the air pumps to fill his tires to the right pressure.

As he got back into his truck, he said, "I worry about Beth."

Lisa glanced at him. "You do?"

"Yeah. She's twenty-five and she's never brought home a guy for me to meet."

"Maybe she's been seeing guys she doesn't want you to meet," Lisa suggested with a smile.

"Maybe. But I'm afraid I haven't given her a

good example of what a relationship should be like. What a marriage should be like."

Lisa nodded. "I know what you mean. I worry, too."

"Do you think it ever stops? The worrying?" Mack asked.

"No. I don't think it ever stops," Lisa replied. "It's hard work, loving someone. But it's what makes life worth living."

Mack glanced over at Lisa with a smile. "True. And sometimes it can be a lot of fun."

And there it was again, the heat between them. The connection.

When they came to her house, he helped her carry her beach bag of leftover cookies and beer to the kitchen door.

"Thanks for the lovely afternoon," Lisa told him. "I feel like summer's almost here." Bashfully, she added, "I think you got some sun."

"So did you. Right here." He touched her cheek and Lisa almost fainted.

"Looks good on you," Mack said. "So, um, work tomorrow. I'll see you first thing."

"Yes, tomorrow," Lisa agreed.

four

Monday morning Lisa was in her bedroom trying to decide what to wear. Something casual and dignified, but sexy. Was that combination even possible? She wanted to crawl back in bed, curl up in the covers, and read. But already she heard Dave and Tom stomping around downstairs, tuning their radio to a rock station.

A knock sounded loudly at her bedroom door.

Lisa usually wore a long T-shirt to bed, which was what she was wearing now. She had no bra on. No shoes, no makeup, and she hadn't dealt with her hair. She reached for her red silk kimono. It would do for a cover-up.

"Come in," she called as she tied the sash.

Mack stuck his head in. "Good morning." He wore carpenter's pants and a flannel shirt.

"Good morning."

"I've brought coffee."

"Oh, thank you."

Mack entered the room. "Can we talk a moment?" he asked as he handed her a to-go cup.

"Of course. Um, should we go downstairs?" When he stood close to her like this, Lisa couldn't think.

"Let's stay up here. I don't want Dave or Tom to interrupt. I'll sit in the chair, okay?"

Lisa laughed. "If you can find room among the clothes. Just toss them on the floor."

Mack sat on the chair. Lisa perched on the side of the bed, waiting.

"Look, Lisa, I don't know exactly how to say this, but I want to get things straight. About us, I mean."

Oh, dear, Lisa thought. Here it came, the kind but firm dismissal.

"I like you, Lisa. A lot. I'm not sure what we've got going, but I don't want to go into it lightly. I think we have fun together. Yesterday at the beach . . . I think we're good for each other. We've both been single for a long time, and . . . I'm not saying I want to be permanent. It's too soon for that. But I want us to be exclusive."

Lisa nearly spilled her coffee. "Yes," she said. He was so handsome. It was his jawline, and his eyes, and his lashes. And his lips. "Me, too."

Mack smiled. "I want us to go out together. I mean to dinner, to movies."

"You want to date," Lisa said, smiling. She felt warm all over.

"Well, and more than date," Mack said.

"Yes."

"I'm too old to play around," Mack said. "I want to make love to you. But I don't want to rush into this."

"Lord!" Lisa exclaimed, losing her cool. She set her cup on the nightstand and stood up, her hands on her red-hot cheeks. Her face must match her robe. "Mack, you're really . . ."

"Blunt? Honest? Candid?"

Lisa walked across the room toward the window, needing the distance. "Yes, all of those things. And I'm glad. I'm grateful. And I want everything you say. But, Mack . . ." Lisa paused and summoned up every speck of bravery in her entire being. "I'm fifty-six years old."

Mack shrugged. "How is that relevant?"

"Because you're only forty-six."

Mack laughed. "I don't think that matters. Do you?"

"Well, yes, yes, I do think it matters. People will talk—"

"People will talk anyway." Mack stood up.

Lisa frowned. How could he not understand how significant the difference in their ages was?

"Let me take you out to dinner Friday night," Mack said. "The Seagrille should be open. We can take our time, drink some nice wine, and get to know each other better. Okay?"

Lisa felt like she was shining. "Okay."

"I'm going down now to talk to the boys. About work."

"I'll be down soon. I need to dress. I feel kind of wobbly," she admitted.

"Drink your coffee," Mack told her with a grin.

Was this happening? Lisa thought after Mack left the room. She wanted to call Rachel and giggle like a little girl. She wanted to break into song and twirl around her room like Julie Andrews in *The Sound of Music*.

She pulled herself together, finished her coffee, and got ready to open her shop.

Not many restaurants were open at the end of May, but the Seagrille was always good, and Lisa hoped she and Mack would be given a booth instead of a table. That way, perhaps, they could have some privacy. They had arrived early because they both had to work the next day.

The waitress, Sally Hardy, knew them both. She did give them a booth, and for a few moments, as Lisa and Mack settled themselves, looked at the menus, and tried to act normally during their first real romantic date, they were alone. But quickly, as other diners entered the restaurant, friends and acquaintances stopped to say hello. Their greetings were short and casual—how are you, the weather's getting better—but Lisa knew that some of the women would start texting their friends the moment they sat down.

She thought she looked pretty, or as pretty as possible. It had been a long time since she'd worn makeup, and it had taken her over an hour to put on foundation, concealer, blush, eye-liner, mascara, and lipstick. And another fifteen minutes to wipe it all off. She ended up wearing light sweepings of blush and a rosy lipstick.

She'd kept her dark hair in its tidy chin-length layered bob. She didn't want to be tossing long locks of hair around as if she thought she was in her twenties.

She was modest in her clothing, too. She had several blouses and light sweaters that dipped low in the front so a lacy camisole peeked through the V. Instead, she wore khakis—not yoga pants, even though she wore them at home and even when doing errands, but she didn't want to seem to be trying to be young tonight—and a light blue sweater with a multicolored swirl of scarf around her neck.

She probably looked like she was going to a PTA meeting.

Mack scrubbed up nicely. He wore a button-down shirt with the sleeves rolled up. His arms were muscular and covered with fine blond hair.

They ordered drinks and considered the menu. Lisa ordered the seafood casserole and Mack ordered a steak.

"Typical, right?" he joked as the waitress went off.

"You work hard physically," Lisa said. "You need red meat." Everything she said seemed like a double entendre.

"True."

They stared at each other for a moment, caught in a web of attraction.

"So," Mack said. "How do we do this? You tell me your favorite book and I tell you my favorite song?"

Lisa smiled. "Sounds like you've been on some dating apps."

The waitress brought their drinks. Mack waited until she left to answer.

"I admit it, I have. I haven't met anyone, though. I've been so busy with work. I'm glad Beth's got her degrees, but college costs money."

"I know. Fortunately, part of the divorce deal was that Erich would pay for the children's college tuition. And both of them worked in the summer to help with expenses."

"So," Mack said, directing his gaze into his glass, "tell me about how you came to have your shop."

A warm rush of satisfaction sped through Lisa. She leaned back against the booth, and smiled. "It's a dream come true. Really. I'm like a child with a box full of toys."

"A very smart child," Mack said. "It's quite impressive that you've run the shop for so long, managing to pay the crushing Main Street rent and still make a profit."

"I took business administration in college," Lisa told him. "I worked for Vesta Mahone and learned a lot from her. I grew up here. I know the cycle of the seasons." Shrugging lightly, she added, "And my kids have lived their own lives for several years now. I'm not distracted from my focus on my shop."

After a moment, Mack asked, "And you never married again?"

Lisa laughed. "I never even dated again!"

The waitress arrived with their appetizers. They both ordered another drink.

"You've been single all this time?" Mack asked.

Lisa felt herself blush. "I was so busy. It was hard, raising two children alone. Also, when they were both in school, I worked at Vestments part-time. And then full-time. And then I had my own shop and it seemed I worked twenty-four hours a day." She paused. "I think I shouldn't have worked full-time, ever, but especially when the kids were adolescents. I should have, could have, maybe, restrained Theo more. But they seemed to need less of me. They certainly seemed to *want* less of me. And we needed extra money. Teenagers are expensive. Although, to give them credit, they both worked in the summer from fourteen on."

Mack asked, with a frown, "Seriously, you never dated since then?"

Lisa laughed. "I was asked out a few times. Sometimes I'd go with a divorced father to see our kids in a play and the four of us would have celebratory ice cream sundaes. But no, I never dated as such. This town . . . this town is so small. I knew I couldn't have a romantic relationship without everyone knowing it, and I didn't want the kids teased in school."

"But the kids are grown. They live off-island now."

"True. They've lived off-island for years." Lisa shrugged. "I suppose I've simply fallen into the habit of living alone and liking it. I'm busy. I like my life. Maybe I like my solitude. Maybe I like . . . not being bothered by a man."

"We'll see about that," Mack said.

Lisa felt her cheeks burn as electricity shivered through her body. The truth was, she'd lived so many years without being the object of scrutiny by anyone, male or female, except her family physician, that this experience of growing closer with Mack, knowing he was now suggesting becoming intimate—well, it was frightening, a little. Or not frightening, but uncomfortable. It wasn't just the physical stuff, an image of herself naked before a younger man's eyes. It was, well, *all* of it.

Being judged. Not pretty enough, not fascinating enough, and certainly not accomplished enough in the art of lovemaking. Until now, until this *date,* she'd enjoyed the mild flirting. It had meant something to her, something flattering and fun, but as she sat at this table in public with

Mack with his gaze fastened on her face and her face certainly bright red, could she tolerate all this? She could back out now. She could tell him simply and firmly that she had no interest in any intimate relationship. She didn't *have* to do this. Whatever it was they were going to do.

But she wanted to do this.

Another thought, and this one she spoke aloud: "Tell me about you."

Mack paused, gathering his thoughts. "I was born here. Grew up here. My dad was a carpenter, so I learned from him. I like the old houses around here. I respect them. The width and length of some of the boards in the older houses, well, they're two hundred years old. Three hundred. They're treasures. So many contractors tear down old houses and ruin the boards, take them to the dump, and build mansions that look like they belong in Vegas. Sorry, don't mean to lecture you."

"No, I like hearing about this."

Mack looked Lisa in the eyes as if he was studying her. "You know, I think you do."

Lisa felt a rush of lust sweep through her. She had to look away. But she wanted to know . . . she needed to know. "What about your personal life?"

"Huh." He set his eyes on his silverware, turning the spoon over and over. "Okay. My personal life, well, it's shrunk down to two people, me and Beth." Flushing, he concentrated on the spoon as if it was fascinating, and said, "I never really *dated.* I never brought another woman into the house. I never introduced Beth to another woman. But . . . I didn't go without female companionship."

A slight prickle of completely inappropriate jealousy pinched at Lisa's heart.

"I never lied to anyone," Mack continued. "I never promised a long-term relationship. I was up front about my situation." His face fell. "And sometimes I'm sure I was a bit of an asshole. I didn't want to get serious."

Lisa waited.

Again, Mack raised his eyes to hers. "But *this* is different. You and I are different. Maybe it's the time. Maybe it's, well, *you.*"

His words took her breath away. At the same time, she imagined those other women, those *sexy* women, their waist-length hair and young shapely bodies, their sophisticated ways . . . she didn't want to imagine how her own body compared.

It was an absolute blessing when their dinners arrived. Their conversation turned back to memories of former restaurants and bars, and then on to former shops, houses, eccentric islanders, back and back into their childhoods.

Mack paid the check and they walked out into the chilly spring evening. As they drove to her house, they didn't talk. When he came around to open the passenger door of his truck for her, she stepped down and waited while he closed the door. Mack put his hand on the door handle and his other on the body of the truck, enclosing Lisa in his arms. She leaned back, looking up at him, and he held himself an inch or two from touching her with his own body.

"Invite me in?" he asked.

Lisa's voice trembled. "Yes. Yes, Mack, come in and I'll make you another cup of coffee."

five

Juliet was twenty-seven years old, lived in a third floor walk-up in Cambridge, Massachusetts, and sat in a cubicle all day long building websites for Kazaam, a large tech company with employees in twenty-seven states. She was heading a seven-member team that specialized in websites devoted to pets: their health, breeding, and of course their hilarious antics. The people she supervised lived all over the map; they communicated through email and Skype. They could be a lot of fun, but Juliet would have preferred to have fun with people in the same room.

At least in the two years she'd worked for Kazaam, she'd made a good friend in Mary, whose cubicle was across from hers. Mary wanted to make money as fast as she could so she and her boyfriend could get married. She was from a large Italian family, and she was friendly and smart and practical, and she'd warned Juliet not to get involved with their supervisor Hugh Jeffers, handsome and in a hurry and wickedly clever. Mary had been right.

Juliet had gotten over a lot of broken romances in her life, at least a lot for a girl who'd gone through high school always considering herself the smart one and her younger brother the attractive one. Having an absent, *totally* absent, father had made her distrust guys from the start, and it had also, oddly, sadly, made her feel she wasn't pretty enough, adorable enough, for her father and therefore for any male.

In college, lots of guys seemed to think she was absolutely the bomb, but she quickly learned that many of them would tell her anything so they could get her into bed. When she was in her early twenties, she'd thought she'd found a lasting relationship with Doug Manchester, but when they both applied for positions at Kazaam and Juliet got hired and Doug didn't, he broke up with her and moved to Chicago. That had been painful.

For the last few years, Juliet forced herself into a routine that worked for her, even if she did think she was becoming a bit eccentric and more than a bit lonely. She worked hard, went to the pub on Saturday nights with her girlfriends, ran three miles four times a week, and spent Sundays like a Victorian spinster, doing laundry, cleaning her apartment, and making a duty call to her darling, hardworking, lonely mother. She'd taken this job at Kazaam in part to be near to her mother, in case Lisa needed her.

Then Hugh Jeffers was sent by New York to take over this office. Brilliant, impatient, critical, he was also elegant and articulate, unlike her caveman brother and her last boyfriend. While all the other men in the office wore long-sleeved L.L.Bean flannel shirts, as if they were leaving momentarily to work as lumberjacks, Hugh wore designer suits with Brooks Brothers shirts that took cuff links. As a hobby he played classical piano.

Mary's opinion was that Hugh had quickly noticed who was the best worker, the most diligent, the most influential, and he'd chosen Juliet to be his lieutenant, standing up for him when there were rebellious mutterings when he wasn't in the office, never failing to carry out an assigned task.

Juliet's opinion was that Hugh had noticed her for her work and then had genuinely fallen in love with her. Certainly he acted that way. When they were sitting in his office discussing website traffic, he suddenly went very quiet. Juliet looked at him, puzzled.

"I want to ask you something," he said, "and I don't want to make you angry."

"Well, that's interesting," Juliet answered honestly.

"Will you be offended if I ask to take you out to dinner?"

She was so surprised, she couldn't answer.

"I mean, socially. I'd like to date you but I wouldn't want you to be insulted. You're too valuable an employee."

In an odd way, it was a romantic moment.

"I'd be delighted to go out to dinner with you," Juliet answered, adding of her own accord, "and it won't change my work habits."

They went to dinner several times. He didn't rush her to bed, but when they finally made love, he was careful and caring. He took her to the symphony, the theater, the ballet. She had to buy new clothes for all these special occasions, and beautiful, luxurious, sexy underwear for after.

He wrote a song about how he loved her and played it for her on the piano. He cooked for her. He brought her flowers. He agreed that when they had time, he would go to Nantucket with her to meet her mother.

Juliet was only slightly bothered by the way he acted toward her at work. He didn't favor her or especially notice her in the office. He seldom looked her way and he never called her in for private meetings. He was out of town many weekends, most often in New York, on business. Those were long weekends for Juliet, because he never called or texted her, and even though she had his number, she was too proud to call him. He had her off balance. She loved her job, and she was good at it, so she had never considered an office relationship. But Hugh told her he loved her. She was expecting a proposal and an engagement ring.

Instead, on a beautiful day in May, Hugh Jeffers walked into the office and announced to the entire staff that he was moving back to New York. Suzanne Daniels would be coming here to Boston to replace him.

Juliet had spent the night with him a week ago, and he hadn't even hinted at such a move. When he made his announcement to the group, his eyes slid over her as if she were nothing but a shadow.

It was all Juliet could do to get through that day. She wanted to corner him and demand to know what he was thinking, what his move meant for her. But she stubbornly kept hold of her dignity and didn't pursue him. Not that night. Not for three days and nights. She'd been certain he would seek her out, or phone her at home, or at least send her an email. But nothing.

Finally, on a Saturday morning, she phoned him and asked him to meet her for lunch, or dinner, or a drink. Hugh told her he didn't have time. So they had a brief and chillingly unpleasant conversation over the phone. She held back her tears. He told her he'd assumed she knew how ambitious he was, and yes, of course he had really loved her, but love could appear in many forms. He thought she knew that he would always love his work more.

Juliet felt like such a fool. How had she allowed herself to be so sappy, so gullible, such a simpering peasant believing the white knight would carry her off on his galloping steed to a castle in happy land?

She hated herself. She was ashamed. She slunk around her apartment all Saturday and Sunday, crying and eating. She talked for hours to Mary. But she didn't phone her mother. She worried about her poor mother, living alone in her big old empty house. Juliet just couldn't dump her troubles on her mom.

She didn't want to go back to the office on Monday because she was afraid the other programmers would look at her with pity. But she forced herself to work, hoping it would distract her from her misery. She pulled on black leggings and a black tank, glad this was her normal outfit. She didn't want to be seen in some bizarre kind of mourning.

She walked to work, bought her usual everything bagel, plastered on a fake *just fine* look and took the elevator to the sixth floor. The long monochromatic space was like any other cubicle farm. People were already here, bent toward their computers. Only Mary gave her a quick hello. Everyone was gearing up to prove they were essential to the new supervisor. Juliet collapsed at her desk and worked in steady despair. No doggie antics made her laugh.

She went through the week in a kind of gloom coma. She faked a smile when necessary, but mostly she kept her head down, and she got a pile of work done.

At the end of the work week, Juliet wanted to go home. Not to her lonely apartment, but to her real home in Nantucket. She had probably driven poor Mary mad every evening with all her weeping and anger. Who else could she turn to? Theo was on the West Coast now. Plus he was such a guy, so unsentimental, he was hopeless. Juliet had gone home for the past Christmas, and Theo stayed in California, so Juliet had her mother all to herself, a real pleasure. They cooked and ate and went for long walks on the stormy beaches and watched old movies together, eating ice cream from the container.

Suddenly, right now, Juliet wanted to go to Nantucket. She wanted all things not digital, not clickable. She wanted to curl up on a sofa with a slice of her mother's red velvet cake, and read anything by Agatha Christie. She wanted to fall asleep in the middle of the night, right there on the sofa. Her mother would gently cover her with a blanket, and in the morning, she would wake her up, laughing at Juliet's wrinkled clothes. She'd fix Juliet an enormous fattening breakfast of eggs and sausage and pancakes instead of the bagel Juliet bought on the way to work, and she'd tell Juliet she'd lost too much weight, and Juliet would eat lots of sweets.

Brainstorm: She actually could go home. All

the work she had to do could be done anywhere there was Wi-Fi.

She arrived at her own city home, a four-story clapboard house, one of the many on the street that needed painting, yanked the front door open, and stepped into the small front hall. She didn't bother to check her mailbox—anything important came on her phone. As she trudged up the stairs and let herself into her apartment, she took out her phone and checked the bus and ferry schedules to Hyannis and Nantucket. If she hurried, she could take the red line to South Station, the Plymouth and Brockton to Hyannis, and the eight o'clock slow ferry to the island. No fast boats were running that night.

She didn't take her leather jacket off. She didn't need to pack—she had clothes in her room at home. She had her wallet in one pocket of her jacket, her phone in another pocket, her charger and computer in her backpack. She went out her door, locked the locks, and ran down three floors of slippery steps to the front door.

She got to the subway, boarded her train, and tapped her fingers impatiently. At South Station, she raced for the bus at terminal number 18, arriving, puffing, just in time for the bus.

She bought her ticket and climbed into the long narrow dimness of the vehicle. It was crowded as usual because it was Friday, so she grabbed the first seat on the bus, where she had a touch more legroom, and settled in for the ride. The portly driver boarded the bus, muttering to himself. The doors wheezed shut. The bus beeped as it backed out, and by the time they were on the road, Juliet was asleep, her head resting on the window.

She woke now and then, blearily staring out the window at the road below. Interstate 93 and Highway 3 glistened with rain. She fell asleep again.

Often a bus driver would take pity on people trying to make the eight o'clock ferry and drive them right to the Steamship Authority. This driver was a good guy, and Juliet stuck a five in his hand in gratitude. She got her ticket in the terminal, slogged out to the ramp leading up into the interior of the *Eagle*, muttering to herself as she did every time, "Why in the bleeping world did they give a ship a bird's name?" She climbed the metal steps to the passenger deck, found a seat at a table, and dumped her backpack.

For a moment, she just sat and caught her breath. She felt as if she'd run the seventy-one miles herself. She was awake now, so she bought herself a bowl of clam chowder and a water (the plastic bottle was recyclable). She opened her laptop and worked on a report on leash laws across the country, answered emails, and nodded to herself: She'd done two day's work tonight. She deserved to play hooky.

The trip wasn't an easy one. The winds had

stirred the ocean into high waves that caused the ferry to rise up and then drop. It was like a roller coaster with an added side to side wobble. Luckily, she didn't have motion sickness, but other passengers were lying down with brown paper napkins soaked in cold water on their foreheads.

At the table directly facing hers, a man sat working on his laptop. He was handsome, older, probably forty, with streaks of white in his dark hair. His jaw was accented with dark stubble. She couldn't see the color of his eyes. His navy blue zip-up sweater looked like cashmere. Juliet thought, Great, another money manager coming to the island. Then she considered her own clothes—skinny jeans, high black leather boots, black turtleneck.

He raised his head and caught her staring. His eyes were blue. Intensely blue with those extra thick black lashes that only guys seemed to get. He smiled at her. Juliet smiled at him. Their gazes held. Juliet felt herself flush and dropped her eyes.

Hello, sunshine! her body said. Stop it, she told herself. He was undoubtedly married with at least two kids. His wife probably had long blond hair, not short dark hair that she hacked off around chin-level whenever she felt like it.

"Bumpy ride," he said.

She looked up. "It is," she agreed.

"It doesn't seem to bother you," he said.

She shrugged. "I'm used to it. I grew up on the island."

"Did you really?"

A woman in the booth behind him snored explosively.

"Do you mind?" He gestured, rising.

"Sure," Juliet replied.

He stood up—he was tall. He moved around to sit across from her. "I'm Ryder Hastings." He held out his hand.

Juliet shook his hand. It was firm, warm, and smooth. So not a manual laborer. "Juliet Hawley."

"And you grew up on Nantucket?"

"I did. My mom still lives here. I'm on my way to visit her. I live in Boston."

"Are you a student?"

"No!" she replied sharply. She hated that he thought she was so young. But she had to admit, dressed as she was, she looked like a student. "I work in tech. For Kazaam." She was not about to tell him she programmed a website about dogs.

"Oh, so you live in Cambridge."

"Yes, well, uh, I always say Boston because some people think Cambridge means I live in England. Cambridge, England." She wanted to slap her forehead because a man who looked this sophisticated would know that Cambridge, Massachusetts, was just across the river from Boston.

Ryder laughed. "Yeah, I know. I live in Marblehead. I'm with Ocean Matters, a group working on changes in coastal towns."

"Tell me more."

"Okay. So, we're private, and privately funded. We're concerned with rising seas, water quality, water pollution, coastal erosion, the loss of eelgrass, that sort of thing. We work with the commonwealth and all of the country's east coast from the top of Maine down to the tip of Florida. It's all one coastline, after all."

"I guess we don't think of ourselves as being part of the East Coast," Juliet mused. "But of course we are."

"By *we,* you mean Nantucket?"

Juliet nodded. *How long are you going to be on the island?* she wanted to ask.

Ryder said, "Nantucket's ecosystem is tied directly to the main coastline. A great white shark has an appetizer near Martha's Vineyard, an entrée at Chatham, and dessert at Great Point."

Juliet grinned. Before she could reply, the captain's voice came over the loudspeaker. "Ladies and Gentlemen, we're now arriving at Nantucket. Would all drivers please return to your cars on the lower deck. Everyone else, please use the stairs on the starboard side."

Through the window, Juliet could see the lights of the town and the cheerful blink of the stubby Brant Point lighthouse. The ferry slowed and groaned as it turned toward the dock.

"I'd better get organized," Ryder said. "It was nice talking to you."

"Nice talking with you, too," Juliet said.

It didn't take long for her to close her computer and slide it into her backpack. She pulled on her leather jacket. Ryder Hastings had already headed toward the stairs, and she was glad. He was too *everything* for her, too old, too posh, too just plain *much.*

The ferry butted the dock, bounced, butted again. Chains clanked, men yelled orders as the crew roped the ramp safely to the boat, and passengers filed off one by one. Juliet was several people behind Ryder, so she took her time getting off, letting others go in front of her. She wanted to see who picked Ryder up, who greeted him, perhaps with a hug and a kiss.

She was pleased to see Ryder walk over to the taxi stand and climb into a Chief's Cab. It was ten-fifteen, and the streets were dark, but Juliet's home was only a few blocks away on Fair Street. She walked. She liked walking through the small town. All the shops were closed, but laughter came from the Brotherhood restaurant and a kid on a skateboard whizzed down Centre Street. She smiled. Here the sidewalks were clear and dry. Possibly, just when everyone thought spring was here, a week of tempests would blitz the island. But tonight it was only cold and windy.

She passed her mother's shop, turned down Fair Street, nodded hello to the handsome stone Episcopal church, and kept on walking toward her home, where she'd bet her mother was lying in bed with a cup of hot cocoa and a good mystery. She had her own key, but she didn't want to alarm her mother by just walking in the door, so Juliet dug out her phone.

"Hi, Mom, hey, you sound out of breath."

"Hi, sweetheart. How are you?"

"Great. I'm on Fair Street. I'll be home in about a minute."

"You what?" Her mother clicked off.

Odd. No point calling again, she was almost there.

Juliet put her key in the lock, opened the door, and stepped inside.

Immediate bliss. Warmth and the perfume of flowers. She called, "I'm home!"

"Hello, darling, what a surprise!" Lisa wore khakis and a light blue sweater with a swirly scarf. She looked exceptionally pretty, and her cheeks were suspiciously red.

"Are you okay, Mom?" Juliet walked forward to embrace her mother. "Do you have the flu?"

Her mother laughed, a little hysterically, Juliet thought.

"No, dear, I'm fine. I was just . . . um, you know I'm having work done on the house, and with this wind I thought I heard a, um, loose window, so I called Mack Whitney, you know, Beth's father, well, he's the carpenter who's helping renovate the house—and he came over to help. Otherwise, you know, I'd be worried all night. Come meet him."

Her mother took her hand and pulled her into the living room where a handsome man sat on the sofa, looking as if he'd been there for quite a while.

Mack rose and shook Juliet's hand. "It's nice to see you."

"Hello, Mr. Whitney," Juliet said politely. She could feel her mother's eyes on her, imploring her to be good. "I thought I'd surprise my mother and come home sort of spontaneously."

"Well, you achieved that goal," her mother said with a laugh. "Mack, I think we left your coat in the kitchen."

"Right," he said. "Right." He strode into the kitchen, came back, slipping his arms into his coat as he walked. "So, Lisa," he said, "I think those shutters are fastened now. They won't slap against the house like they were doing."

"Thanks, Mack. I'll see you and the guys tomorrow morning."

Juliet kept her eyes on her mother as Lisa walked Mack to the front door. When it was shut, she waited a few beats, and then said, "You said you had trouble with a window and he said you had trouble with shutters. So which is it? Or are you *sleeping* with him?"

Lisa hesitated. She walked into the living room and sat down, patting the chair across from her. She didn't speak until Juliet dumped her backpack and sat down.

"Mack is the general contractor here. We've become good friends." Lisa blushed crimson. "Actually, it's true, we're dating, seeing each other, whatever it's called now."

"But, Mom, I'm pretty sure you're older than he is."

"I *am* older than he is. By ten years."

"Oh, Mom!" Juliet stood up as if to walk out of the room. Instead, she sat back down. "Mom, are you sure this is wise?"

"Wise?" Lisa smiled. "Why are you worried about that?"

"Because you've got to know he's going to drop you for someone younger and you'll get your heart broken and I don't want you to be hurt."

Lisa leaned back in her chair, crossed her arms over her chest, and tightened her lips. "Somehow you've managed to be both loving and insulting at the same time. Look, Juliet, all this is really none of your business. You don't want me checking on who you're sleeping with. You've been out of this house for almost ten years. I don't break into your apartment at ten o'clock at night, do I?"

Juliet flushed. "Mommy, are you saying this isn't my home anymore?"

"Of course not. Don't be ridiculous. Sweetheart, this will always be your home." Lisa walked into the kitchen. "Come on. Let me make you some hot chocolate."

Juliet followed her mother into the kitchen. "I'd rather have a glass of wine."

Lisa said, "Oh, good. I wasn't really up for making cocoa." She settled into a chair and leaned her arms on the kitchen table. "The red wine is already open. There, on the counter."

"Would you like a glass?" Juliet asked her mother.

"No, thanks. I've already had some."

Juliet poured a glass and sipped the wine.

Lisa gave Juliet an appraising look. "So, how are you, darling? Why the surprise visit?"

Juliet cleared her throat. "Work can be . . . stressful. My boss is leaving for New York, so we'll all have to get used to some new boss, but that's not such a big deal. I just wanted, I don't know, to spend some time at home."

"How long are you planning to stay?" Lisa asked.

Juliet bridled. "What, is there a time limit now? Because you want to be alone with your boy toy?"

Lisa smiled gently. "Juliet. Of course not."

Juliet sat across from her. For a moment, Juliet noticed the gray streaks in her mother's hair, and a rush of love swirled through her. When she was in her early teens, Juliet had seen a therapist who had helped her understand that because Juliet couldn't take her anger out on her shit of an absent father, she took her anger out on her mother. Juliet understood, but that didn't make her anger disappear.

"It's the weekend and I'm done with my work, or I can finish it from here, and I, um, thought I was getting a cold." Juliet didn't want to tell her mother that her heart had been broken, but here in her childhood home, with her darling mother looking so concerned, the words spilled out. "Okay, I'm not getting a cold. I've been dumped. Brutally." Tears rose to her eyes.

"Tell me," Lisa said.

"He was my boss. Hugh Jeffers. He's smart and sophisticated. When he asked me out, I was thrilled. He's so—*superior.* He took me to ballets and operas, and he has a piano in his apartment. He wrote a song about me." At this, Juliet broke into sobs. "I thought he loved me. Then a week ago, he suddenly announced to the entire office that he was moving to New York and a new administrator would take his place. Oh, Mom, he didn't even tell me in person! He didn't call me. I had to call him, and he was so *cold.*"

Lisa rose from her chair, moved around the table, and bent to hug Juliet tightly. "I'm sorry, Juliet. So sorry."

Juliet leaned into her mother's sympathy and cried until she felt all emptied out. "Thanks, Mom." She reached across the table for a paper napkin and blew her nose.

"Honey, use a tissue," Juliet said. She moved the box of tissues from the small desk area to the table. "A tissue's softer. That napkin will chafe your skin."

Juliet burst out laughing. "Oh, Mom, you're always such a mom!"

Lisa returned to her chair. "I guess I am."

"Well, thank you." Juliet wiped her eyes and sat up straight. "Sorry to be so pathetic. I suppose I thought I'd come home and sleep in my own bed and spend the days watching television in my flannel pajamas snuggled in a quilt on the sofa."

Lisa smiled. "And I would bring you grilled cheese sandwiches and make a big pot of vegetable soup."

"Yeah. That, too."

"I can certainly do that, but you might want to watch TV in my room. I bought a wide-screen since you were here last. The downstairs is going to be filled with hammers and saws and music."

"I'll probably keep to my room. I can watch stuff on my computer."

"I think we should go to bed. We've both had a long day. Sleep is a great healer."

Juliet and her mother went through the

comforting routines they'd had for years. Double-checking the front and back doors. Turning off all the lights except the small nightlight in the kitchen. Going upstairs to their rooms, calling good night.

At the door to her bedroom, Lisa turned. "Juliet?"

Juliet answered, "Yes?"

"How old was this Hugh Jeffers?"

Juliet shrugged. "Thirty-six. Maybe thirty-seven."

"Right." Lisa smiled. "Good night, sweetheart." She went into her room.

Juliet cocked her head. What did her mother mean?

As soon as she asked herself the question, she knew the answer. Juliet had fallen for a man ten years older than she was. So was it wrong that her mother fell in love with a man ten years younger than she was?

Well, Juliet decided, he'd better not break her mother's heart.

Lisa had an en suite bathroom but Juliet and Theo shared the bathroom at the top of the stairs. Lord, the arguments Juliet and Theo had had. He was such a guy. Tiny whiskers all over the sink after he shaved. They looked like bugs. Why couldn't he use a paper towel and leave the sink clean? Not to mention the soggy towels and sweaty sports clothes he left on the floor.

In high school, when Theo was such a god, so gorgeous, so hunky, with girls swarming around him, Juliet had threatened to take photos of the way he left his bedroom and their bathroom, but Theo only laughed, not worried at all.

In her old bedroom, Juliet stripped off her city clothes and pulled on a pair of old pajamas she'd left in her chest of drawers. Her bed was neatly made up, her nightstand stacked as usual with a pile of books and a box of tissues. A small high-tech reading light was attached to the post of her bed. She turned off the overhead light and the reading light cast a clear white glow onto her pillow. A little full moon. She crawled in, pulled up the covers, gazed at her familiar walls, and lay thinking about physical attraction, the whims of fate, and if there really was anything like true love.

six

Six weeks ago, Theo had ended a spectacular ride at Newport Beach getting slammed by The Wedge to the bottom of the sea. Massive adrenaline rush, but he'd fractured his humerus and yes, he was bored of humorous puns, and he also had a minor concussion. After the X-ray, the doctors assured him he didn't need surgery, but he'd been in the hospital for a few days, then in a clamshell brace (a clamshell brace, so how could he not think of Nantucket?) for almost a month, and now he wore a sling. The swelling was gone but he still took the oxy. His doctor said to keep taking the oxy and gradually switch out to Tylenol as the pain eased.

You're supposed to get away from home, right? Theo had done the best he could to start his own life anew. But the oxycodone that the doctor prescribed for him made him think of Atticus, and Atticus made him think of his home clear across the continent, which made him think of Beth, who he had loved all his life and who never knew it.

But what a douche he was to be feeling sorry for himself here, when he was still alive, a short walk to the Pacific Ocean, with only a pretty much healed fractured humerus. And Atticus was dead. Had been dead for too many years.

Theo had been best friends with Atticus ever since they were kids. They walked into the Small Friends preschool, bonded immediately, and kept on like that into middle school. Both were handsome (both knew it, how could they not, with the attention they got from girls), energetic, and smart. Theo was the blond jock. Atticus was the black-haired stormy intellectual with the Heathcliff vibe that made girls crazy for him. They'd been best friends, not really interested in girls.

In eighth grade, it started to change. They had talked about girls, made dumb crass jokes that they could never say in front of their parents, but slowly they both became more respectful. Partly because of the mandatory life science class, partly because of their own turbulent hormones.

They noticed Beth Whitney at the same time. Well, they'd known her forever, of course, but they *really* noticed her the summer after ninth grade when they were all swimming at Surfside. She'd gone from little girl to gorgeous overnight, it seemed. When she peeled off her shirt and ran down to the water in her bikini, Theo said, "Well, damn," and Atticus said, "Agreed."

It wasn't just teenage lust, it was also that Beth was so nice, and funny, and smart, and well, sunny. They both had classes with her, and their high school was relatively small, so they said hi when they passed in the halls, but one day Theo went to get something out of his locker and he saw Atticus in the hall and Beth standing next to him, looking up at him, smiling.

Theo and Atticus had always walked home together. By that spring, Beth walked with them. Atticus was always in the middle, and often he and Beth held hands. Theo wondered if this was how it felt to have a broken heart, a searing pain from his collarbone to his guts that burned him even as he smiled and joked with the other two. Maybe it was also raging jealousy. He stopped walking home with them, staying late for a game of basketball or just goofing around, anything to let them have their space. By their junior year, Atticus and Beth were a definite couple. Theo started seeing other girls. He could pretty much see any girl he wanted, which was vain of him, he knew, but it was also true, and it also sucked because the only girl he wanted was Beth.

Late on a Saturday morning in the early spring of his senior year, his mother rapped on his bedroom door. "You've got a visitor."

"Fine," Theo called, yawning. He was just lying there staring at the ceiling, feeling sorry for himself. "Let him in."

The door opened and there was Beth.

"Hey!" Theo cried, scrambling to sit up in bed.

He wore only his boxers to sleep in, so he was naked from his waist up.

"Sorry to wake you," Beth said. She was all long blond hair and big green eyes and tight jeans and a loose sweater. "Can we talk for a moment?"

"Um, sure."

Beth perched on the end of his bed. "It's about Atticus."

Of course it was about Atticus, Theo thought. "What about him?"

"You are his best friend. His closest friend. You've been avoiding him lately, and so you probably haven't noticed, but he's gotten kind of . . . depressed."

"You think it's because I'm avoiding him?"

"I don't know. I mean, he told me he has these moods sometimes. His parents want him to see a psychiatrist, but of course he won't. So maybe it's not you, but I think he might talk more honestly to you."

Theo was having trouble simply dealing with the fact that Beth Whitney, in all her beauty, was sitting on the end of his bed. He couldn't get his, um, mind past that. "What do you want me to do?"

"Call him up. Hang out with him. Like even tonight. I'm going to a sleepover with friends. It would be the perfect time to see him."

Theo brought his knees to his chest, keeping

the sheet over them, and folded his arms on his knees. “You really love him, don’t you?”

Beth turned bright pink. “Sure, I love him, I mean I care for him, but he’s not . . . not my one true love.” She couldn’t look at Theo. “I mean, he’s so smart and he can be so funny, but he can be hard work at times, and I feel more like his, oh, psychiatric nurse than his girlfriend.” She covered her face with her hands. “That’s an awful thing to say, isn’t it?”

“So would you ever, um, date someone else?”

Beth looked at Theo. She was still bright pink. “I couldn’t, Theo, not while Atticus is so unhappy.”

For one long moment, Theo’s eyes met Beth’s, and a warmth spread through his chest, through his limbs, through his face.

They both looked away.

“I’ll call Atticus and see about tonight,” Theo promised.

“Thanks, Theo.” Beth flashed him a quick smile as she rose. As she went out his door, she turned back. “Bye.”

After he heard the front door shut, Theo rose, showered, dressed, and went into the kitchen to have breakfast.

Then he called Atticus.

“Hey, I haven’t seen you in forever. Can I pull you away from your girlfriend and hang out tonight?”

There was a long pause. "I don't know, Theo. I'm kind of in a bad mood."

"Oh, and this is something new?" Theo taunted.

"Fine. Let's meet at the Jetties."

They met at the playground in the dunes. In his backpack Theo carried a six-pack of beer he'd stolen from his mother's supply. They sat on the swings for a while, idly drinking.

"How's Beth?" Theo asked, hoping he sounded casual.

Atticus shrugged. "Annoying."

"What?"

"Maybe it's not her fault. Maybe I think everyone's annoying these days."

"What do your parents say?"

"They want me to see a shrink."

"That might be a good idea." Theo gazed out at the water as he spoke, not wanting to get too intense about Atticus's depression.

"I've got a better idea."

"Oh?"

"Let's walk." Atticus rose and headed around the turn where the sharp dark rocks of the jetties began.

Theo ambled along beside him. The water was calm, the waves splashing quietly on the beach. Far in the distance a ferry light glowed. It was spring, but it was still cold. Both guys wore jackets.

"Here's a good place," Atticus said. He dropped down in the shallow sand between two dunes.

Theo sat next to him. "Want another beer?"

"Not yet. No. I want you to try this." Atticus reached into his pocket, pulled out a plastic vial, and shook a couple of white pills into his hand.

"What is it?"

"Oxy."

"Oh, man." Theo shook his head. "Don't do that."

"Hey, I do it almost every night, and believe me, it's the best high I've ever had."

"It's addictive, Atticus."

"It's addictive, Atticus," Atticus mocked in a whiny voice. "Look, try one. One won't get you hooked. If you want to know what I've been up to, this is it."

"Atticus, come on."

"You come on. Don't be a wuss."

Reluctantly, Theo took a pill.

"Chew it up. It will get in your system faster. Doesn't taste good, but wash it down with some beer."

Theo obeyed. "So you'd rather be out here doing this with me than be with Beth?" he asked.

"Beth's too conservative. She won't try it with me. She's become a real nag."

"That's a shit thing to say, Atticus," Theo said. "What's wrong with you? She's a . . ." The rush hit him. "Wow," he said. "I've got to lie down."

Theo fell back against the sand and lay there with an odd gentle ecstasy rushing through his veins. "I really love you, man," he said to Atticus.

"Yeah, bro. Me, too."

Maybe an hour later, Theo woke up to find himself alone in the dune. He called for Atticus, but no answer came. He sat for a while, thinking about the experience. He'd been drunk before, and in high school his sister had brought home some pot and they'd smoked it out in the yard while their mom was at a friend's house. Unfortunately, they both discovered pot made them anxious, a terrible gripping anxiety causing them to think they couldn't breathe. They sat outside trying to calm each other, laughing hysterically as the marijuana faded, and Theo vowed he'd never try it again.

Well, oxy was different. He'd totally found that out, and it had been a rush, but not one he wanted to repeat. He liked being in charge of himself. He was learning to surf, and surfing was a natural high, an exhilaration and sense of triumph and a feeling of being truly plugged in to the world.

Eventually Theo pulled himself together and went home. The next morning, Atticus phoned.

Without preamble, Atticus asked, "How did you like *that?*"

"Truthfully? It was cool. But not for me. I

don't want to get addicted. I want to get better at surfing this summer. I—"

Atticus interrupted. "You know what? You are the most boring guy I've ever met. Screw you."

"Wait, what?" Theo asked.

But Atticus had ended the call.

Theo was miserable all that Sunday, wondering if he should call Beth and tell her what happened, then hating himself for using Atticus as a reason to call Beth, and wondering if he should just go over to Atticus's house and talk to him, but remembering the times Atticus had been in a funk before, and nothing but time had cured him.

"Is anything wrong?" his mom asked late in the afternoon.

"Yeah. I'm worried about Atticus. He's kind of depressed." Theo seldom talked intimately with his mother these days, but he thought he might explode if he didn't.

"Yes, we're all worried about him," his mom said.

Theo, who'd been slumped on the sofa, watching TV, sat up straight. "You are?"

"Sweetie, it's no secret that Atticus struggles with depression. It's not anyone's fault. He might need to be on some kind of medication."

He *is* on some kind of medication, Theo thought. But he didn't tell his mom that. He didn't want to rat out his friend.

• • •

Theo was too busy with sports to see much of Atticus that spring and in a flash, high school was over. The high school graduation ceremony was liberating and terrifying, like being pushed out of a plane for a parachute fall when you weren't quite ready to jump. Atticus graduated, but he didn't show up at the ceremony or the parties, and he never answered Theo's calls. Theo was pumped to go out to California for surfing and college, and he was pretty much all about himself and getting off the island. So he gave up on trying to connect with Atticus.

That summer, Theo got a job at Young's Bicycle Shop on the strip. He liked the work. He was good at fixing bikes, good at dealing with people. On his time off, he surfed, when the waves were good enough.

One hot summer day when clouds turned the sky gray and it was one hundred percent humidity but no rain, the kind of day that made everyone grumpy, Theo was working and he saw Atticus walking by himself.

"AT!" he'd yelled. "Atticus!"

It was around noon. Most people had rented their bikes and most wouldn't return them until later, and plenty of other guys were working there, so Theo raced off down South Beach Street yelling Atticus's name.

He grabbed his friend's shoulder. "Hey, wait a minute!"

Atticus stopped.

Theo got a good look at him. "You look like Edgar Allan Poe," Theo said.

"Thanks," Atticus said, but a bit of his mouth turned up in a grin.

"What's going on with you, man?" Theo stationed himself in front of Atticus, making Atticus face him.

"Bad patch," Atticus said. "Just going through a bad patch. I broke up with Beth."

"You did? Why?"

Atticus shrugged. "She was getting on my nerves."

"Be serious."

"I am. It's for her own good, Theo. I'm no good for anyone these days. She's all excited about going off to college. I can't find the energy to write my name."

"You should see a therapist."

"I am. He told me to exercise. That's what I'm doing. Walking."

"Your parents—"

"They're doing their best. Mom smiles so much I bet her face hurts. Makes my favorite dinner every night, and I can hardly eat it." Atticus looked down at the pavement. "It's the oxy I want, Theo. I need more oxy."

"Sounds like you need rehab, not more drugs."

"Oh, man, don't get on me, too. Be my friend, okay?"

"Okay. Sure. What can I do?"

Atticus looked up, his face hopeful. "Get me some oxy?"

"Come on, Atticus. Man, you don't want to keep on this way. Tell me what I can do to help. I'll quit my job and shadow you every moment of your life, telling you jokes and making you surf and we can get drunk and you can get off the oxy."

Atticus smiled. "You're the best."

"So let's—let's meet for burgers at the Jetties tonight, okay?"

"Sorry. I've got a date with a dealer."

"Atticus, stop it!" Theo held his friend by the shoulders. "You're better than this."

Atticus kept smiling, a strange, dark, dead-eyed smile. "Actually, Theo, I'm not."

Theo dropped his hands.

Atticus walked away.

And why had Theo let him go? Why hadn't Theo done something to keep Atticus alive? Atticus was so obviously caught in the claws of a depression—or an addiction—and still he let Atticus walk away.

A few days later, Atticus committed suicide, overdosing on OxyContin. He was smart enough to know how much oxy was too much, so anyone who knew Atticus would have known he'd overdosed on purpose. And his parents informed the police and their friends that Atticus had left a suicide letter.

Theo had been grief-stricken and furious at himself and at his friend. He burned the anger and the time away by working two jobs that summer, drinking enough to help him sleep at night. In August, he drove clear across the country to attend the University of California at San Diego. He'd chosen the school because it was a short drive to some of the best surfing in the world. He took the necessary college courses, only barely passing them, because he was concentrating on surfing. Still, he graduated. Barely.

After college, he bartended all night, surfed all day, had plenty of friends and a batch of sizzling hot girlfriends who also surfed and who did not need a long-term, committed relationship. For a long time, he thought he'd died and gone to heaven.

Then, the wipeout. He felt like the ocean had betrayed him. He was in pain, and he was embarrassed.

And he was grounded. He shared an apartment with a couple of other surfer guys who were much younger than Theo. After his crash, sitting in his pajama bottoms and brace in their dark, crappy, beer-fumed apartment while the two eighteen-year-olds sauntered out in the morning with their boards ("Hey, man") and came in at night reeking of booze and weed ("Peace, man") became less and less pleasant for Theo. He began to feel righteously sorry for himself. He studied himself in the mirror and thought he already looked bloated from not getting any exercise. He checked the refrigerator and saw several six-packs of local beer—San Diego was famous for its craft beer—and a moldy chunk of cheese that he ate anyway, because he was so hungry. He could go out and find a friend or he could buy himself breakfast. He wasn't pathetic but he was acting pathetic and he hated himself for taking OxyContin, which helped with the pain but made him think of Atticus. He vowed not to take it any more, but to rely on Tylenol. Okay, Tylenol and beer. He opened the freezer door and saw nothing but a half-empty bottle of vodka so he drank some because he couldn't take more Tylenol for another two hours.

He just plain totally wanted his mother. He wanted Nantucket. He wanted to go home.

seven

Saturday afternoon, Lisa asked Juliet to attend a lecture with her. "If you don't want to come, sweetie, that's okay. I'll find someone to sit with."

"I'll come, Mom. I'd like to go." Juliet got dressed and walked down to the library with Lisa.

The lecture was held in the Great Hall of the Nantucket Atheneum. Juliet and Lisa went up the curving carpeted stairs, past the cat's eye and the figurehead, and into the main room. Almost all the chairs were filled. Juliet and Lisa hurried to take two chairs on the side. Lisa saw Mack and his daughter, Beth, several rows in front of them. How complicated—Beth was home. But how lovely, Lisa thought, smiling to herself—she could look at the beautiful back of Mack's neck during the lecture.

Sandra Martin, the director of the library, went up the four steps to the stage and the podium. It was a sign of the importance of the speaker that Sandra introduced him, but Lisa let the introduction blur past her because she was thinking of Mack.

"Ryder Hastings has a doctorate in environmental science, specializing in coastal affairs. He has served on several environmental boards, including the Harvard Environmental Science and Public Policy Board of Tutors, the Massachusetts Ocean Management Initiative, and the U.S. Coastal Research Program. He's here today to speak with us about his new organization, Ocean Matters."

Lisa straightened in her seat to see the speaker. He was tall and handsome, probably in his thirties. Were there no single men in their fifties?

Ryder thanked Sandra and began his talk with the usual how-nice-of-you-to-come-out-today, allowing Lisa time to stare frankly at the man. After all, everyone else was.

He said, "I'd like to begin my talk with a quote from the National Geographic Explorer-in-Residence, Sylvia Earle. Sylvia is a marine biologist and legendary oceanographer whose documentary *Mission Blue* is available on Netflix.

"Sylvia Earle said: *'If we fail to take care of the ocean, nothing else matters.'*"

Ryder waited as his audience muttered agreement. For the next half hour, he spoke passionately about how seventy-one percent of the planet was ocean, and how too many creatures and plants in the ocean were dying. How the ocean was the world's largest carbon dioxide sink. Ninety-three percent of the planet's carbon dioxide was stored in vegetation, algae, and coral under the sea. But it couldn't keep up with the carbon that man's use of fossil fuels was adding to the atmosphere. Added to that was the problem of plastics, pollution, and overfishing.

Ryder illustrated his speech with PowerPoint images, and he ended by listing the ways people could help the ocean. He mentioned his organization, Ocean Matters, and told them how to join up, how to find the website, and the names of several relevant sites.

The applause at the end of his talk was enthusiastic, not a great surprise because he was talking to people who lived on an island. Afterward, people gathered around the hospitality table to pour themselves a paper cup of lemonade and take a cookie or two. Others stood in line to talk with Ryder, including Juliet and Lisa, waiting their turn.

When they reached the lecturer, Ryder said, "Hi, Juliet. It's great to see you here."

"Hi, Ryder." Juliet nodded toward Lisa. "This is my mother, Lisa Hawley. She lives here year-round."

"Yes," Lisa said, "and I'm most interested in your ideas and your organization."

"Let me give you my card," Ryder said. "I'd like to find someone to head a chapter of Ocean Matters here on the island."

Lisa took the card. "I'm sorry I can't do it,

because I support everything you said. But I own a shop on Main Street and summer is crazy."

From behind her shoulder, Prudence Starbuck, an island native in her seventies, spoke up. "I'd be glad to help."

"Nice meeting you," Lisa said to Ryder as she moved away.

"Nice meeting you," Ryder answered. "And nice seeing you again, Juliet."

Juliet flushed at the warmth in his gaze. She hurried off to speak to a friend. Lisa spotted Mack at the round table with the punch bowl in the middle. She headed his way.

"Hey," she said. "How are you?"

"Good." Leaning forward, he said in a low voice, "You look very kissable."

Lisa grinned. "So do you. But my daughter's here."

"And so is mine."

"I thought I saw her sitting with you. When did she get here?"

"Last night. With her master's finished, she's home and looking for a job."

"We're headed into tourist season. She'll have no trouble finding work." Lisa turned to search for Beth. "I haven't seen her for years."

"She's there. In the blue dress."

"Oh, she's lovely." Lisa sighed. "Theo's been in California for seven years. I'm not sure he'll ever come back."

"Actually," Mack said with a grin, "that's fine with me. I'd like to be the only male in your life."

Lisa felt herself blush. "Mack—" She wanted to tell him to *stop* because other people crowded next to the table for punch. She almost hated it when Mack spoke seductively. It reminded her of Erich, who'd been a magician with words and an adulterous husband and a cruelly absent father. She couldn't say all this to Mack, not here, not now. It almost made her dizzy, feeling so attracted to him and at the same time so frightened.

From across the room, Lisa met her daughter's eye and understood the slight sideways motion of her head. Time to leave.

"I've got to go," Lisa told Mack. She was aware of several Nantucket acquaintances watching them, so she said politely, "Good to see you." She slipped from the group and joined her daughter.

"Do you want to say hello to anyone else?" Lisa asked.

Juliet shook her head. "No, thanks."

They went down the curving stairs, out the tall white doors, and down the steps to the brick sidewalk.

"How do you know Ryder Hastings?" Lisa asked.

"I met him on the boat coming over," Juliet said.

"He seems nice."

Juliet shrugged. “His work is certainly important.”

“I wish I had the time to help out.”

Juliet said, “I would help if I spent more time here.”

“You know you’re always welcome.”

The wind was rising, whispering through their hair.

“We should drive out to Surfside tomorrow to see the waves,” Juliet said. Immediately she corrected herself. “I mean, I should. I don’t want to mess up your schedule. I mean, if you’re planning something with Mack.”

“Oh, I think Mack and I can resist each other for a day or two,” Lisa answered, laughter in her voice.

“Good,” Juliet said churlishly. “Sorry to be so childish.”

Lisa linked arms with Juliet. “You *are* a child. You are *my* child. I love you and Theo best of all. You know that.” As they turned the corner onto Fair Street, Lisa said, “Let’s get a pizza and watch a movie tonight.”

“Great idea,” Juliet agreed.

eight

The next morning, Lisa and Juliet drove out to Surfside. The south beach had always been Juliet's go-to place when she had a problem. The yielding sand, the flashing light of the waves, the whirling wind, all cleared her thoughts.

Today, though, Ryder Hastings's lecture ran through her mind. Of course when she was a kid in school she'd learned about the ocean, about plastics caught in fish stomachs, in turtle throats. She'd seen films of dead whales with a frightening assortment of human-created debris in their stomachs. She'd seen the birds and fish helplessly trapped in a thick coat of oil in the Gulf of Mexico from the BP oil spill. She'd taken tests on the information, and aced the tests, but she hadn't become a crusader. Looking out at the gleaming blue waves that replenished her soul, she experienced a pang of guilt.

She wondered what her brother thought about all this. Theo lived for surfing out there on the California coast. He must care. Maybe he was involved in some kind of protest or clean-water effort. He could act brainless, but he had a good heart. They talked or texted now and then, but they weren't close. She kind of missed him. She'd text him sometime, maybe tonight.

On their way from the beach, Juliet thought about bus schedules to Boston. She'd love to stay on the island, but she really had to get back to Kazaam. Although . . . she often worked at home when she didn't feel like fighting through a blizzard, and that was never a problem. Maybe . . .

When they walked in the front door, Juliet could smell the delicious aroma of tomato, garlic, and olive oil. Her mother's spaghetti sauce was simmering in the slow cooker.

"That smells fantastic," Juliet said, giving her mother a hug.

"Thanks, sweetie. I've made an extra batch for you to take home."

But this *is home,* Juliet thought.

Before she could think twice, she said, "Mom, what if I came here for the summer?"

Lisa was in the kitchen, stirring the sauce. "Could you do that? I mean, with your work?"

"Sure. Almost everything I do is online, even communicating with the others in our office. Well, I'd have to okay it with the new boss, and I'd probably have to go back a couple of times, but I'm sure I could make it work from here." As she talked, Juliet's spirits rose. "I'd love to work all morning and swim all afternoon. I could see my old friends. And I could help you. Summer is the busiest time at your shop. I could take over buying groceries and cooking."

Lisa settled the lid back on the slow cooker. Leaning against the counter, she folded her arms. "Does this have anything to do with Mack? Do you feel you need to keep an eye on me in case I do something stupid?"

"Honestly, that never crossed my mind." Juliet grinned. "But now that you mention it . . ."

"It would be nice to have you here for a while," Lisa said. "But wouldn't the noise of the carpenters drive you crazy?"

"It gets noisy in the office, you know. And I could hole up with my laptop in my room and wear headphones."

"Well, think about it. You know you're always welcome."

"Thanks, Mom." Juliet crossed the room and hugged her mother. Feeling the comfort of her mother's embrace, Juliet said, "Going back into the office makes me so sad. It would be so much better if I came home for a while."

Lisa held Juliet away from her, but kept her hands on Juliet's shoulders. "You're a brilliant woman, Juliet. You can walk into that office like a star."

Juliet pouted. "So you don't want me here?"

Lisa gave Juliet one of her *Mom* looks—affection mixed with exasperation. "You know that's not what I said."

Juliet smiled. "I know. And I will go back into the office tomorrow. But forget being dumped, it's fun to think of spending most of the summer here."

"Then that's what you should do."

Later, with a jar of her mother's spaghetti sauce in a padded carrier, Juliet climbed the ramp to the afternoon fast ferry to Hyannis. She settled in a booth, set up her laptop, and worked all the way over. When the ferry pulled into the harbor, she packed up and got in line with the crowd of other passengers.

As she was walking down the ramp, a familiar voice called her name. She turned.

"Ryder!"

She was glad he was a few people behind her so she could take a moment to pull herself together.

"Hey," he said. "Going to Boston? Want to ride with me? I've got a car in the lot."

"Oh, um, thanks, but I'm taking the bus."

"But I'll get you there faster, and you won't have to ride with a lot of smelly strangers."

Her natural sarcasm took over. She sniffed loud and long, pretending to recoil. "Well, not with strangers."

Ryder laughed. "Come on. I'm over here." He went ahead of her, threading his way between other travelers with rolling suitcases, wailing children, and dogs making the most of their long leashes while their owners shouldered their bags.

Juliet followed him, unable to resist studying his backside. He wore faded jeans, a white shirt, and a lightweight navy blue blazer. His thick shaggy hair covered his neck. His shoulders were broad, his long legs moved easily. She wanted to drop her backpack, race across the tarmac, and tackle him from behind, covering him with kisses right there in front of everyone.

But she was done with men.

I'll bet he drives a Mercedes, she thought, trying to chill herself away from her heated emotions.

Ryder stopped next to something resembling a spacecraft.

He drives a Tesla, Juliet said under her breath. *Of course he drives an electric car.*

Ryder turned, grinning, as if he'd heard her. "Ever been in one of these before?"

"Oh, often," Juliet retorted sarcastically, although why she had to be sarcastic she didn't understand. It was as if her mind was trying to shove her away from this man while her body wanted to jump him.

"You'll like it. It's quiet." He reached out his hand.

Juliet took a step back.

"Let me put your bag in the back," Ryder said, amused.

Juliet slid the straps off her shoulders and

handed it to him. She opened the passenger door and stepped into the car. “Wow,” she said aloud. The interior was impressively spacious.

“Like it?” Ryder asked as he slid into the driver’s seat.

“Very much.” Juliet tried to keep a hard edge. “It must have cost a fortune.”

“Maybe. But every little bit helps the environment.” Ryder spoke casually, but met her gaze. There it was, that spark between them. With a smile, he added, “Electric is good.”

Juliet wondered if he was acknowledging the connection between them or just talking about his car.

They drove out of the parking lot, through Hyannis, and onto the highway, where the car accelerated swiftly and smoothly.

“I feel like I’m in a vehicle that’s half Aladdin’s carpet and half spaceship,” Juliet said.

“I know, right? It’s the car of the future. Within five years, there will be more electric cars on the roads than internal combustion cars.”

Juliet didn’t respond. She always chose not to talk about matters she really knew nothing about, and sitting next to Ryder Hastings, it seemed she knew nothing about almost everything.

After a comfortable silence, Ryder asked, “Music?”

“Sure.”

Ryder chose a classical station and the car filled

with such lilting, peaceful music Juliet felt lifted to another sphere. What an irresistible man, she thought, who could combine the future and the past so effortlessly.

"What did you think of my talk?" Ryder asked.

"I thought it was great. Important. Your organization sounds like it will make a significant change around here."

"We're certainly going to try," Ryder said. "And not just on the East Coast."

"Isn't there a new boat that trawls for plastic?"

"There is. But it disturbs the ocean environment."

"Wow." Juliet slumped, feeling sad. "The human animal is a bad creature."

Ryder quietly disagreed. "Not always. Not all of us."

She shot him a cynical look. "Like you, for instance?"

"And like you."

Juliet snorted. "I work for Kazaam. I build websites about cute domestic animals. I keep the websites running and organize teams all over the country. Fun, but not what you'd call environmental work."

Ryder gave her a warm glance. "I read a study that watching cute animal videos can lower blood pressure. So you can consider yourself a health worker."

Juliet laughed. "Right. And what do you

consider yourself? A saint?" As soon as she spoke the word, she cringed.

"You seem kind of antagonistic toward me," Ryder said calmly.

Juliet bristled. She took a deep annoying breath as various yoga friends had advised her. "I suppose I do," she answered honestly. "I apologize. I guess it's the typical islander reaction to a wealthy new know-it-all setting foot on Nantucket and telling us what to do, and then doing it because you have so much money regardless of what we think."

"Yeah," Ryder said. "I get that." He was quiet a moment, thinking. "Or," he said, "it could be something else."

With a smooth roll of his wrist, he steered the car into a rest stop. He shut off the ignition, unfastened his seatbelt, and twisted in his seat, facing her.

"What are you doing?" Juliet asked.

"This." Ryder put his hand on Juliet's chin, tilted her face to meet his, bent forward, and kissed her mouth.

It was sugar. It was satin. It was fire.

Juliet couldn't pull away, didn't want to pull away. She leaned into the kiss, closing her eyes, drinking in the pleasure with all her senses.

Ryder sat back, giving her space, his eyes on hers. "I've been wanting to do that since I saw you on the ferry."

Juliet was trembling, and she'd never been quite so terrified in her life. "So this is the way you attract people to your causes."

"Right," Ryder agreed with a grin. "I found it especially effective on Prudence Starbuck."

Juliet smiled at the thought of Ryder kissing the starchy old Puritan. "I don't know you."

"You haven't googled me?"

Proudly, truthfully, she said, "No." Had she ever wanted anyone this much? No. Not even Hugh Jeffers. Part of that attraction, she had to admit, had been that he was her boss. She'd believed he thought she was the smartest employee, the cream of the crop, a future team leader. Their relationship had been secretive and she'd liked that, too. It made her feel more special.

But love? She wasn't sure she'd ever really been in love, and what she felt for Ryder was like the achingly powerful crushes she'd had on Justin Timberlake and Chris Hemsworth. Part infatuation mixed with the knowledge that it was hopeless.

Ryder told her, "I'm thirty-five. Divorced. Clementine has remarried and is happy. I live alone in my family's house in Marblehead. Oh, Greta also lives with me." He waited for her to ask who Greta was. When she didn't, he continued, "She's our housekeeper. In her sixties, now, but my mother calls her 'a wonder.' I travel a lot, mostly up and down the East Coast, but really anywhere I can get a group to listen to me." He paused. "I'm not seeing anyone else. I haven't been interested in anyone for a long time. Not until I saw you."

"So you want to take me to bed," Juliet said bluntly.

Ryder's gaze was intense. "Of course I want to take you to bed. But I'm in no rush. I want to get to know you."

I'm way in over my head, Juliet thought. She kept her tone light, sassy. "Okay, what do you want to know?"

Ryder turned on the engine and checked his rearview mirror. The traffic was steady but not congested. He pulled back onto the highway. "Tell me about your family. Your parents."

"This feels like a therapy session."

"All right, then, I'll tell you about mine. They're charming, cultured, well-traveled alcoholics. They both inherited money. They support each other's drinking. They have friends who also drink. They live in Boston and Boca Raton and London. We are not estranged, but we're not close."

"Do you have any siblings?"

"I do. One sister. Two years older. She's become a sort of free spirit. With her inheritance money, she bought a farm in Vermont where she raises alpaca. Her name is Eugenie, but she calls herself Engine, because she wants to be an engine of change. She's living with a woman, Kate, now, but for a long time she had a male partner. She doesn't drink alcohol but she certainly does eat food. She's a big girl, and she says so herself, and she's happy with that. Actually, she's very beautiful, like the goddess of the harvest. Long black hair in braids tied with string or rope. No makeup, very tan even in winter, carries herself like a queen. She's got lots of friends who stay in some of her guest houses and help with the farm."

"You love your sister," Juliet observed with silent envy. How would Theo describe *her?* She could imagine: *smart with sharp edges.*

"I adore her. She's so emotionally strong. So certain. She wants to—well, what we jokingly call 'save the world'—she wants to help the world, too, but she's chosen to do it in a way that makes her happy. She has an idyllic home."

"Your own home isn't idyllic?"

Ryder drove for a while without speaking. "As I've told you, I'm divorced. It was a short, unpleasant marriage that made our parents ecstatic and made us miserable. So, I've been single for years. I've seen other women now and then. No one special."

An unexpected flash of jealousy surprised Juliet when Ryder mentioned other women.

"Your turn now," Ryder said.

"Hmm." Juliet leaned back against the headrest. "My mother, Lisa, well, you met her. She's wonderful. Especially admirable because our father left her for another woman when were young. So basically, we're a three-person family."

"Do you ever visit your father?"

"No. We've never been invited. I haven't even seen a picture of him for years. When we were kids, Mom used to show us photos of our father holding us when we were babies, and she impressed upon us what an intelligent man he was. He's a banker, and he also inherited a nice chunk of money, so he always made the child support payments on time. Mother appreciated that. But when you're little, you don't get it about the money. You don't understand why your dad doesn't want to see you."

"I'm sorry."

Juliet shrugged. "It was harder on Theo, not having a dad around. It made us both feel . . . not exactly worthless, but not worth much. Theo had a tough time in high school and thank heavens, he discovered surfing. I think he got rid of his anger that way. Now he's out in San Diego, a chill surfer dude."

"And you?"

"Me." Juliet thought. "You could say I have a problem trusting men. The last relationship I had was bizarre. He had to move to New York, and he didn't tell me in advance or ask me to go with him. Well, I don't suppose I would have wanted to go. We weren't *crazy* for each other. I was hurt when he left, but mostly I was so insulted. So, well, there's that."

"He sounds like an idiot."

"I think he was more of a user." Juliet watched the road fly past, all the cars and trucks changing lanes to go faster. Something about Ryder's words, the way he made her feel admired and comfortable, helped her think. "And you know? I'm not sure I want to love anyone. My mother, who is totally wonderful, got dumped by our father and we were abandoned, too. So I'm not comfortable trusting anyone. But I'm fine. I'm really good at my job. It's fun. It pays well. I can work from anywhere as long as I have a computer. I've got a good apartment and great friends in Cambridge." She paused, laughing. "Could I sound any more boring? All I lack is the cliché cat."

"I don't think you're boring. And from my point of view, I don't think anyone on the island thinks you're boring, either. I've seen people look at you with envy. Admiration."

"Really?" Juliet was shocked. "Where?"

"At my lecture at the Atheneum. I saw some guys checking you out."

"Ryder, lower the volume, please. I know those guys. They were probably trying to see if I've become a lesbian."

"Oh, you can tell that by looking?"

Juliet laughed.

"We're almost there," Ryder said. "Let me take you out to dinner Tuesday night. Just dinner, nothing else."

"Fine," she answered carelessly, hoping she didn't sound as frightened, amazed, and attracted as she felt. "That will be fun."

nine

Sometimes, Beth thought, a person really needs life to give them a sign.

When she woke on the first day of June, her third morning home, her bed and her childhood bedroom had seemed odd, as if they belonged to another person, and in a way, they had. Of course if she had to, she could walk through the entire house blindfolded, but this house had belonged to a different person, a girl who had been knocked down by fate before she had time to grow up.

On her bedside table was the framed photo of her as a little girl with her father and her mother. She'd been only two when the picture was taken, and she didn't remember that moment, but she cherished the photograph that proved it had existed. Her mother had existed, had loved her, so long ago, and might even be somewhere loving her still.

Next to that picture was one of Atticus. The glass was cracked because one day years ago, in a fit of rage at Atticus for killing himself, she had picked up the photo and carried it out to the trash barrel and tossed it in, slamming down the lid as hard as she could. That night she hadn't been able to fall asleep until she quietly retrieved the picture. She would never see him alive again, but she needed to have him with her somehow. And the cracked glass over his face seemed somehow appropriate, because he was broken. She never got a new one.

Beth pulled on a light summer dress and flip-flops. Her father called out to her, "See you tonight!" and left for work. She found fresh coffee waiting for her, and in the middle of the kitchen table, a box of Cinnamon Toast Crunch, which had been her favorite cereal when she was a child.

"Sweet!" she said aloud, smiling at her father's thoughtfulness.

But what she really craved was an onion bagel with cream cheese. She didn't want to hurt her father's feelings, but no way was she going to eat that sugary cereal. She wasn't a little girl anymore.

Carrying her mug, Beth walked through her home as if it were a museum. In a way it was a museum. Nothing had changed since she went away to college, seven years ago. No new furniture, no new carpet, no new drapes—one new thing, a large flat-screen on the wall in the den. Other than that, she didn't think her father had changed a thing.

But why should he? Old Persian rugs that were once his family's softened the wood floors, and the mix-and-match furniture was welcoming. The most modern place was his kitchen, with its gleaming chrome appliances and the rack over the stove, which was hung with copper-bottomed pans. The only art on the walls were three pictures Beth had painted at various times in her life. Her father had had them framed and hung around the large room.

He needed some good art. He could use a new armchair—the one he clearly favored was slightly sagging. She had usually come home from college at Thanksgiving and Christmas, and she'd also spent every summer at home, but she'd never considered the state of the house because she was working two jobs to make money for college and then for grad school and working for her master's.

And now? She wanted to brighten up the place.

First things first. She needed to get a job. She wanted to work for the Nantucket Historical Association, but they were fully staffed and now that summer was here, they would have plenty of volunteers. There were museums all over the country that needed qualified help, but Beth wanted to live and work on Nantucket. At least she thought she did. Now that she'd earned her master's degree, she had no one to report to, no deadlines to meet, no papers to write, and it seemed only natural to return to her island home.

That didn't mean she had to stay here. She wasn't locked in.

But actually, she was locked in, by her own emotions. She wanted to see Theo again.

Theo. It had always been Theo for her, but he was so popular, dating a different girl every weekend, she'd assumed he had no interest in her. Atticus was Theo's best friend, and Atticus had been in love with Beth. He had told her that, and that had tied her to him. She had *cared* for him, she'd worried about him and tried to help when his dark depressions came over him. Somehow they had become a couple, and she believed, she was *certain* that she had made him happy, or at least less depressed. From time to time in classes or walking in the hallway, Beth caught Theo looking at her, and his look was like a song calling her home, and then he'd flush and turn away. So she had believed that Theo liked her, that he might actually want her in the way she wanted him—not simply sexually, but spiritually, too, as if he was missing part of himself, and if only she would go to him, he could be complete. That was how she felt about him.

They never talked about it. Once, at a school dance, when he held her as they moved to a slow song and the desire between them was so obvious, so strong, Theo had smiled down at her and asked, "Beth. What are we going to do?"

"What can we do?" Beth asked, and there was

no answer, or not the answer they wanted. She was Atticus's girl, and he needed her in a serious way—so serious that his mother had actually taken Beth for coffee so they could talk about Atticus and his problem.

"You know," Paula Barnes had said, "Atticus is afraid you will leave him for Theo."

Beth had nearly knocked over her mug. "Why would he think that?"

"Atticus is very sensitive," his mother had replied.

"Yes, I'm aware of that," Beth snapped, because she wanted to say, good grief, every moment of every day when I'm with him, I have to be attuned to his precious sensitivity, and sometimes I want to run away and be free or do something that will offend that sensitivity! Immediately, she apologized for snapping at his mother. "I'm sorry. I know it's hard for him. I wish someone could help."

"He's seeing a therapist. And he's on medication. And, Beth, Atticus's father and I are so grateful to you for being there for him, for doing all you do. That's why I asked to meet you. To thank you. To tell you we know he can be hard work, but we believe he'll get better, he'll get well. He's so awfully brilliant, and he has a wonderful future in front of him—if we can just get him there."

Mrs. Barnes was crying, quietly, gently. Beth

knew what she had to say, and she said it, "I care for Atticus very much, Mrs. Barnes. I'll be there for him as much as I can be. You can trust me."

Often, it wasn't a hardship, dealing with Atticus. For one thing, he was amazingly handsome, in a doomed-poet sort of way, with long tousled black hair and blue eyes with black lashes. He was tall and too thin, and he always wore button-down shirts to school, so he looked like an aristocrat among the grungy peasants. At his best, he could be smart and funny and quick-witted. At his best, he always had Beth laughing.

At his worst, he didn't laugh. He hardly spoke. He had dark circles beneath his eyes from not sleeping and he grew increasingly paranoid, thinking the teachers were trying to flunk him out, thinking that Beth and Theo were in love. It became too unpleasant for the three of them to walk home together, so Theo walked home another way. With other girls.

Even when he was at his worst, Beth never suspected that he might actually commit suicide.

When Atticus was found dead from an overdose, everyone who knew him or his family was shocked. Many were overwhelmed by grief, but a few people were angered, and their anger at this senseless loss had driven them to bring therapists over to the island to talk at a town meeting. The police department had bulked up its presence. The mental health organizations had spread the word that they were there to help. Beth's father insisted she spend an hour a week with a counselor. And that helped, a little, because Beth felt so guilty about Atticus's suicide. Had she not loved him enough? She'd never had sex with him, but he had never urged her to, and she knew Atticus didn't often have the energy or the desire for much of anything. Dr. Moore helped release some of the guilt she carried, and Paula Barnes had written a brief note to Beth telling her that Atticus's suicide was not in any way Beth's fault, that it might have happened sooner if Atticus hadn't had Beth's companionship and love.

Over time, the town went on. The Barnes family moved off-island. Beth and her classmates went off to college.

With a kind of jolt, Beth came out of her reverie. She was here, now, staring out the kitchen window, lost in her thoughts. She wanted to go forward, but where?

She gathered up her purse, redid her lipstick, and was headed out the door when the house phone rang.

"Beth? Is that you? You are exactly the person I'm looking for!" Prudence Starbuck didn't need to introduce herself. Her sterling silver voice was unforgettable. "Listen, darling, I'd like to take you to lunch to talk about a job that might interest you now that you're home."

"Oh, Mrs. Starbuck, that's very nice—"

"It concerns this new organization, Ocean Matters. I saw you at Ryder Hastings's lecture. I've agreed to be his point man on the island. We need someone young and energetic and savvy to do the social media for our Nantucket chapter."

"I'd be glad to volunteer my free time, Mrs. Starbuck, but I need to get a job—"

"Darling, this *is* a job. You'll have an office on Easy Street, and a computer and all that sort of thing, and of course you will have a very considerable salary. Now, what are you doing for lunch today? May I take you to lunch at Cru?"

Maybe this was the sign from fate that Beth was looking for! Anyway, Beth liked Mrs. Starbuck's brisk can-do energy.

"I'd be happy to meet you at Cru," Beth said. "What time?"

ten

Monday morning, Lisa unlocked the door to her shop. Every time she entered, moving around the space, turning on lights, waking her computer, she felt a surge of pride. *She* had built this business. *She* had made it happen.

She set her go-cup on the shelf behind the counter. She was behind on ordering, and because Monday mornings were always slow, she expected to get a lot of work done.

She was arranging a new shipment of summery jewelry—turquoise, blue, coral—when Moxie Breinberg entered the shop.

"Hi, Moxie," Lisa called. "Let me know if I can help you."

"Sure thing." Moxie fastened her attention on a rack of new sleeveless dresses, pulling one out and holding it to her while she looked in the full-length mirror, putting it back, choosing another one. "Could I try this on?" she asked Lisa.

"Of course," Lisa said, leading Moxie to the dressing room.

For a good thirty minutes, Moxie tried on dresses. Moxie was divorced, with one child in college. An extremely pretty woman, she spent a lot of time keeping in shape and trying to look young. Lisa knew Moxie the way she knew many islanders, from seeing her at community events, school plays, summer parties, so she knew that Moxie was around forty-five—around Mack's age—but she wore cropped tops and short shorts and very short dresses with plunging halter tops in the summer. Lisa didn't think Moxie had ever bought anything from her shop, and her curiosity grew.

Moxie made her decision and brought a light peach pashmina to the counter.

"I think I'll take this. It's so pretty."

"It is. And you'll look beautiful in it."

"So," Moxie said, "I heard that you're seeing Mack Whitney."

Lisa focused her attention on the credit card machine. Now she knew why Moxie had come in. "He's working on my house," Lisa explained. "I have to have some ceilings replaced and my bathroom renovated."

"Oh! How nice." Moxie toyed with the other pashminas displayed on a nearby table. "So that's why he took you to the Seagrille?"

"Right. Last Friday. I didn't see you there, Moxie."

"Oh, I wasn't . . ." Moxie laughed a tinkly laugh. "Someone told me you two were there. Together."

Lisa took great care wrapping the pashmina in tissue and slipping it into a bag.

When Lisa didn't answer, Moxie said, "He's a lot younger than you are, isn't he?"

Lisa hadn't thought this kind of inquisition would happen so soon. *Put on your big girl panties,* she told herself, and with a sweet smile, she said, "Why, yes, he is, and so are you. In fact, you're around the same age, right? Of course, you look so much younger, Moxie. You could be in your thirties. Your *early* thirties." Lisa handed Moxie the small paper shopping bag holding the pashmina. "If you'd like to look, well, not older, but more sophisticated, I could help you build the right wardrobe." Lisa moved around the counter toward her summer dress rack. "For example, this long-sleeved silk dress would be elegant on you. And it's only a bit over four hundred dollars."

"Oh, thanks," Moxie stuttered, heading for the door. "Maybe another time." She fled.

Lisa grinned. If there was anything she'd learned from her ex-husband and his mother, it was how to be critical in the sweetest possible way. She felt slightly guilty, but she mentally replayed their conversation, and decided she hadn't insulted Moxie really, she had only smothered her with compliments. And, as announcers said about sports events, Lisa had won the field.

She returned to her computer and her spreadsheets, but she couldn't stop thinking about the brief exchange with Moxie. It had been spontaneous, and Lisa had defended herself and her relationship with Mack without thinking. What did that mean? Did she think she could have a relationship with this man who was ten years younger?

She certainly wanted it.

The phone rang.

"I can't believe you didn't tell me," Rachel said.

"And good morning to you, too," Lisa replied. "What was I supposed to tell you?"

"Lisa! I thought I was your best friend. The whole town knows you're dating Mack Whitney! And you didn't even call me."

"Oh, Rachel, I'm sorry, but I don't even know if 'dating' is the right word, and it's happened so fast, and then Juliet came home with a broken heart, and just this moment Moxie came to the shop to get a dig in about the age difference between me and Mack."

"Well, he *is* an entire decade younger than you."

"Rachel! Don't be mean."

"I'm not being mean. I'm being factual. I'm worried about you."

Lisa sighed. "I'm worried about me, too. I know I'm too old for him, but he seems to like me, and we have amazing chemistry."

"So I heard."

"Oh, for heaven's sake. All we've done is have dinner at the Seagrille."

"And . . . ?" Rachel coaxed.

"And we talked. We got to know each other. He told me about Marla and I told him about Erich. It was a good conversation."

"And . . . ?"

Lisa paused to look through her shop window at the street. No one was coming toward her shop. "Okay, Rachel, but this goes no further than you, right? I don't want to be the subject of gossip."

"Oh, my God, Lisa! Did you go to bed with him?"

"Of course not!"

"Then what?"

Lisa felt her face flame as she talked. "So he drove me home and I invited him in for coffee, and we sat on the sofa, and he kissed me." She closed her eyes, remembering how he had put his hand on her cheek and gently tilted her mouth to his. The kiss had lasted. She had responded, putting her arms around his neck and leaning against him.

"Lisa, are you still there?"

"Yes, Rachel. Mack kissed me, and it was wonderful, and our ages didn't matter, all that mattered was right there between us—"

"And?"

"And," Lisa said, bursting out with laughter,

"and then Juliet came walking in the door. We jumped apart and we both made excuses for why Mack was there, which was ridiculous, and the nicest thing, Rachel, the *nicest* thing was the way Mack looked at me when he left, smiling with his eyes, showing me we shared a secret now."

"He said all that with his eyes?"

"Yes," Lisa said dreamily.

"Oh, honey, you sound down for the count."

"That sounds terrible."

"Well, do you think it's good?"

"Rachel, I hardly know what to think yet. All this is so new, and I've never been in this place before, where I feel attracted to a man, and terrified at the same time. I mean, I *know* I'm older than he is. I *know* I've had babies and gotten stretch marks and I'm not all fit and toned like younger women. But come on, I'm not decrepit! I still have all my teeth!"

"Lisa, stop. I'm sorry I got you so worked up. I'm not implying that you're not gorgeous enough for him, because you are. I'm only worried about you. You're not the kind of person to have affairs, or dalliances or whatever they're called."

"And you think that Mack and I couldn't possibly have a serious, long-term relationship."

Rachel didn't answer for a moment. "Do you think the two of you could?"

"To be honest, Rachel, until the last few days I didn't think Mack and I could have *any* kind of relationship. And I still don't know what the future holds. We've talked honestly about our past lives—Erich, Marla—but we haven't talked about the future. It's too early to do that. You don't have to warn me, Rachel. I'm scared. I'm afraid of being hurt when he dumps me, which I have to assume he will, but don't I deserve some pleasure until then? Because I think he really likes me."

"Of course he likes you. You're wonderful. And of course—"

A customer entered the shop. "Rachel, I have to go. Talk later." Lisa quickly ended the call. "May I help you?"

"Just browsing," the woman said. She was young and slim and wore four-inch Manolo Blahniks.

Thank heavens, Lisa thought. A summer person. She wouldn't know about Lisa and Mack, and if she did, she wouldn't care.

eleven

Theo had just flown all the way from California, and he was beat. He really wanted to go home, but getting to Nantucket was never easy or cheap, and at the moment, he was tired of traveling. His arm was healing nicely, the doctor had said, but he still wore his sling, and took Tylenol for the pain. He had some oxy left but he didn't want to take it. He didn't want to get addicted, plus it made him think of Atticus and then he got sad.

When he got his aching bones off the plane at Logan, he took a moment to contemplate making the bus ride to Hyannis and the slow ferry to Nantucket, but he was just too tired, and his head hurt. So he thought of calling Juliet to ask her if he could spend the night at her place. True, they didn't keep in touch regularly, but still, he was her brother. He was her younger brother, so shouldn't she be willing to take care of him? After all, Juliet had been the responsible good kid, getting all A's, helping in the kitchen, never doing anything wrong, and somehow not being a nerd. When they were little, Juliet had adored him, playing with him as if he were a pet or a doll, but as they grew older, she had seemed to resent him, probably because their mother had put the burden of cooking the evening meals on her. They all knew Theo couldn't be relied on for dinner—he was always at basketball practice or surfing.

Now Juliet would probably hate having him around being injured and pathetic and pretty much penniless, but he was too tired to think of an alternate plan, and he knew Cambridge from going there with friends on high school holidays. He had her address so he caught a bus into South Station and then the T to Harvard Square. He walked to her apartment, hoping she'd be home. If not, he'd lie down right outside her door and fall asleep.

He climbed the stairs to her apartment. He knocked, politely, on the door. He heard footsteps padding toward him.

Juliet opened the door.

"Theo!"

Theo grinned his trademark little boy grin. For a few moments, he was golden.

She hugged him, pulled him into her apartment, and slammed the door. "What are you doing here?"

"I broke my arm."

"Oh, Theo!"

"It's not that bad." Theo dropped his duffel bag on the floor and loped over to the sofa. "Only a pain in the ass. I mean the arm. I got slammed by a wave and my humerus was fractured so I have to wear this sling. Do you have any beer? Or vodka?"

"I've got wine."

"Wine. Really."

Juliet went into her galley kitchen and stuck her head in the refrigerator. "Found a couple!" She brought back two bottles of golden liquid.

"Hey, let me have the beers. You go get yourself your precious wine."

Juliet paused. "It's seven o'clock here. What time is it in California?"

"It's beer time," Theo told her. "Who cares? I've been flying for hours and I haven't had anything to eat or drink except a small pack of nuts and a Coke."

She rolled her eyes, handed him the beers, got herself the wine, and sank on the chair across from him. "So tell me. What are you doing here?" She squinted at him. "Want pizza?"

"Oh, man, I'd love pizza. But no pineapple!"

"Broccoli? Red pepper? Any kind of vegetable? A salad on the side?"

"Do I look like I need vegetables?" Theo asked.

Juliet made a face at him. "You are still so vain."

"Five cheese," Theo told her.

She phoned in two large five-cheese pizzas.

"So how are you?" Theo asked, tossing back a beer.

"I'm good. I'm fine."

"Boyfriend?"

Juliet sagged against the sofa. "Don't ask."

"So, basically, no boyfriend."

"You say that with such relish."

Theo held back a grin. He'd bet that all brothers could irritate their sisters and feel sympathy for them at the same time. "Sorry, Juliet, really. Want to tell me what happened?"

Juliet shook her head. "No. It's over. He's moved to New York." She took a sip of wine. "What about you?"

"No one serious. Lots of surfer babes, but no one's looking for anything long-term." He drained his bottle of beer. "So how's Mom?"

"Actually, I'm concerned about her. I was down there yesterday. She's having an affair with a guy ten years younger than she is."

"Go, Mom!" Theo toasted her with another gulp of beer.

"It's not funny. She's got that big house, and she's divorced and emotionally vulnerable, and I just know he's going to find a way to get at her money, at least he'll charge her double what he should for the work he's doing on the house."

"Okay. Slow down. Who's the guy?"

"Mack Whitney."

"Jeez, Juliet, Beth Whitney's dad? When I was in high school, I was over at his house a lot. He's a good guy. I've never heard anything bad about him. What makes you think they're having an affair?"

"His crew is doing work on the house—"

"About time. What's Mom having done?"

"Oh, the dining room ceiling and the living room walls and her bathroom, it doesn't matter. He's there all the time working, but after work he's still there."

"Sleeping over?"

Juliet shrugged. "I don't know. I went down on the spur of the moment, got in on the late boat, walked to the house. I phoned Mom just before I got there. I thought she'd be thrilled. But it was ten-thirty at night and she and Mack were sitting on the sofa, and Mom's clothes were rumpled! Plus, I saw the way Mom looked at him. The last night I was there, I asked her what was going on, and she said she was 'seeing' Mack and she liked him a lot and he was terrifically smart, *smart* I don't think being the important quality."

"So you think he's hot." Theo grinned wickedly.

"What? You are so gross. I don't think he's *hot,* but I think he's good-looking, and he is a lot younger than Mom!"

"Well." Theo hesitated, not sure what to say because he wasn't sure how he felt. "Mom's good-looking."

"I know that. She's beautiful. But she's fifty-six years old! Mack Whitney should date someone his age, hell, he could date someone thirty-six years old."

"How old is Mack?"

"Forty-six. I looked it up in the town register."

Theo laughed so hard he choked on his beer. "Nancy Drew."

"You are so immature."

"Come on, Jules, why are you so worked up about this? Mom deserves to have a little fun."

"I'm worked up about this, Theo, because I'm afraid that people will laugh at her, an older woman with her boy toy, and second, and most of all, I'm afraid she'll get a broken heart when he dumps her for someone else. Also I just know he's trying to get his hands on her money."

"Mom doesn't have that much money. If Mack Whitney was trolling for some big bucks, he could find dozens of women on the island who are way richer than Mom." Theo gave Juliet a look. "You're thinking that money is going to be our money someday and Mack might get it."

Juliet crossed her arms defensively. "For one thing, yeah. But honestly, Theo, I'm more concerned about her . . . her sense of self-worth. Our father left her cold when we were kids. She hasn't had a serious relationship in years. How is she going to feel when Mack Whitney drops her for the first cute waitress off the boat this summer?"

Theo nodded. He liked the idea of traveling

to his mom's to help her instead of dragging his sorry ass home to Mommy. "Okay. Let's go see her. And let's make it a surprise."

Juliet woke early—she always did. Her left arm was crushed up against her head. It took her a moment to remember that she'd let Theo have her nice comfy double bed. He'd played the sympathy card—his arm, and he hadn't slept in a comfortable bed for five years. And whose fault is that? Juliet had wanted to say, but she was so glad he was here, she said she'd sleep on the sofa. It also allowed her a chance to catch him if he sneaked out to get into her stash of hard liquor, which was nothing much really, only some vodka and rum. In high school, Theo had partied plenty, but sports during school and surfing all summer had kept him clean.

She heard thunderous snoring from her bedroom. When had she last had a man in her bed? Oh, right. Hugh. Hugh who now lived in New York. Who hadn't bothered to say goodbye. Her girlfriends said guys like him liked to "seduce and abandon." Why were men like this? Why had Juliet been so naïve?

Enough. Tossing back the blanket she'd been wrapped in, she stood and stretched and did a few yoga morning exercises. From the window, the blue sky promised a sunny day. She slipped into the bathroom, took a quick shower, and wrapped herself in her toweling robe. Padding into the kitchen, she started coffee brewing. The aroma was bound to wake Theo. If he didn't get up by her second cup, she'd wake him herself.

She opened her computer on her kitchen table and worked for a while. When it was nine, in Juliet's mind, nearly lunchtime, she called, "Theo! Time to wake up!"

No answer. No sounds of movement.

She knocked on the bedroom door, pushed it open, and called, "Theo! Get up!"

No reply but the snarl of snoring. She always had been the bossy older sister, so it was a natural act to open the door and enter the room. Besides, it was her apartment.

Theo lay on her bed like an angel dropped flat on his back. Juliet was grateful a sheet covered his torso. She went forward, intending to shake him, but stopped when she saw the Tylenol on the bedside table. And the beer. Obviously he'd found another beer at the back of her fridge and washed the pills down with the beer.

When did Theo say he fractured his arm? Tylenol and beer, not so good together.

"Theo." She leaned over the bed and shook him. "Theo. Wake up."

"Uh?" Theo blearily opened his eyes. "Go away."

"Theo, it's morning. We're going to see Mom."

"For God's sake, let me sleep. I flew across the

continent yesterday, my arm's screwed up, I'm supposed to rest. The doctor told me I have to rest."

Theo turned onto his good side, his back to Juliet.

"Two more hours, and then we're going." Juliet shut the door, her thoughts all over the place. Her mother with a boyfriend, her careless brother back on the East Coast. She was sitting down at her laptop when she realized she'd forgotten she had dinner with Ryder tonight.

She would have to cancel it. Maybe that would be the wise thing to do, anyway.

She texted Ryder: *Sorry, Ryder, I can't do dinner tonight. My brother just arrived with a broken arm and we've got to go to Nantucket to see Mom. Some other time, I hope.* After agonizing over the words, she ended the text with a friendly but neutral *OXJ.*

twelve

Lisa woke feeling like a schoolgirl on the first day of vacation. Which she certainly was not. She had to shower, dress, make some sort of breakfast, and open her shop. But she allowed herself another few moments to lie in bed remembering the phone conversation she'd had with Mack the night before.

She'd left her bedroom windows open slightly. She could hear the birds chirping on the magnolia tree and far away, high in the sky, the hum of an airplane coming to the island. More and more planes would be coming as they brought back the summer people.

And her shop would be more and more busy.

She'd talked on the phone with Mack about this last night, one business owner to another. Mack was a restoration carpenter, specializing in old houses, but the big money was made by construction companies tossing up brand-new McMansions. Millionaires eager to live for a couple of summer months in a home with a hot tub, a home movie theater, and a swimming pool often approached him, offering him enormous sums of money if he could build their house, *right now.* When Beth was in high school, with college tuition on the horizon, Mack had accepted some of the offers. He'd built spacious houses on beautiful lots, but the work didn't seem true to who he was and why he was living on the island. Now Mack wanted to do the work he loved, restoring old venerable houses instead of building vanity castles.

"I understand," Lisa had said. She was curled up on her sofa in her comfy robe, leaning on pillows. She'd turned off most of the lights, because she liked the sense of intimacy she felt while they were talking. "When I first worked for Vesta, before you were born—"

"Stop that," Mack interrupted.

Lisa was determined to keep them both aware of the difference in their ages before they got too close. Before she got hurt.

"Okay," Lisa said. "Anyway, Vestments sold clothing for the young and chic and sexy. Very short skirts. Plunging necklines. Skintight and revealing."

"I'd like to see you in something tight and revealing," Mack said.

She ignored him. "I suggested we sell more traditional apparel. Blazers, silk shirts, long-sleeved dresses. More women came in, and younger women also bought some of the more tasteful clothing. Hermès scarves. That sort of thing."

"What do you sell now?"

"The same stuff, really. Classy clothing. Elegance never goes out of style."

"Does Juliet wear what you sell?"

"Heavens, no. She's very NYC urban. Lots of black, knee-high boots."

"I'll bet Beth would buy your clothes more often if she could afford them. She's always liked the clothing you carry." Mack laughed. "Listen to me, as if I know anything about fashion."

"But that's interesting," Lisa told him, and it was. Speaking about clothing led them to talking about their children, what they'd been like as children, what their goals were now.

As they talked, Lisa settled more deeply into the sofa cushions. Somehow this conversation made her feel more comfortable with Mack. Neither one of them went to bars, and Mack never really had, since he became a father at twenty-one. They had the work ethic ingrained in them, and that didn't bother them one single bit. They both loved their work, the routine, their everyday life.

"Oh, Lord," Lisa said after they'd talked for over an hour, "I'm afraid you're as much of a stick-in-the-mud as I am."

"Yes, I think we're very much alike," Mack agreed.

Lisa paused, wondering about the consequences of this conversation. Before she could speak,

Mack said, “So the age thing shouldn’t bother us, right?” Again, before Lisa could speak, he said in a joking tone, “I can put up with you being more sophisticated and better traveled than I am, and you can put up with me being callow and inexperienced.”

Lisa’s heart went into overdrive. *I’m frightened!* she wanted to say. But Mack was . . . endearing. She wanted to spend more time with him. She wanted to do more with him. “Yes, I think we can put up with each other, at least for a while.”

“Great. Okay, let’s go to the movie tomorrow night.”

“I’d like that,” Lisa said.

“Then it’s a date. I’ll get tickets in advance and pick you up at six-thirty.”

“Lovely. Thank you, Mack. See you then.”

“I might see you before then.”

“Really?” Lisa’s heart raced.

“I’m working on your house with my crew, you know.” Mack laughed as he spoke.

“Oh, right. This conversation took me to another sphere of reality.”

“And I haven’t even gotten started,” Mack told her with a smile in his voice.

The movie playing at Dreamland, the only theater on the island, was a biographical drama about a famous singer whose star had faded. It was oddly exciting to sit in the dark room with

Mack's shoulder touching hers, and when Mack reached for Lisa's hand, and held it until the movie ended, Lisa was almost too overwhelmed to pay attention to the screen.

But when the movie drew to its conclusion, Lisa wanted to sink in her seat and disappear before the lights came on and the audience saw her with Mack.

To her surprise, as the lights exposed the room, Mack leaned over and whispered, "Did your high school boyfriend ever kiss you in the movie theater?"

"Not with the lights on," she whispered back, her mouth only inches from his ear.

"Let's go to your house," he said.

The theater was only half full. No teens. As they filed out into the foyer, some people said hello to Mack, some to Lisa, and Lisa's friends grinned and did a thumbs-up which Lisa hoped Mack didn't see. Women who were Mack's age spoke to him before giving Lisa a brief up-and-down glance.

And Mack put his hand on Lisa's waist, gently guiding her to the door.

They walked instead of driving to Lisa's house. It was a beautiful night, calm, windless, with the moon riding high in the sky. Main Street was bright with businesses staying open late now that summer was here. They held hands and window-shopped as they walked. Art galleries, real estate companies, clothing shops, the bookstore, the pharmacy. Brick sidewalks and a cobblestone street. No stoplights, no neon, only old-fashioned streetlights and tall trees full and heavy with summer leaves.

"When I walk here, I sometimes think of all the people in past generations who have walked just like this," Mack said.

"Yes. I do that, too," Lisa replied. "I've read that you're either a future person or a past person."

"I guess I'm both," Mack said. "I revere the past, which is why I try to restore old houses, so they'll be lived in in the future."

"But some things can never be returned to the perfect state they were in when they were young," Lisa said awkwardly.

"And some things get better as they grow old," Mack said. "Many people, for example, become more beautiful. Softer. So a person wants to sink right into them."

Lisa couldn't get her breath.

Mack stopped walking. They were only a block from her house, and on Fair Street many of the homes had not yet been opened for the summer, so only the moonlight illuminated their faces. Mack gently embraced Lisa, turning her to face him. He stared at her for a long moment, his eyes silver in the soft light, and Lisa knew her eyes must look silver, too. He bent and kissed her. The air was very quiet. No cars passed, no dogs barked, even the leaves didn't rustle on the trees. Mack's mouth was warm and insistent. Lisa raised her arms around his neck and pulled him closer.

When they broke apart, they were both out of breath.

"I'll race you to the house," Mack said.

Lisa let her head fall back as she broke into laughter. At this moment, age did not matter. Desire mattered, and it was overwhelming her, so she took Mack's hand and pulled him along to her house, both of them laughing.

She'd left one light burning in the living room and the door unlocked—she seldom locked it, here on this small island. They stepped inside and as soon as Mack pushed the door shut, he moved Lisa against the wall. He pressed himself against her, held her wrists in his hands, pulled her arms above her head, and kissed her exposed neck and collarbone and then returned to her mouth. She shook with desire. She brought her arms down and pulled his body even more closely to her. She wanted to crawl inside him, she wanted him to crawl inside her, she needed to be totally with him.

"Let's go upstairs," she whispered.

The front door flew open, nearly slamming Mack in the back.

Juliet came inside, and behind her, there was Theo!

"Mom!" Juliet said scoldingly.

"Mom," Theo said lovingly.

Lisa's breasts were heaving as powerfully as if they were right out of a romance novel. Her poor senses jammed together. Desire made her heart thud even as it slowly evaporated, and anger at being interrupted at this particular moment battled with joy at seeing her son again. She couldn't catch her breath to speak.

Mack stepped back as the children, the grown children, entered the hall. He held out his hand to Theo. "Hi. I'm Mack. Remember me?" He nodded at Juliet. "Hello again."

"Hi," Theo said, with a smile for Mack. "Nice to see you. You're Beth Whitney's dad, right?"

"Right."

"Could we *possibly* move out of the hall so we're not all right on top of each other?" Juliet asked, her voice going falsetto in her strangled attempt to be polite.

"I have to be going," Mack said. "Working day tomorrow." He winked at Lisa.

"Thanks, Mack, see you tomorrow," Lisa said, and suddenly she leaned up and kissed him quickly right on the mouth. She held his gaze for a moment, letting him know what she'd rather be doing.

Really? she thought, as Mack went out the door. She'd rather be in bed with Mack than spend time with her two children?

Yes, she thought guiltily, she would.

Mack left.

"Let's go to the kitchen," Lisa said. "I'm sure you're hungry, Theo."

Theo slung an affectionate arm over Lisa's shoulders. "So Mom's got a boyfriend, *hmm?*"

"Yes," Lisa told him, holding her head high. "Yes, I do." She detached herself from Theo's arm, walked to the refrigerator, and surveyed the contents. She'd been eating for one for so many months—years!—except when Juliet or Theo came home, which wasn't often. "Theo, I can make a Western omelet for you. Eggs, cheese, tomato, and onion. Does that sound good?"

"Sounds great, Mom, thanks." Theo threw himself into a kitchen chair.

"Do you have enough to make me an omelet, too?" Juliet asked, her voice strained.

"Of course," Lisa replied cheerfully. As she worked, deftly setting the tomato, cheese, and onion on the chopping board, taking all seven eggs left in their little cups in the refrigerator door and settling them in a bowl, she kept her back to her children. "So, Theo," she said as she worked, "what a surprise! I don't know when I last had both of my children here together."

"Yeah, I'm glad to be home," Theo said. "I had an accident, got slammed by a wave, had a fractured humerus—"

"Oh, Theo!" Lisa turned from the stove.

"Darling, so that's why you're wearing a sling! How do you feel now?"

"It's nothing, Mom, really. I probably don't even need the sling anymore. I just use it to remind myself to go carefully."

"Poor guy. That must have hurt. Were you frightened? Under all that water? You'll have to tell me about it sometime."

"I know I don't want to do that again." Theo was rubbing his arm, almost proudly. "I'm kind of off surfing. For a while, at least." He cleared his throat. "I thought maybe I could spend the summer here, get a job, make some money, decide what to do."

Lisa slowly poured the egg mixture into the cast-iron skillet hissing with hot butter. She lowered the heat, waited a few moments, then added the chopped cheese and veggies. She was glad to have something to focus on, something nurturing to her son, because her immediate reaction, to her own surprise, was certainly not unfettered joy at Theo's news. And it wasn't, she mused, only that it would make it difficult for her to be alone in the house with Mack. It was also the knowledge that Theo, being Theo, would expect her to do his laundry, buy his groceries, and cook his meals, as she was doing now.

But maybe this was a good thing. Maybe this was fate's way of pulling Lisa away from what Juliet considered a disastrous affair. The eggs were done. Lisa hefted the skillet to slide the omelets onto two plates.

"I'm thinking I'll stay here for the summer, too," Juliet said.

Lisa almost dropped the skillet. "You're sure?"

"Well, don't go overboard with the enthusiasm," Juliet snapped.

Lisa ignored her daughter's mood. She knew her children loved each other but most often Juliet acted like a green-eyed cat, jealous of her brother.

"Here we go," Lisa said to Theo. "Do you want some juice?"

"Mom," Theo said, "I want a beer."

"Me, too," Juliet echoed.

Lisa set the plates in front of her children. "And will there be anything else, sir and madam?" she said, half-jokingly, half-sarcastically.

Juliet stood up. "I'll get the beers, Theo. You get the silverware." Before Theo could respond, she said, "I know you hurt your arm, but I'm sure you can carry two forks."

Lisa poured herself a glass of wine and settled at the table. Juliet sat at one end, Theo on the other, so she had to turn her head to study her children. Oh, they were so beautiful. Even now, it gave Lisa such a deep, primal pleasure to watch them eating.

"So, Juliet, you decided your job will allow you to be here for the summer?"

"Of course. I'll go back every now and then for a face meeting."

"Ah." Lisa turned toward her son. "And, Theo, I'm sure your employer will be missing you out in California."

Theo talked with his mouth full. "Haven't worked for six weeks. Because of my arm. Plus I was bartending and giving surf lessons. Lots of guys can take my place."

Lisa nodded. *So when will I have private time with Mack?* she wanted to ask. Instead, she said, "It will be wonderful to have you both here. But you know, I have my shop to run, and summer's always the busiest time, so I'll need you to pitch in and help me with the chores. Like buying groceries, cooking, and doing your own laundry. That sort of thing."

"Sure," Juliet said. "I do it all for myself in Cambridge."

"Do you think you'll get a job here?" Lisa asked her son.

"I want to give myself another week to rest my arm," Theo said. "Just traveling back from California wiped me out. I mean, not just my arm was hurt, but my entire body, and my head took quite a knock—"

Juliet interrupted. "Oh, come off it, Theo. That was six weeks ago. Don't be a baby."

"It's early in the season," Theo said reasonably. "I'll look for a job this week. But give me a break, okay?" Before anyone could respond, Theo stood up. "This was delicious, Mom. Thanks. But hey, I think I'd like a couple pieces of toast." He walked to the bread drawer and took out a loaf. "Would you like some, too, Juliet?"

Juliet hesitated. She knew she'd been outplayed. "Yes, please."

Theo made putting the bread into the four-slot toaster using only one arm an Oscar-worthy act of courage and skill. Lisa wanted to applaud, but he'd only just arrived home. She would humor him. He put two pieces on a plate and brought it to Juliet, and set the butter dish in front of her.

"You good, Mom?" he asked.

Lisa smiled at her son. "I'm fine, thanks."

And I really am, she thought.

thirteen

Why did someone else's cooking always taste better than his own? Theo finished his toast and wanted to lick his plate.

"I've got to get some sleep," his mom said, rising from the table. "First, let me show you what Mack's doing on the house."

"I'll tidy the kitchen," Juliet said. She smirked at Theo.

Theo smirked back and followed his mom. The downstairs rooms were all weird, either the furniture moved or covered in drop cloths. He only half listened to his mother describe the cracks in the ceilings, the bizarre plaster stilts, the dust, and a zillion minor problems. The loose panes on the tops of the inner doors that his mom had, she said laughingly, making it a humorous tale, tried to fix herself. The scuffed floorboards, the worn rugs, the ancient wooden kitchen floor. The broken dishwasher—it was easy, Lisa had said, doing dishes for only one person.

His mom's bedroom had changed. Once in sixth grade he'd done a really cool, if he said so himself and he did, painting of himself, Juliet, and his mom. His mom had loved it so much she'd framed it and hung it on the wall across from her bed. While he was gone, she'd taken it down and replaced it with a large flat-screen television. The thought of his poor mom lying in bed watching television all alone made him oddly melancholy. Plus, didn't she like his painting anymore? He didn't see it anywhere.

He entered his room, which he'd held in his mind as a kind of private shrine. And found mountains of clutter. Clutter that wasn't *his.*

"I'm going to turn your room into a guest room slash crafts room," his mother told him.

Theo stood in his room, gawking. His bed was there, more neatly made up than he'd ever had it. Still, there were his chest of drawers, his desk, his desk chair, his shelves of books, trophies, games, and balls. But his posters of the Foo Fighters and Britney Spears in not much more than fringe had been taken down. And cardboard boxes—so many of them!—were piled in the room. On top of his desk. In the corner. At the end of his bed.

"Whoa," Theo said. "That's radical."

"Why is it radical?" Juliet demanded, coming up the stairs. Juliet always wanted to be the favorite, and she never would be, Theo thought smugly. "You haven't even been home for *years.*"

"Yeah, well, I'm here now," Theo shot back.

"Good night, sweetiepies," his mom said, kissing him and Juliet on the cheek before disappearing into her room and firmly shutting the door.

"Good night, *sweetiepie,*" Juliet echoed over her shoulder at Theo as she went to her own room.

In his room, Theo moved the boxes around, kind of noisily, as if he wanted to kick them out into the hall. He expected his mom to stick her head in the door and tell him they'd move the boxes somewhere else tomorrow, but she didn't. He brushed his teeth in the bathroom he shared with Juliet, who'd left one hundred cosmetic items on her side of the sink. He shut his door, got into bed, and immediately felt at home.

The mattress had a trough in the middle. He was torn between being grateful that it was there, one thing that held his mark, and being pissed off that such an old, lumpy, and undoubtedly stained mattress hadn't been replaced.

This mattress had seen a lot of action. The memories made him smile. He'd hated being a teenager, unable to have power over anything in his life, but he'd had quite a bit of power over high school girls and footballs.

Well, every girl except the girl he wanted most. Beth Whitney. She had been all about Atticus, and when the three of them were together, Beth never even looked at Theo.

That had been hard. High school had been hard.

Every day he'd wakened to an anger simmering

deep in his chest. Anger at his mother for letting them live like they did, driving an old sedan, not even four-wheel drive, it was embarrassing. His mother had insisted on teaching him to drive, and sometimes he'd wanted to howl at her. He *knew* how to drive a car, his high school friends had taught him out on the dirt roads in the moors. His mother was so not fun when she gave him lessons. If he'd had a father, a guy to teach him to drive—and all the other things a father could have taught him—that would have been fun.

Theo kind of remembered his father. A shade, a shadow, tall and broad and handsome. Theo's mom always said, "I'm so glad you're a big gorgeous guy like your father."

She was always saying nice things about his father, this man who hadn't seen him at all since Theo was a little kid. So many times he'd wished his father was dead. A lot of times, when people asked, Theo told them his father was dead. Then he'd put on a sad face and look at the ground and refuse to talk about it anymore.

Why had his mom never cursed his father, wept with hatred? She probably thought that in some twisted way she was protecting him. But Theo knew plenty of guys in school whose father had moved away, divorced, that stuff. He'd seen a mom throwing dishes in a fit of anger at her ex-husband.

Jeez, he was getting totally *morbid* lying here

like this, where old memories drifted out of the walls to haunt him.

He needed something. Something to ease the pain. He'd brought some oxy with him from California, in case his arm went bad again, but this pain wasn't physical.

He reached under his mattress to see if the porn magazine was still there. That would cheer him up. He felt the flutter of paper and pulled out *Golf* magazine. He'd always *hated* golf, it was boring. How did this mag get here, in his room, under his mattress?

His mom, he realized. His mom had played a trick on him. Which meant she'd known he'd be back home someday.

He heaved out a large breath and lay back on his pillow and looked at the May 2015 cover. A minute later, he was asleep.

fourteen

Beth woke to discover that her father, as usual, had made coffee, left her a note on the refrigerator, and gone off to work. She drank her coffee while she showered and dressed, eager to start her own job. The day was brilliant, warm and bright. Beth walked from her home to the new Ocean Matters office on Easy Street. What a location, right on the waterfront next to the Steamship Authority docks! For a moment, she studied the front of the office. It had a large picture window. She'd find a great poster to put there to lure people in. This space had been an antiques shop years ago, and then a real estate agency. Now it was the Nantucket headquarters for Ocean Matters, and wasn't that change? Didn't that show that people were beginning to care about the environment?

She unlocked the door with the shiny brass keys Prudence had given her, along with several folders of documents and a scribbled list of Beth's duties.

First things first, Beth thought, as she surveyed the large room. A desk, two large tables, a computer and printer, and a storage locker had been carelessly brought in, along with several boxes of supplies. The office looked disorganized—well, it *was* disorganized, but now she was fresh and full of ideas and optimism after her conversation with Prudence. She needed to find someone to build the website. She could work on a draft of the mission statement, and a list of people who should receive an invitation to join Ocean Matters.

Prudence had given her a list of the more environmentally aware people with money who should be at the top of the appeal. But certainly, Beth thought, they needed young people, too, people her age who were optimistic about the future because honestly, they had to be. She typed in a few names. She hadn't been on the island for years and she'd lost touch with old friends. She was still living in a sort of dream world, transitioning from her life as a graduate student to life back in the town and the house where she'd grown up. She had planned to take a week to renew her familiarity with the island, to spend some time with her father, who must have been so lonely without her. But so quickly she had a job, and one she believed in!

Her fingers were on the keyboard when Ryder strode into the room. She'd met him briefly at the lecture, and she had spoken with him on the phone after Prudence hired her, but he was still new to her, and in a way, larger than life.

"Come with me," he said without even saying hello. "We're going out to Cisco. There's a seal stranded on the beach. Neck caught in a plastic net. The Marine Mammal Stranding Team just phoned. I want to see this. I want you to see it. My island ride is out on the street. We'll go in that."

Beth jumped up. She grabbed her phone, her purse, the keys.

"I should lock up."

"Hurry."

Beth double-checked the door and raced out to climb into the passenger seat of his Range Rover. Ryder hit the gas the moment she'd shut her door. She clicked on her seatbelt.

They rode up to Washington Street, over Dover, and turned right at Five Corners, heading for Hummock Pond Road.

"It's not far," Ryder said, as much to himself as to Beth.

"I know," she answered. "Do you want me to video it?"

"Good idea. Yes."

She was outrageously pleased with herself. She looked straight ahead, feeling important and purposeful.

After a few moments of silence, she sneaked a look at Ryder's hands on the steering wheel. They looked strong and tan, as if he was a man who sailed boats. Carefully, she slid her eyes up to settle on the side of his face. He had a handsome, strong profile, like a king or the commander of a ship. His nose and cheeks were red from the sun and his forehead was paler than the rest of his face, like so many men who wore their scalloper's caps all the time. When Prudence hired Beth for the job, she'd informed Beth that Ryder was divorced, lived in Boston, and was president of the board of Ocean Matters.

She jumped a bit when he asked, "Where are you from?"

"Nantucket."

"I mean, where did you grow up?"

"On Nantucket. I'm a real native. Born here, went to high school here, went to college at Wheaton, and got a master's in museum studies at BU. But all along I knew I wanted to come back here. I'd like to be director of the Nantucket Historical Association someday." Beth blushed when she told him her deepest dream.

Ryder took his eyes off the road to look at her. "You're really extraordinary, Beth, and a very lucky woman to know where you want to live and what you want to do. So many people your age have no idea. I know I didn't. It took me a long time to find out and I did a lot of stupid things on the way."

"Well, doing stupid things is half the fun, isn't it?" Beth joked and almost covered her mouth, shocked that such a carefree sentiment had come from her own voice. But something about Ryder, maybe simply his age, or maybe his calm very controlled presence, made her feel safe. If she'd said something like that to her father, he'd have given her a lecture about safe driving and the use of contraceptives.

Ryder leaned forward, concentrating as they bumped over the rutted dirt road to Cisco Beach. He parked at the top of the bluff leading down to the water. They both jumped out.

"There," Ryder said, pointing.

They slid down the sandy bluff to the beach. A man in shorts, work boots, and T-shirt was straddling a harbor seal, who was wallowing side to side, trying to escape and getting nowhere.

"Leo," Ryder said.

"Ryder, hey. Stand over this little lady and hold her steady while I cut the plastic off."

Ryder straddled the animal, gripping it with his calves, holding it firmly with his hands.

The seal was about five feet long, its fat body covered with soft speckled gray fur. Beth stayed a few feet away, knowing that the presence of people stressed these animals. She positioned herself to the side of the seal's face. It looked like a puppy, a sad puppy, its short snout bewhiskered and spotted and its black nose shaped like a black button.

She clicked pictures and moved to the side to

video the men struggling to free the seal from the net of turquoise plastic that ringed the seal's neck, choking it.

Something about the bulk of the creature and those wide dark eyes made her think of the last time she had seen Atticus, even though then his eyes had been blank and staring.

She shook it off. This was now. This animal would live.

As the plastic was cut away, the seal lifted its head and cried out. It wasn't a bark or a groan, it was more like a song, a long note held, expressing its fear . . . and its hope. After Leo sliced the last plastic cord away, he turned the seal's head to check the neck for injuries—none—and said "Okay" to Ryder. Ryder released the struggling seal. Immediately, it humped its ungraceful way down to the ocean and disappeared beneath the waves.

The two men shook hands and congratulated each other. Both were out of breath, and Leo actually dropped right to the ground.

"Thanks for coming so quickly," Leo said to Ryder. "I tried to deal with her myself, but she fought me. She really wanted to bite me."

"I was glad to help," Ryder said. "Beth, did you get it all on video?"

She double-checked. "I did!"

"Great," Ryder told her. "We'll get it up on Facebook and Instagram right away."

"Send me a copy," Leo said. "We'll post it on our marine mammal rescue site."

"So," Ryder said as they got back into his SUV, "first thing, get a Facebook and an Instagram account. Claim a domain and start building our website. We need to get this up fast."

"I can design the website but I'll need someone else to build it."

"Fine. Get someone right away."

His Bluetooth phone buzzed, the number flashing on the dashboard panel. As they drove back to town, Ryder talked with his secretary in Boston and there was no way Beth could not overhear the conversation. Ryder had a lot of meetings scheduled, including one with the governor. She was impressed, and she was glad that this new organization she was starting to work for was gaining support. It made her even more excited and eager to do her job.

They reached Easy Street, Ryder pulling into a parking space near the small grassy park that overlooked the harbor.

As Beth started to open her door, Ryder put his hand lightly on her arm. She turned back to look at him.

"Beth, what we did today was important. We were only three people, and we can't save the entire ocean. But think how that seal feels now, free of that plastic noose. We're starting a grassroots movement—" He stopped and corrected himself. "An eelgrass movement," he continued with a smile. "That seal was lucky, but so were we. We've got the perfect iconic video for what's happening out there in the ocean and how people can help. Think about that when you design the website."

Beth blinked as Ryder spoke, so passionately, a fire in his eyes and his hand so warm and restraining on her arm. As if he might draw her closer.

God! she thought, what was she even thinking? He was old! But he didn't look old and he didn't seem old. He was energetic, fiery, strong. She wanted to throw herself into his embrace and kiss him. Her heart was racing. She hoped he couldn't feel it through her arm. It was so many things at once, the excitement of doing something significant, the attraction of this frighteningly brilliant man, the opportunity to use her own skills and intelligence . . . and the chance of humiliation if she failed.

Beth said, "You know, different groups are already doing research here, on the loss of eelgrass, on water quality."

"Good," Ryder said absentmindedly, glancing at his watch. He lifted his hand from Beth's arm, and straightened in his seat. "I've got a meeting. Keep working on this. This seal did us a great favor. Email me."

"Sure," Beth said, smiling, and stepped down from the SUV.

Back in the office, Beth was energized. She sat down in her comfortable executive chair, pulled up a pad of lined yellow paper, and started a list. She studied her video of the men with the seal and decided it was really pretty awesome. For an hour she worked in a kind of cool-minded, emotion-hot intensity, until she paused, emotionally punched by the realization that her home, her island, was a kind of canary in the mine for the future of the coasts. Suddenly, this was very personal.

It was odd, difficult, to read the daily weather reports and mix that news with her memories of growing up on the island. She'd been so very happy, and sometimes she felt guilty about that happiness, because she had lost her mother, so shouldn't she always be sad? But the loss had happened when she was so young, she hadn't known what was normal, she didn't comprehend what she had lost. Her father had been her world, and she was his.

Her father loved the island. On weekends Mack took her hiking around the wild, lonely barrier beach called Coskata-Coatue that protected the Nantucket Harbor from the more savage waters of Nantucket Sound. He woke her early Sunday mornings to go to uninhabited island preserves to join the group of bird-watchers; he drove through a snowstorm to Coskata so she could see the snowy owl perched majestically on an evergreen. He taught her how to handle a Boston Whaler, how to fish, how to gut and dress the fish. He explained how the Wampanoag tribes had hunted whales from a canoe and gathered wild blueberries and beach plums from the moors to keep them healthy through the winters. He'd taken her with friends to spend the night on the nearby lonely island, Tuckernuck, and he'd shown her all the exquisite Main Street homes once built by the whaling captains. He'd impressed on her that this environment was fragile, the history of the island was unique, the beauty of the island unsurpassed.

Beth grew up knowing, deep in her heart where words could not go, that she was part of the island. She belonged to it.

And now, with the arrival of Ocean Matters and Ryder Hastings, she glimpsed an opportunity to help it. She had not been able to help her mother, and although Beth took as many chemistry and science courses as she could tolerate, she knew that she would never be the person to cure cancer, not the kind of cancer that had taken her mother. She'd never obsessed about that, she couldn't control the past. But when Atticus died, Beth had carried a kind of guilt with her that weighed heavily on her heart. She had not loved him enough to make him love his life. No one blamed

Beth for this, and she never spoke with anyone about it, because she knew with the rational part of her mind that she couldn't have saved Atticus, even if she'd stayed by his side every moment of every day. But she was determined to do *something* life-affirming, something that helped, that mattered.

And working for Ocean Matters made her believe she could do that. Would do that.

I am doing that, she thought as she looked at the work she'd done, as she saw more and more comments about the seal landing on the Facebook page. She was getting the word out. In her own small way, she was part of something larger, this island and the waters around it.

But what she'd done was only the beginning. She'd created a Facebook page and an Instagram page, but she needed help in order to build a website. She'd gone as far as she could go without technical help. Leaning back in her chair, she wondered what her next step should be.

fifteen

Juliet woke early, her mental alarm clock set to work time. For a while she allowed herself to look around her room, her *childhood* room. She'd been away for so long, first college, then her job with Kazaam. When she'd returned home for Christmas, for a week in the summer, she hadn't paid attention to her bedroom, but now she was almost twenty-eight, which in her mind meant she was almost thirty, and here she was, in bed alone, gazing at a poster of Ashton Kutcher on the wall.

Well, he *was* nice to look at.

Ryder Hastings was nice to look at, too.

She reached for her phone on the bedside table. Yesterday he had answered her text canceling dinner with a brief: *Maybe sometime next week?*

She had texted: *I'll probably be on Nantucket.*

So will I, he replied.

Since then, nothing new from him, and why should there be, she hadn't contacted him. Would she? Closing her eyes, she remembered how he had kissed her in his Tesla. What she'd felt for Ryder Hastings as they kissed, and what had lingered during the drive to Boston, was deeper than what she'd ever felt before. More *dimensional.*

Ha, Juliet said to herself, throwing back the covers and sitting up in bed. More *delusional* would be the correct word. She'd always known she didn't want to follow the traditional path, love, marriage, children. She'd always wanted to make a difference in the world, and while Kazaam hadn't actually brought world peace, she knew from comments on the website that her posts of dogs who had been mistreated and rescued and given a good home had brought a moment of joy and belief in the goodness of people. Maybe that was an event of little significance, but still, it counted.

She pulled on a pair of leggings to wear with the Red Sox tee she slept in, slid her feet into flip-flops, and went down the stairs, carrying her laptop with her. In Cambridge, she often waited until noon to dress, working in bed or on her sofa in a robe and slippers. She smelled the tantalizing aroma of coffee coming from the kitchen and headed toward it.

Her mother was in the kitchen.

"You look nice, Mom," Juliet said, kissing Lisa on the cheek.

"Nice," Lisa echoed, and smiled.

"What? You want your daughter to say you look like a babe?" Juliet poured herself a cup of coffee and settled in a kitchen chair. “Speaking of men—”

Lisa interrupted. “I didn’t realize we were speaking of men. And I need to open the shop.”

“So you don’t want to hear about the time I spent with Ryder Hastings?”

“The time you spent with Ryder Hastings?” Lisa echoed. “I do want to hear about that.”

“After his lecture, somehow we were on the same boat back and he offered to drive me up to Cambridge in his *Tesla.*”

“Go on.” Lisa folded her arms and leaned against the sink.

“He asked me out to dinner. I accepted. But then Theo arrived and we wanted to come down here, so I texted him to cancel.”

“And that’s it?”

“That’s it. He hasn’t called back.”

“Do you want him to?”

“Of course I want him to! He’s all the things, Mom. Smart and rich and charming.”

Lisa looked worried.

Oh God, Juliet thought, *she’s going to get all anxious and tell me that smart and rich and charming aren’t the best qualities in a husband, my father was smart, rich, and charming and look what happened to them . . .*

“Isn’t he a lot older than you are?” Lisa asked, making herself all bright-eyed and chirpy, like a sweet bird on a branch.

"Isn't Mack a lot younger than you are?" Juliet countered.

"Touché," Lisa said, with a genuine smile. She pulled her large leather bag over her shoulder and kissed Juliet on the forehead. "I do have to open the shop. We'll talk more, later." She went out the back door into the day.

Juliet stood at the open door, soaking in the sweetness of the morning.

"Must run," she told herself and tore up the stairs to put on a sports bra, a loose T-shirt, and running shoes. No iPod, no music in her earbuds. Simplicity.

This was what she needed. It worked every time, clearing her head, getting away from electronics, enjoying the weather on this beautiful island. She hurried downstairs, opened the front door, checked her Fitbit, and headed off.

It felt good to run. June was a gentle time, with hydrangea blooming and roses budding. She zigzagged along the narrow streets down the hill to the town pier where sailboats, Boston Whalers, and fishing boats bobbed in the breezy waters. And now she was home, really back home. When she was younger, she went to Cisco and Dionis with her friends for parties, but the town pier and the small beach patrolled by gulls and mallards felt like her very own. Here, the water was translucent, the ducks paddling along complacently, the wooden dock scattered with shells the gulls had dropped from a great height to break open so they could swoop down and seize the sweet meat inside. From here she could see the small chubby Brant Point lighthouse and a fast ferry slowing as it came into the harbor. Here, between the beach and the street, wild roses were already in bloom, perfuming the air. Across the harbor, on the Monomoy beach, someone was flying a red kite.

She sat on the sand to catch her breath, then untied her shoes and walked down the cool sand and into the water. It was very cold, and yet she wanted to fall into the water, as if being baptized by the bliss of being alive. Instead, she went back to her shoes, retied them, and stood, looking in all directions. She decided to walk the docks, up and down Swain's Wharf, Old South Wharf, Straight Wharf, and Old North Wharf until she was across from the Harborside Stop & Shop and headed up Main Street.

At the corner of Main and South Water, she paused as a large Range Rover drove past. Beth Whitney was in the passenger seat, and Ryder was driving.

The shock stopped her dead. She bent over with her hands on her knees, shaking her head in dismay. Ryder was with beautiful Beth. Juliet groaned. A woman walking her spaniel gave her a curious glance, but Juliet ignored her.

Juliet turned around, picked up speed, ignored

the rest of her route, and raced to her house, wanting to get to her phone. She hated having it with her all the time, but if she didn't have it, that seemed to be when she needed it.

She crashed into the house, leaving the door open behind her. For a moment she put her hands on her knees again, catching her breath.

"Juliet? Is that you?" Theo called from the kitchen.

"Yes," Juliet called back. "Give me a moment."

"I want coffee," Theo said.

Juliet staggered into the kitchen and collapsed on a chair. "So have some. The Keurig's right there."

Theo searched the countertops. "Where are the pods?"

"We don't use the pods. They aren't recyclable. They don't biodegrade. There's a basket in the drainer, and ground coffee in the pottery canister that says 'sugar.' "

Theo found a spoon, filled the basket, grumbling under his breath. "How can anyone fill this damn thing when you've just woken up? You need caffeine before you can do this kind of teeny-weeny tiny hands operation."

Juliet snorted. "So, fill it the night before."

"You're such a hard-ass." Theo waited while the machine boiled the water and filled his cup. He carried it over to the kitchen table and sat down.

"Theo, you talk like a fifteen-year-old. Stop it. You're too old to be so crude."

"Well, you're too pretty to be so cranky."

Surprised, Juliet let down her guard. "I just saw Beth Whitney in the car with Ryder Hastings."

"Who's Ryder Hastings?"

"The new rich guy who's come to save our island."

"And that's a bad thing? Because, you sound bitter." Theo poured three teaspoons of sugar into his mug and stirred.

"I thought we were . . . starting a thing," Juliet admitted.

"Well, just because Beth was in his car . . ." Theo asked casually, "How did Beth look?"

"Right," Juliet said. "I'd forgotten. You like Beth."

"Everyone likes Beth," Theo said miserably.

Juliet gazed at her handsome, softhearted brother, and she wanted to put her arms around him and cuddle him as she had when he was very small and had hurt himself on his bike. Now he looked like a Greek god, but a very downhearted Greek god.

"We're not going to know what's going on sitting here like a pair of burst balloons," she said. "I'll go take a shower and get some Kazaam work done on my laptop. You should shower and get dressed, and maybe go through the stuff in your chest of drawers, find out if you've got anything here that will fit you."

"Mom put a ton of her stuff in my room."

"Oh, poor baby. I'm sure you had much better accommodations in California. So put it out in the hall if it bothers you. And start a load of laundry. Cheer up. When I've got some work done, we'll go into town and I'll buy you lunch."

Theo lifted his head and smiled. "Thanks, sis."

Juliet headed up the stairs to shower. She was in a better mood after talking with Theo. He was such a good guy and he seldom got upset when she bossed him around. Plus, he still had a crush on Beth, and Juliet could remember the high school years when she'd caught Beth staring at Theo as if he were a hot fudge sundae on a scorching summer day. A Beth-Theo romance was not out of the question. And Beth was two years younger than Juliet, which would make Ryder seem even older to Beth.

Juliet sang in the shower.

sixteen

As they strolled down the brick sidewalks of Main Street, Theo said he thought the town hadn't changed much.

"Are you kidding? A lot has changed," Juliet said.

"Huh?"

"Congdon's Pharmacy is gone. Arno's is gone. Tonkin's."

They turned down Federal. Theo said, "The Catholic church is still here. Hey, and the post office and library."

Across from the brick town buildings stood a white clapboard structure that had once been a home, then a series of offices. The Mooney Building. Now it had a patio out back and steps led down to a bright café.

"The Corner Table Café," Juliet told him. "It has it all. Healthy food and Wi-Fi."

Theo laughed. "Checking out the crowd included?"

She ignored him. He followed her to the refrigerated cabinet stretching along one wall. Juliet was right, the food looked fresh and delicious. Theo chose a container of mac and cheese and one of lasagna.

"Please," Juliet said. "Could you eat a salad? Maybe some roasted broccoli?"

Theo stacked the container of roasted broccoli on top of the others. Juliet had salmon on arugula. At the register, she took out her credit card. Theo reached out for some cookies.

Juliet said, "You don't want those."

"Give me a break," Theo snapped.

She looked exasperated. "*Those* are gluten free. The ones *you* want are at the left."

"Oh, right. Thanks," Theo muttered.

They settled in at a corner table. The café wasn't crowded but it was busy. Theo's food had been heated up in handsome black bowls. They had real utensils, not bendy plastic ones, and free carbonated water. Theo dug in.

"Juliet!"

Theo, still chewing, stared up at the voice. Beth was walking their way. Unlike Juliet, who looked like any Silicon Valley techie with her cropped hair and black clothes, Beth was classy, silky blond hair waving over her shoulders, white shirt, tan skirt, sandals. He swallowed his food without tasting it.

"Beth." He actually stood up, the way he'd been taught to do when a woman approached a table. He hadn't done that in a long time.

"Hi, Theo." Leaning over, she kissed him on the cheek. "You're back on the island again. And you're here, too, Juliet!"

"I am." Juliet forced a smile. "Maybe for a while. We just got here."

"Want to join us?" Theo asked.

"Sure," Beth said. She set her laptop on the bench. "I'll get some lunch and be right back."

Juliet murmured, "Theo. You're drooling."

"Am not." Still, just in case, he ran his hand over his chin. "She didn't look like that in high school."

Juliet rolled her eyes. "Men are so easy."

Theo concentrated on eating before Beth returned. He didn't want her to see him masticating away on the damned broccoli like a horse.

Theo had taken the bench side and Juliet was in a chair across from him. Beth pulled out a chair next to Juliet and sat down, arranging her bowl of salad and couscous, her knife and fork, and her glass of water on the table, and her napkin in her lap.

"Theo, it's wonderful to see you!" Beth said. "Are you back for good?"

"No, I kind of came home to recover. I wiped out when I was surfing. A bad fracture. I was in the hospital for a while. Then in a brace. For a while, a sling."

"Oh, too bad. Does it hurt?"

"Not so much now," Theo said bravely.

"You were in California, right?"

"Right. I got my degree at UCSD. Since then,

I've been surfing and working near San Diego. I don't know how long I'll be here."

Beth looked disappointed. "Yes, the surfing here can't compete with the Pacific."

"What about you, Beth? What are you doing?" Theo asked.

She told him about her degree in museum studies. "I was going to apply at some of the museums, but after Saturday, when Ryder Hastings spoke here, I've agreed to work for the Nantucket chapter of Ocean Matters."

"What's that?" Theo asked.

Juliet interrupted. "You're working for Ocean Matters? What are you doing?"

"I'm their operations manager, and probably general gofer. We've set up office on Easy Street. I've got it furnished enough to work in, and I'm going to design a website. I need someone to build it for me. Oh, Juliet, you build websites, don't you?"

Warily, Juliet admitted she did. "But I don't know how long I'll be on-island, or how much more work I can take on."

"Oh, please help me build the website. I already have an amazing video to put on. Ryder and I went out to Cisco this morning to rescue a seal that was choked with plastic around its neck. It was very emotional. I've posted on Instagram and Facebook, but I really need to build a website for Ocean Matters."

"You and Ryder?" Theo asked, not daring to look at her. "That sounds very chummy."

Juliet held her breath.

"Don't be weird," Beth said. "I work for Ryder. For Ocean Matters. It's about our oceans, Theo, which you of all people should care about since you're such a big surfer."

"Yeah, sorry," Theo said. "Just checking to see if you were, um, going with Ryder."

Beth leaned across the table, close to him. "No, Theo. I'm not going with Ryder. Not with anyone."

Theo smiled. He couldn't stop gazing into her eyes.

Juliet broke in. "How did you get your job, Beth?"

Beth sat back in her chair. "Prudence Starbuck, you know, the bossy old heiress on Main Street. Prudence has agreed to be the head of the Nantucket branch of Ocean Matters. I'm their employee."

"With pay?" Juliet asked.

"Yes. And I've got a lot of work to do." Beth blushed as she turned to Theo. "Could you help me unpack the computers and printers? They're so heavy. Oh, but your arm . . ."

Quickly, Theo said, "It's okay, mostly healed. I'll use my other arm. We'll work together." He had never been more self-sacrificing.

"Our office is near the Steamship Authority," Beth told him.

"Cool. I'm ready whenever you are."

"Let's go!" Beth said. "I'll take my lunch with me to eat later."

Theo nearly knocked over the table as he rose to follow Beth to the door.

"Men," Juliet whispered as her brother followed Beth out of the café. Theo had been in love with Beth since high school. He'd broken many hearts. Juliet hoped Beth didn't break his.

"Hello, there."

Juliet looked up. Ryder Hastings was standing next to her table.

"Hello," she answered warily.

"I've been trying to reach you," he said.

"Yes," Juliet replied coolly. "I know. I heard about your adventure with the seal at Cisco today."

Ryder slid onto the bench where Theo had been sitting only moments before. He was Theo's height, but much slimmer than muscular Theo. He had a mug of coffee in his hand, and a muffin on a plate.

"It was a moving experience." He laughed. "In all meanings of the word. Once we got the plastic off, that seal scooted into the water faster than I thought seals could go on land."

Juliet toyed with her food. The man was

frustratingly handsome. Dark hair, thick and shaggy, as if he was too busy to visit the barbershop. Blue eyes full of curiosity and what looked like a whole lot of mischief. His nose and cheeks were red from the sun. Didn't the man own sunblock, or was he too busy to apply it?

Aware of how she looked in her black yoga pants and sleeveless black tee, aware that her brown hair was rumpled and almost the same careless length as Ryder's, aware that she wore no mascara or lipstick but only her naked, natural face, Juliet raised her chin and said, "That's a wonderful thing you did. Beth told me about it. She's posting on social media, but, um, she asked me to help build a website."

"You're going to help? Great!"

The air between them danced like lights from a disco ball. Juliet couldn't take her eyes away from his. She wanted to freeze him there across from her so she could stare at him, at his blue eyes, his black hair, the furry hair on his arms—he wore a blue button-down shirt with the sleeves rolled up. She thought what she felt must be kind of like being tasered.

"There you are!" a man said, clapping Ryder on the back. Without an invitation, Leo Johns slid onto the bench next to Ryder. "Hey Juliet, did you hear about Ryder helping me save a seal this morning?" He sensed the change in atmosphere as he sat down. "Sorry, Juliet, I don't mean to interrupt your conversation but Ryder and I have a meeting scheduled for now. About Ocean Matters. Would you like to join us? We can use all the hands we can get."

Juliet couldn't think straight. It all whirled: the abrupt jump from intimate desire to the outer reality, the cup in her hand, the one in Ryder's hand, the hard table between them, the buzz of other people laughing and chatting, all around her in the bright room, Leo Johns with his jug ears and round belly like a short Santa Claus in tennis shorts, a nice man, a retired lawyer who gave his time and money to island causes.

"No, thanks," she said. "I've got to be somewhere. See you."

Ryder took her wrist in his hand. "We didn't get to have our dinner. Can I take you out tonight?"

Run away, an inner voice warned. *Are you kidding?* another inner voice said.

"I can't do it tonight," she said.

"Tomorrow night?"

His hand was warm on her wrist. His grip was light, and electric. She knew Leo Johns was watching.

"Okay, I guess, tomorrow night." She picked up her wallet and left quickly, before they could make plans.

It wasn't until she was all the way to the Hub that she remembered she hadn't put her cup in the tub for used china. The omission stopped her in her tracks. She went hot all over. What would Ryder think of her, of her ability to care about the ocean, if she couldn't even remember to remove her cup from the table to the bin? Should she go back and move the cup? No, that would be insane.

"What is going on?" Juliet muttered.

Shaken, she walked down to the harbor, taking long strides, cutting through other walkers as if she was on roller skates. The walk helped her catch her breath. The sight of the blue water, so clear even where motorboats were docked, calmed her even more.

She sat on a bench and watched the fishermen prepare their Boston Whalers. Real life was hard work, she decided. Her apartment and office in Cambridge suddenly seemed like a refuge to her. A hiding place.

But with much of her heart and all of her body, she didn't want to hide.

So, she wouldn't hide! She'd flirt like a male peacock, using all the colors of the rainbow. Okay, that might be too much, but she knew exactly where to find the perfect outfit to wear to dinner with Ryder.

She walked past the post office, the Catholic church, and the Hub, where people were buying magazines, newspapers, and coffee. She crossed the cobblestone street and stopped in front of *Sail*, her mother's store. A darling turquoise dress with a sexy halter-top was in the window, and Juliet's reflection in her all-black Athleta tee and yoga pants wavered over the dress like a crow floating on a flower.

She pushed the door open and went inside. The air was cool and dry and fragrant, and upbeat music drifted through the air from a local radio station. Lisa was bending over her jewelry counter. No one else was in the shop.

"Hi, Mom!"

"Darling!" Lisa came from behind the counter and hugged Juliet. "Not that I'm complaining, but what brings you here?"

"I want to buy a dress to wear out to dinner with Ryder Hastings," Juliet said.

"Really? Oh, what fun!"

Seeing her mother's face brighten sent rockets of emotions through Juliet's heart. Guilt, because she'd always been critical of Lisa's store and in fact, in her teenage years, she'd been really snotty and insulting about it. Pleasure, because this simple act was making her mother so happy. How hard it must be to be a mother, whose happiness was so tightly bound up in her children.

And finally, an emotion she hadn't experienced often—*anticipation.*

"Can I try on that turquoise dress in the window?" Juliet asked.

Lisa laughed. "Of course. You must be a size six." She walked over to the rack, lifted the dress down, and told her daughter, “Let’s go into a dressing room. While you’re trying this on, I’ll see if I’ve got anything else you might like.”

Juliet stepped into the small room with its gold hooks and little flouncy stool and large mirror. She peeled off her pants and tee, unzipped the turquoise dress, and slid into it. It took a few seconds for her to understand what she saw in the mirror. She looked very, very feminine, and the dress was cut to make her breasts seem enormous. This was not who she was. Was this who she should try to be?

Her mother’s voice floated through the curtain. “Juliet, I’m hanging some dresses on the rod. You don’t have to try them on, but I think they’d look great on you.”

“Thanks, Mom.” Already, Juliet was discouraged. She couldn’t wear this dress.

She lifted another dress off the curtain rod and held it up to her. It was navy blue, short sleeved, with a square, slightly low neckline trimmed with white piping. Summery, nautical, undeniably classy. It fit perfectly, showing off her trim figure, and the hem was slightly flippy, which Juliet loved.

Stepping outside the cubicle, Juliet held up her arms. “Ta-da!”

Before her mother could speak, two women in Lilly Pulitzer dresses and straw hats trimmed with ribbon entered the store. They wandered over to the Ralph Lauren rack and flipped through the hanging clothes, exchanging comments—"Oh, this is darling!" "Oh, you'd look stunning in this!"

Juliet ducked back into her pretty stall. Lifting the dresses her mother had brought over for her to try, she concentrated on trying them on. She couldn't help but overhear the others.

Her mother said, "May I carry some things to a dressing room for you?"

"Yes, please. Your clothes are *darling!*" one of the women said.

"Thank you," Lisa told them.

The two women—Juliet figured out that their names were Zoe and Cynthia—called to each other as they tried on the dresses.

"Oooh, sexy!"

"Maybe too plunging?"

"Excuse me, miss? Could I try this in a size four?" Zoe flung a dress over the curtain rod.

"Of course," Lisa said. "I'll see if we have it in that size."

Juliet tried on an ivory tank dress that would look fabulous if she ever got a tan, but with her winter working-girl pale skin didn't work.

"Hey," said Zoe, "have you seen Ryder Hastings? The Boston guy who's heading up Save the Water? He's gorgeous, rich, and single!"

"Yes," Cynthia said lazily, "he's on-island. He

called me about his environmental group. He is handsome . . .”

Juliet froze, all her senses focused on that conversation.

“I don’t think it’s called Save the Water. That’s hilarious. I think it’s Ocean Affairs.”

Juliet almost had to clamp her hand over her mouth to keep from correcting the women.

“Whatever. I think they’re going to have a big fundraising gala in August.”

“I hope they have it somewhere inside. I hate when my heels get stuck in the grass.”

“Want to offer your house for the gala? You might get to know him better then . . .”

Juliet sat down on the stool, taking deep breaths.

“So these are adorable!” Zoe cooed. “I’ll take them all. Wrap them in tissue, will you?”

“I’m taking these,” Cynthia said.

“Oh, no,” Zoe said, “you’re not getting the same dress I am, are you?”

“Just the one. The others are all different. I’ll check with you every time to be sure I don’t wear it to the same event. Besides, we text each other every day.”

Feeling like a total idiot, Juliet watched through a sliver of space between the curtains as her mother wrapped the dresses in tissue, slipped them into bags, and rang up the sales. Zoe and Cynthia checked their phones and then dropped their platinum credit cards on the counter and signed the receipts.

"Thank you," Lisa called, as the women left her shop.

Juliet stepped out of her cubicle wearing the navy dress. "What do you think?"

"Oh, darling! You look absolutely elegant."

"Right, that would be me," Juliet said, but she was flattered. She knew her mother wouldn't let her buy anything that was wrong for her. "I'll take it."

"I'll give you the family discount," Lisa told her.

"Good, because your stuff is expensive," Juliet said.

"Did you hear my customers talking about Ocean Matters?" Lisa asked, as she delicately folded the dress in tissue.

"Ocean Affairs," Juliet snorted. Then she straightened, hit by a thought. "Of course everyone will get the name wrong until I get the website built. I've got to go back and talk with Beth." She picked up her pretty lemon-colored bag with *Sail* on it in navy blue. "Thanks, Mom!"

Juliet strode down the brick sidewalk, swinging her bag and buzzing with excitement about her new dress. Oh, God, she was such a girl. She could understand statistics and write code, but she was so totally a girl.

And she kind of liked it.

She reached Beth's office on Easy Street. The door was open, and the office had been set up so that it looked professional and welcoming.

Beth was at a table, eating her salad. "Your brother left about ten minutes ago," she said.

"It's you I want to talk to." Juliet pulled out a folding chair and sat across from Beth, carefully setting her bag on the floor. "We need to get the website up as soon as possible. Can we discuss its design, colors, and so on? We can always add and change, but we've got to get it up. I just heard someone call it Ocean Affairs."

Beth laughed. "I know. We do have to get busy. Theo was so helpful with the furniture—" She saw Juliet's impatient scowl. "So now, let's get going on the website."

"I want to use GoDaddy, because it's the fastest," Juliet told her. "But I need to know what you want the general appearance to be. Colors. Logo? Contact box."

"I think blues for the colors, don't you?"

Beth spun her chair over to her laptop. Juliet carried her chair over next to her. Beth was young, educated, smart, slow to anger, quick to understand, very quick to laugh. Plus she smelled good. This was more fun than working at Kazaam, Juliet decided. Beth moved back so Juliet could work, and Juliet's fingers flew over the keys.

seventeen

Lisa closed her shop at five on the dot and hurried home. The guys were still plastering somewhere on the first floor, but she didn't stop to say hello. Theo and Juliet weren't around, which was a blessing. She had time to focus on herself.

She took a long hot soaking bath. When she got out, she dried carefully and spent a luxurious time rubbing creams and lotions into her skin, everywhere on her skin, bum and inner thighs as well as feet and neck. After double-checking that she'd locked the bathroom door, she dropped her towel and studied herself in the mirror.

She saw a perfectly healthy woman with a not unattractive body. She still had a waist. Her hips were larger than they once had been, but in general, she looked okay. She'd never been embarrassed when she wore a bathing suit to the beach.

But tonight would be different. *Could* be different. Tonight she was going to Mack's for dinner.

Wrapped in a towel, Lisa left the bathroom and headed for her underwear drawer. She wore ivory or black bras, with cups to conceal her nipples, wide straps for support. There wasn't an inch of sexiness about them. And her panties! She always wore cotton for comfort, and the waistbands were stretched and the fabric was tired from hundreds of washings. And they were so huge! Lisa had never been comfortable in bikini panties. Once, years ago, she and Rachel had experimented with thongs. That had been hilarious. Why would any woman wear them? You certainly couldn't when you had your period and in the past few menopausal years—dear God, she was in menopause! Several times, with no reason or warning whatsoever, Lisa's period showed up and then she had to race to the bathroom for a pad.

But younger women had to deal with periods every month, Lisa thought, and felt a little better. She found an old pair of black panties to go with a black bra. She put them on and thought she needed to start doing sit-ups. *Crunches.* The thought of that torture was enough to make her consider, briefly, forgetting about men for the rest of her life.

Oh, she looked fine, she told herself, and no one was going to see her underwear tonight. If she had time, she'd order some new undies. With lace.

In a green sundress and sandals, she walked to Mack's house. It felt good to stretch her legs, and it calmed her nerves to walk through this charming town, plus no one would see her car parked in front of his house.

She'd wondered what his house would look like, feel like. He was a hard worker, and from what she'd seen of his truck and the way his employees left her house at the end of the working day, she expected a tidy minimalist interior with few possessions and all of them in their appropriate places. His house was a large Cape with a simple lawn and no flowers, but his door was a cheery yellow with a brass whale for a knocker.

"Come in," Mack said, holding the door wide.

"Wow." She stepped into the hall and immediately into a long open plan room serving as living room, dining room, kitchen and den.

"I knocked some walls down," Mack told her, giving her time to look around. "Remember, I had a little girl to raise, and I wanted her to have friends over, and this way I could keep an eye on her while I cooked dinner."

Lisa walked around the long room. The glossy wooden floors were covered with thick Persian rugs, subtly marking different areas. The walls were ivory, and bare except for a few pictures that were probably done by Beth as a child. The furniture was mix and match, inviting armchairs with soft cushions, an heirloom mahogany dining table with diverse chairs—antique wood, pale white Ikea-ish, light oak, all with non-matching quilted chair pads that made the area colorful.

The kitchen was modern. Gleaming chrome

appliances, a long granite work counter, a cork floor, and the ceiling hung with a rack of copper-bottomed pans.

"Beautiful home," she told him.

"Thanks. I thought we'd eat outside if that's okay with you," Mack said.

"Of course."

Mack poured her a glass of red wine—he'd learned her preferences—and led her to the patio. It was brick, with bright blue tubs of red geraniums set around the edge. "Beth's contribution," Mack said. A large state-of-the-art grill stood at one side.

Mack lifted the lid to test the roast. "Hungry?"

"Very."

"About fifteen minutes more," Mack told her.

They sat at a round patio table in canvas chairs next to each other, sipping a delicious pinot noir. The striped sun umbrella had been closed, and for a while they made light talk while they watched the sky change over the neighboring trees. Mack's backyard was as plain as his front yard, simply a lawn with untamed shrubbery around the perimeter.

"I used to have a swing set here," Mack said. "Then a large wading pool. Beth and I discussed putting in a real swimming pool, but somehow I never got around to it, and she prefers going to the beach with her friends." He sighed. "At least she used to. She grew up so fast."

Lisa swiveled in her chair to look up at the back of the house. "You have a large house."

"I do. Well, we did, my wife and I. We planned on having several kids. But that didn't happen. When she died, I thought I'd move from this house, but the therapist told me it would be good for Beth to remain in a place she knew, where she felt comfortable, rather than changing her young life even more. But I had to make some kind of visible acknowledgment of Marla's life and death, I wanted Beth to feel her mother was with her still in some way. So I turned the master bedroom into a playroom for Beth. I got rid of the bed and most of Marla's belongings. I put Beth's toys in the dresser and turned the closet into a dress-up space, a hiding space, storage for whatever stuffed animals she'd lost interest in. I knocked out the wall between the two rooms and built a small three-fourths wall with shelves on it holding Beth's books and separating her bed and bedside table from the larger area so she could have her own private space. It might sound like a strange thing to do, but it worked well for her."

"It sounds like a unique way to deal with such a major change in a child's life. And Beth has grown into a lovely, successful young woman."

"Thank you," Mack said. His voice softened, his gaze settled on Lisa. "After dinner maybe you'll come upstairs with me and I can show you the rooms."

Lisa said, "I'd like that," and she knew he understood exactly what she meant.

When the roast was ready, Mack attended to unskewering it and deftly carving it on the carving board attached to the grill. He had already set the table with placemats and plates and cutlery.

"What can I do?" Lisa asked.

"Bring out the bottle of wine?"

Lisa fetched the wine and filled their glasses. Mack had broiled Brussels sprouts coated with olive oil and salt on the grill in an aluminum package, and he transferred them into a serving dish. They ate as if starving, feasting on the meal, using the bread to sop up the peppery juice of the meat.

"This is amazing," Lisa told him. "You'll have to stop me or I'll eat the entire roast."

"Oh, I'll stop you," Mack said with a smile. "I have other pleasures planned."

And that did bring her to a halt. The words *I haven't, I can't,* flashed through her mind but her body strongly reminded her that she certainly could, and after they'd brought the food and dishes in and quickly put everything away, she was ready for him when he turned to face her.

"Now for dessert," he said.

"Oh?" Her heart was pounding hard.

"What a cliché, right?" he asked. "I should

have a curly pointed mustache to twirl. Ah, my pretty, want to see my etchings?"

She smiled. She thought he was as nervous about all this as she was. Mack wasn't yet fifty, but years of manual labor had taken its toll on his beautiful body. The fourth finger of his right hand had been knocked out of line with a careless blow of someone's hammer. He was solid and muscular—she'd studied his body thoroughly when he was working on her house—and he was beautiful, but he wasn't young.

But he was ten years younger than she was.

He took her hand, leading her up the stairs to the several bedrooms and baths. They passed Beth's rooms quickly, neither in the mood for the sweetness of childhood or the turbulence of adolescence. They wanted their own particular sweetness and turbulence.

Mack's bedroom was large but plain. A queen-sized bed with clean white sheets and a light quilt at the bottom. A modern ergonomic reading chair with a standing light behind it. A long dresser. A flat-screen television on the wall.

It wasn't quite sunset, and the light from the two windows was an indigo blue, a kind of iridescent darkness. They stepped into the bedroom. Mack closed the bedroom door. The harsh yellow hall light vanished and they saw each other in the kinder, more romantic dusk that revealed and hid so perfectly that it was as if this light, this time of day, had been created exactly for making love.

Lisa stood still. Mack moved toward her, put his arms around her, pulled her against him, and bent to kiss her. At the kiss, they both changed, in a kind of magic, from reasonable friends to ravenous beings who had been denied what they craved for far too long. Lisa had forgotten what desire felt like—had she ever felt *this?*

But when Mack ran his hands down her body, Lisa pulled away. "I'm sorry. I can't."

"Lisa—"

"Please."

"Don't be frightened." Mack took a step back, giving her space.

"I'm not frightened," Lisa said. She saw the concern in his eyes and admitted, "I'm *terrified.*"

And wonderfully, after a tense second, they both smiled.

"Come over here," Mack said, patting the side of the bed. "Sit. Just sit. Let's talk."

She carefully sat on the edge of the bed. "Mack, it's not just the . . . sex. I haven't been with a man since Erich. Maybe that's odd, but it's the truth. But it's more than the sex. I don't know how to explain it. I don't know if this, whatever it is, between us, is temporary or . . ."

"Or permanent," Mack finished for her.

Shocked, Lisa said, "Well, *that*'s a frightening word, isn't it?"

Mack nodded. "It is." Reaching over, he took

her hand. "I guess this is happening all too fast. We're like a couple of teenagers."

Lisa smiled ruefully. "I know. But I'm certainly not a teenager."

"Nor am I."

"Mack, I have to say this." Lisa took a deep breath. "I worry about the difference in our ages. I'm so much older than you."

"Lisa," Mack said seriously, "I've gone so many years without meeting the right woman. Now I've found you. I don't care about our ages. I want to be with you."

"Yes," Lisa said. "I want that, too. But I still need time . . ."

"I can wait. I'm not a kid anymore. I know who I am and what I want. I want you. But look. No one knows how long he has to live. All the wisdom says to seize the day. I want to seize each day with you. Actually," he said with a smile, "I want to seize you."

Lisa smiled. "I want that, too." Reluctantly, she added, "Just not yet."

"I'll be ready whenever you want," Mack said. He stood up. "Let's go back downstairs. Sitting on this bed with you is keeping me from thinking logically."

Because she was shaking, Lisa held on to the banister as they went downstairs. She hoped this didn't make her seem like a little old lady who was afraid of falling, and as she turned to explain this to Mack, who was right behind her, she thought, But I *am* afraid of falling, afraid of falling in love.

They went into the kitchen. Lisa sat at the table while Mack brewed two cups of decaf.

"If I have real coffee after eight o'clock, I can't sleep," Mack explained.

"I know. I'm the same way."

He set her cup before her and sat down across from her. Lisa stared into her cup, stirring it as if her life depended on it.

"I'm sorry," she murmured.

"Don't be," Mack said. "Look, Lisa, whatever is happening between us is something rare, I think. I certainly haven't felt this way before."

"No, I haven't, either. It's not only physical, Mack."

"I know. And it's new. But it's strong. And it's real."

Lisa lifted her eyes to meet his. "So what do we do?"

Mack smiled. "I guess we slow down. I mean, on the physical part. I think I've got a lot to learn about you and a lot I want you to know about me, and something about you makes me want to be around you, even if it's just walking on the beach."

The front door slammed.

"Hey, Dad!"

Lisa froze.

Mack said, “She said she was going out with the girls. I was sure she’d be gone all evening.”

“Dad?” Beth strode through the large room, a shining princess with her long blond hair and willowy frame. When she spotted Lisa, she stopped dead, blushing crimson, wide-eyed. “Oh, Lisa.”

“I invited Lisa to dinner,” Mack told her.

“Oh! Oh, wow, so that’s why you were marinating that giant roast.”

“Hi, Beth.” Suddenly Lisa was grateful for the years of practice her own children had given her with awkward situations. “Your father’s been working on my old house and we’ve become good friends. He invited me to dinner, and what a surprise! He cooks as well as he restores old homes.”

Beth smiled uncertainly. “Oh,” she said again, obviously struggling through her emotions to find words.

“I thought you were having a girls’ night out,” Mack said.

“I did, kind of. I left early because I have to work tomorrow.”

“Want a cup of decaf?” Mack asked.

“No thanks. I’m good.” His question eased the situation, and Beth joined them at the table. Shyly, she turned to Lisa. “I saw Theo today. At the Corner Table Café. He came over to the Ocean Matters office and helped me unload and hook up the computers and printers." Quickly, Beth brightened. "Oh, and I saw Juliet and asked her to help build a website for Ocean Matters and she agreed."

"That's great," Lisa said, but secretly thought, *and now Mack's daughter is going to be involved with both of my children.* So much had happened in the last half hour that Lisa couldn't think straight. *I've just been kissing your father,* she thought giddily and she glanced over at Mack. He was smiling at her. Lisa was dazzled, and frustrated that she couldn't continue the intimate conversation with Mack, and all she could do, really, was leave. "I should go home. I've got my shop to open tomorrow."

Mack stood up. "And I've got your ceilings to finish." He put a hand on her waist as they walked toward the front door.

Lisa paused at the door. "Thanks so much for the delicious dinner. That roast was almost the best thing I've ever tasted."

"Yeah," Mack said with an intimate wicked grin. "For me, too."

eighteen

When her father returned to the kitchen, Beth asked, "Are you dating her?"

She knew her father would be slow to answer. He was a thoughtful man, wanting not to be misunderstood.

"I'm not sure," he said at last. "I think for now we're friends."

"You two looked more than friendly to me."

Mack put his hands on the back of a chair. "Would that be a problem for you? I know you liked Theo in high school."

"Oh, Dad, come on, that was high school!"

"Theo is back in town. He helped you in the office today."

"True," Beth responded with exaggerated patience. "But that was a one-time thing." She was distressed and couldn't figure out her own emotions.

Her father said, "Well, you're upset about something."

How could Beth tell her dad that what was really driving her out of her mind was Theo?

She'd felt so close to Theo when he was unpacking the computers. He'd seemed so *real,* not just a handsome goofball. But what was going on with Lisa and her dad? It would be impossible to date Theo if his mom was dating her dad!

"Thanks," she said, when her father handed her a warm cup of cocoa with a marshmallow on top. "This is awesome." She took a breath. "But please. Are you seriously seeing Lisa, like, romantically?"

Mack grinned. "Are you, like, ten years old?"

"I mean, Dad, come on. Isn't she a lot older than you?"

Mack's face changed. She could tell her father's sense of humor had disappeared. "She's ten years older than I am. We're both adults. I don't see the problem."

"Well . . . won't people talk?"

"For God's sake, Beth. When have we ever cared about people talking? I thought I raised you to be more open-minded than that. So what if people talk?"

Beth flushed. She'd made her father angry, and that was an indication of how he felt about Lisa Hawley. When she was a little girl, she'd wanted, in a vague misty Disney sort of way, to have a new mother who would love her and help her choose the right clothes and make her bedroom lavender instead of the dazzling pink her father had painted it. By the time she was twelve, her feelings had changed. She didn't want another woman to break into the happy twosome she'd become with her father. Whenever she caught him flirting with another woman at a school ballgame or play, she'd plunge into a dark mood for days. She'd pretty much hated him during high school because he wouldn't let her go places or have boys spend the night like her other friends' parents did.

But now she was older, and she could guess at how lonely her father had been all these years. Lisa was nice. She was pretty, even beautiful, she was smart, and she was kind. Beth could understand why her father liked Lisa.

But Lisa was Theo's mom. Would Beth be as upset about her father dating Lisa if Theo was still out on the West Coast or married to someone else? And why was Beth so adolescent over Theo anyway? He was handsome, but was she shallow to care about that? No. No, even in high school she'd crushed on Theo Hawley. He was kind, never a bully. He was smart, too, though not a super brain like his sister. If anything, now that Beth was searching her memories, she thought Theo had been kind of . . . lost. He'd been everything—prom king, football quarterback leading the team to victory, head of the Clean Team that walked Nantucket's beaches and streets, picking up litter. But she remembered an occasional melancholy in his eyes.

It had always been Theo for her, but she'd hidden it, because she didn't dare let anyone know her feelings. Atticus chose Beth, and all her girlfriends were crazy with envy and curiosity, because Atticus was mysterious, the dark prince, the tortured poet, his black curls hiding half his eyes, those eyes as blue and deep as the sky. He needed her, and that was a powerful pull. Atticus had confessed to her his most secret fears, his depressions, his anxieties, and toward the end, his discovery of OxyContin.

After Atticus died, Beth discovered that for her, grief felt like fear, as if she herself were trapped in the earth, but alive, unable to claw her way to air. For a long time, she lived every hour and minute with the words *if only* scratching through her mind. If only she had slept with Atticus, would that have kept him from wanting to die? If only she had pressured Theo to help Atticus, maybe together they could have saved him? If only she had told Atticus's parents that he was using OxyContin, buying it from some older guy who hung around the high school, shooting hoops. If only she hadn't really wanted to be with Theo, because Atticus had been so sensitive, he probably had guessed her true feelings.

Now here they all were, so many years later, and when she'd been alone with Theo in the Ocean Matters office, she had wanted so much to touch him. To take his hands and talk to him for hours, about everything. To kiss him.

He'd seemed pleased enough to be around her.

Sometimes when their eyes met, his look stopped her heart. But Theo stopped every woman's heart. She was too serious and he was too lighthearted to make a long-term relationship work.

She came out of her reverie to see her father sitting there, waiting for a response.

"You're right, Dad," Beth said softly. "It's cool that you're happy." She rose from the couch, took her mug to the sink, dutifully rinsed it and put it in the dishwasher, kissed her father good night, and went up the stairs to her room.

She wouldn't allow herself to be involved with Theo—big freaking chance. Theo could have any woman he wanted, plus he loved the ocean on the other side of the country and would no doubt return there where the women were all fit and tanned. She needed to knock herself sideways, off her obsession with Theo, and she had to find a way to do it.

In her bedroom, she studied herself in her full-length mirror. She was on the slim side and she was pretty enough. She was not completely unexperienced with men. There had been two, and she had almost loved them. Just not quite. Besides, she planned to live here all her life, though that didn't mean she had to settle down right now. She could play around, she could experiment, she could be frivolous—maybe she could have an affair with Ryder! He was handsome, and they'd be seeing each other often, and there wasn't a chance that he'd be serious with her, but she didn't want serious, she wanted fun. Summer fun, just like everyone else!

nineteen

Theo slept late again and woke grumpy. He showered and pulled on board shorts and a tee. He was aware of Juliet in her bedroom talking to someone on the phone. In the kitchen, he brewed himself a cup of coffee, made toast, and used up most of the jar of strawberry jam. As he ate, he heard Dave and Tom chatting and laughing in the living room.

Loneliness and a sense of uselessness nibbled at him. He put his toast back on the plate, suddenly ashamed of pigging out on the great glob of jam.

The only thing Theo considered himself good at was surfing, and he was hardly an ace at that. Surfing was always challenging, even dangerous, and while they might look the same, each wave was different. A few times, Theo had caught the tube, surfing inside the barrel of a humongous wave, with water around him in a loop as he sped just in front of the crash. In those moments, he'd experienced the almost religious high of being part of the spectacular unnamable energy that created the wave and lit the wave from the sun and made his body and the sun and the wave one quantum whole. Those few times he'd felt exalted, way out of body at the same time he was totally in his body. He'd felt touched. Chosen. Blessed.

But those rides in the tube were few and far between. He'd never belong to the elite core of surfers, no matter how many years he tried. And when he was slammed into the ocean floor, he'd felt more than hurt—he'd felt rejected. Dismissed. Damned.

Without surfing, what was he? He worried about whether or not he would ever feel brave enough to surf again. His mind played over and over in an endless loop the shock of that monster wave slamming him into the ocean floor. The knockout punch bashed the wind and all sense out of him, and for a long moment he'd squeezed his eyes shut, knowing he was about to die. He didn't die. The water lifted him up, and he swam to the shore, his leash tugging his board with him. Everything hurt. He'd never wiped out like that before, and he was embarrassed and angry at his weakness.

Often when someone wiped out, the guys gathered around, slapping one another on the back, shouting encouragement or sarcastic insults meant to get a surfer back up and in. This time, Theo's left arm hurt like hell, and he couldn't shake it off. Finally, Eddie drove him to a hospital where the fracture was diagnosed and his arm set in a brace and a sling, and he was actually glad, because Eddie could tell the others that the wave that slammed Theo had broken his arm, allowing him to retain some kind of dignity.

The doctors said not to try to surf until he'd had his arm x-rayed to check that the fracture was healed. That had been fine with Theo, but now he hated himself for just sitting around doing nothing.

For being a coward.

He was afraid of going into the ocean. The waves on the east side of the country were tame compared to San Diego, but still, Theo felt no pull. He didn't even want to swim at Sesachacha, which was a waveless pond. The summer was getting hotter but he had no urge to cool off even in the shallow shores of Jetties Beach.

Maybe this fear was temporary. Maybe.

Pushing away from the table, Theo rose and wandered into the living room. "Hey, guys." He was impressed by Dave and Tom, how contained they were, how deliberately they moved. They looked to be in their early forties, probably married with children, and Theo felt like a douche around them.

"What do you think of the ceilings?" Dave asked, nodding upward.

"Good. They look good." Theo had no idea how to judge ceilings. "What's next?"

"Your mom's bathroom. We've got to renovate it, take out that old bathtub—"

"But hey, doesn't it have claw feet?" Theo asked.

"It does. It also has the cast iron showing through the porcelain because so much has worn off over the years. We've got to put in a new floor, fix up the window, paint the walls, put in a new tub."

"We've found a new claw-foot tub for her," Tom added.

"I suppose you need a plumber's license," Theo said.

"We have them. Mack has a contractor's license but no one needs carpenter's licenses. We like working for Mack because we get to do a lot of different stuff."

"Huh. Well, let me know if I can help," Theo said. "I can't do the plumbing stuff but I can help carry."

Dave and Tom exchanged looks. "Man, you don't need a license to carry a tub. After we detach the plumbing, you can help us carry it down the stairs and out to our truck."

"Great." Theo gave a thumbs-up.

"Do you have some time to do it now?" Dave asked.

Let me check my calendar, Theo thought.

"I absolutely have the time," Theo told him.

They hiked up the stairs to his mother's bathroom. It didn't take long for the men to disconnect the plumbing.

"Okay," Dave said. He was tall and burly, with a bandana around his forehead to catch sweat from dripping down his face. It was actually a very cool look, and Theo wanted his own bandana because sweat dripped down his face, too, but he thought he'd probably look like an asshole if he wore one. "This tub weighs three or four hundred pounds. Theo, you and I will take one end. Tom can take the other."

Tom was a small, wiry little dude. He saw Theo's flash of consternation and grinned. "Theo, I could take you in a fight."

Theo nodded. "I'm sure you could."

They positioned themselves. "On the count of three," Dave said.

At three, Theo heaved upward with the other two, and the tub was off the floor.

It weighed more than a rhino.

Slowly Theo and Dave backed out of the bathroom and down the hall to the stairs. The worst part was going backward down the steps. Then the full weight seemed to be on him and Dave. Theo had strong thighs and pecs, but mother of pearl, this bathtub was a monster. He was aware of Dave straining and grunting, swearing, as he set the pace, slowly, purposefully, setting one foot down a stair, and then the other, waiting for Theo to match his movements. And Theo flashed on his quarterback days, when he had been part of a team, and on their best days they had moved collectively like one creature composed of several parts. Those days had been the best.

They continued, step by step, down to the front hall, where they set it on the floor and took a breather. Like the other two men, Theo put his hands on his knees and bent forward, huffing.

"Okay," Dave said. "Open the door as wide as you can. We'll take it out to the truck."

When they had finally loaded the tub in the truck, Dave and Tom walked around, shaking their arms, stretching their backs, cursing, and laughing. Theo copied them, but instead of shaking his arms, he rubbed his left upper arm where the pain was. The pain didn't go away.

"You okay, Theo?" Dave asked.

"Yeah. Wow. That was a mother."

"It was. Couldn't have done it without you. Thanks."

Dave turned to Tom and said something about installing the new window in the bathroom. Theo waved, went into the house, and up the stairs, as if he had a hundred projects waiting for him.

What he had waiting for him was a vial of OxyContin. A *doctor* had prescribed it for him.

"No," Theo had argued. "I don't want Oxy-Contin."

"Look," the doctor had said, exasperated. "Bone fractures hurt. Oxy helps with the pain. If you're not in pain, it will make you high. You're an adult. When the pain has lessened, gradually take fewer pills, and then quit altogether. I'm not renewing this prescription, and you're not going to become addicted if you follow my instructions."

Theo had taken the oxy, but after two weeks, he changed to Tylenol four times a day. His arm still hurt, but not much more than it had in high school after getting slammed in football. He hated oxy. It had killed Atticus. It was the enemy.

But now his arm hurt like hell. He shut his bedroom door tight and threw himself down on the bed. Damn, his arm burned with pain. *Heating pad,* he told himself. *Tylenol.*

Beth would never date him, never speak to him again if he used oxy.

Would Beth ever date him at all?

Dave and Tom were stomping up the stairs and then working in his mom's bathroom, muttering and guffawing and pounding and dragging.

Theo wanted to disappear from the planet. He did not want to lie in here like a baby, whining about his poor wittle arm. He needed to do something practical. Something real.

He grabbed his cell, tucked it in the back pocket of his shorts, and opened his bedroom door.

He went to the bathroom. "Hey, guys, can I help you with anything else?"

Dave and Tom eyed him up and down.

"We can't pay you without Mack's permission," Dave said.

"I don't need paying. Just, I've got nothing scheduled today."

"Great. See those metal pipes we've cut? Take them out to the truck. Then you can come back and help us move the toilet."

Theo gathered up a bunch of pipes. The ends were jagged and they were small but not light. His arm hurt like hell, but he was grinning as he headed down the stairs.

twenty

Juliet put on the navy blue dress her mother had helped her choose in Sail. Her mother loaned her pearl earrings to Juliet, and with a touch of lipstick and a smidgen less eyeliner and mascara than she usually wore, Juliet looked, she was surprised to see, maybe kind of elegant. She and her mom had battled through clothing wars during her teenage years, when Juliet wanted to wear black, brown, or gray, and her mother kept giving her pastels that would delight a five-year-old. Now Juliet realized she had finally aged enough mentally and physically that she could accept her mother's taste. There was nothing much she could do with her hair, but if she brushed it a certain way, she looked rather Audrey Hepburn-ish.

Her mother had the only full-length mirror in the house, so Juliet went into Lisa's room to get the complete view. Turning this way and that in front of the mirror, Juliet remembered how she never wanted to dress like her mother and she absolutely *never* wanted to get married and have two children and be left alone to raise them. Juliet had determined she would be smart and focus on her work, on math and computers, digital black and white, nothing soft, fuzzy, and compromising.

Yet this summer, something about this summer, was softening her or softening the world around her so that the air was gentler, and she was happier. Light was more sparkling and magic so close by. When she looked at herself in the mirror in the navy blue dress, she realized she looked very much like a woman that a handsome, educated man would want to spend time with. The knowledge surprised her and made her do something she hadn't done since she was thirteen. She put her arms around herself and twirled around in a circle, laughing.

She knew Ryder planned to take her somewhere posh for dinner, and she was sure he'd wear a blazer. Nantucket was an island of cobblestones, bricks, and sprained ankles, so she wore low heels. No bracelet or necklace, although she had a jewelry box full of those. Her dress and earrings and shoes said *proper,* but her black eyeliner, delicately and artistically applied, said *sex.* Her small black clutch was in her hand when Ryder knocked on the door of her mother's house.

"Wow," he said when he saw her.

"You clean up pretty well yourself," Juliet told him saucily. She was right. He wore a Brooks Brothers blue-and-white striped button-down shirt and a navy blue blazer with Nantucket Yacht Club brass buttons.

For a lingering moment, they stood looking at each other so intensely, so intently, that Juliet thought Ryder was going to take her in his arms, carry her into her mother's house, and ravish her. Yes, ravish. That was the message in his eyes.

"Yeah," Ryder said, as if she'd asked a question. "We have to go. We have a reservation."

Seated in his Range Rover, they rode out to the Chanticleer, one of the priciest and most fabled restaurants on the island. They talked idly about current news, the weather, their days, but the air between them was languorous, heavy with unspoken words.

The maître d' greeted Ryder by name. "Good evening, Mr. Hastings, we have your table ready. Please follow me."

Juliet was aware of the glances of other diners. No one she knew was seated at any of the other tables, but she would bet one of her high school chums was working in the kitchen.

The maître d' pulled out her chair for her. A waiter came over and Ryder went through the complicated discussion of whether to start with wine or a cocktail.

Juliet asked for a martini.

The room was handsome, the tables set far enough away from one another that no one would worry about being overheard. Nantucket had many fine restaurants, but this one was known worldwide.

"Why did you bring me here?" Juliet asked archly.

Ryder looked puzzled. "So we could have dinner."

"Stop it. You're a complicated man. I already know you're wealthy, so there's got to be some other reason than impressing me."

Ryder waggled his eyebrows theatrically. "So you're already impressed with me?"

"How could I not be? Electric car? Saving the oceans?"

"I'm no saint, believe me. And I brought you here because the food is good. I like the atmosphere."

Out of the corner of her eye, Juliet saw the waiter approaching with their drinks on a tray. She waited until he'd set their drinks down. She took a sip of her bracingly cold martini.

Tilting her head, smiling a Mona Lisa smile, Juliet said, "I think you should be impressed with me."

"Oh, I am," Ryder answered, leaning forward to put his hand over hers.

She pulled her hand away. "Not that way. Well, not only that way. I spent several hours at the Ocean Matters office yesterday. Beth asked me to help build a website. This is my field of expertise. I know what I'm doing and I work fast."

"Is it up yet?"

Juliet laughed, a throaty laugh full of confidence. "It can take weeks, even months, to build a website. I've got a good start, and when I get home tonight, I'll go back to work on it."

"Not exactly how I saw this evening ending," Ryder said.

She ignored him. "I can work all night, if necessary. I can super-focus. Beth gave me a general idea of how it should look, the background an azure ocean with sea creatures and a menu that includes the mission statement, the names of board members, and an easy link to become members and receive the newsletter. Also, an ocean album page where people can scroll through gorgeous underwater shots." She settled back in her chair, smiling triumphantly.

"Good Lord," Ryder said. "I could kiss you. Well, I want to kiss you anyway, but this is great news."

"We're only in the beginning phase. I mean Beth is. I'm obviously helping out on a freelance basis."

"Tell me how you know Beth."

"Because we grew up on the island, of course." The martini was performing wonders with her mind, conjuring up marvelous memories of life on the island, summer parties, school dances. "I'm two years older than she is, but my brother, Theo, hung out with her sometimes, and with

Atticus." That name made her heart drop like an anchor. For a moment, she was caught on the sorrow of his death. She took a small sip of her martini, steadying herself.

Ryder said, "It must have been magical, growing up on this island."

Juliet paused to gather her thoughts. "It's wonderful and terrible," she replied. "I mean, the ocean, the beaches, the history, and so on are fun when you're a kid. When you're a teenager, it's different and not in a good way. You know we have no chain businesses here. No McDonald's, Starbucks, no malls, no place to hang out. The winters are long and dark and there's no place to go unless you ice skate. We do have a rink. We start feeling . . . isolated . . . and some of us go off-island for college, some can't deal with the hugeness of the real world, and come home." She shook her head. "Could I sound more depressing?"

"You're not depressing. You're honest. That's what I wanted."

"I should probably extol the beauty of the island, the golden beaches, the profound connection with the ocean, and there's that, too, of course. It's not possible *not* to feel that connection even when it's unpleasant. I mean, getting to and from our hometown relies on what the ocean's doing. Gale force wind? No boats running, no planes flying, not that we could afford the airfare. Some of the major football games are off-island but half the passengers toss their chowder on the way because of high seas, and when you try to return, boats are canceled."

"Frustrating."

"And don't mention *Moby-Dick*!" Juliet faked choking herself. "That's like the school's bible. If I have to read another word about the anatomy of a whale . . ."

"Time changes things," Ryder said. "A century ago, Nantucketers hunted whales. Now, we protect them."

"Things don't always change for the better. For example, Ezra Noble. He's been making his living all his life, fishing these waters. Restaurants buy from him, and if you get to the dock on time, he'll sell to individual customers. Now his boat is disgraceful. Ezra can't afford to paint it or overhaul the engine. He can barely afford the docking fee. He's old. He doesn't have a pension. In the past few years, as the seal population has exploded, there are fewer fish for Ezra to catch. Ezra has a daughter with cystic fibrosis. He's got a lot of family here, siblings, aunts and uncles, and they all do what they can. He can't leave this island. It's been his family's home for generations. But he may not be able to afford to stay."

Ryder said, "You're very passionate about this island, aren't you?"

Please don't say passionate, Juliet thought. She wanted to kiss him. She wanted him to kiss her.

Reining herself in, she said, "I really should order. After this martini, I may be passionate, but one more sip and I'll be under the table."

"I'd like to see that," Ryder joked, nodding at the waiter.

After they ordered oysters as starters and salmon as an entrée, Ryder said, "So we have something in common. We like seafood."

"I grew up eating fresh oysters I found myself at the Jetties or out at Coskata," Juliet told him. "The hard part is opening the shell." She looked down at her hand. "I cut myself more than once."

"I like to go out sport fishing with friends and bring back a nice big tuna," Ryder said. "Of course now that I've met Sylvia Earle, I worry every time I eat fish, because so much of the population of tuna has been diminished by overfishing."

"Please, no guilt talk while I'm enjoying these oysters," Juliet said, as they were set before them.

For a while they focused on holding the oysters by the hinge end, sipping in the liquid, and chewing the sweet fish thoroughly to release the variety of delicate flavors. As they ate their salmon, Ryder told Juliet more about his work.

"I'm flying to China for a week later this summer," he said.

"China? Why?"

"Because about three-fourths of the human beings on this planet who will be affected by rising waters live in China. Shanghai, Beijing. Cities along the Yangtze River Basin. The Chinese are reacting quickly. They're far ahead of the United States. They've developed something called the 'sponge city initiative.' "

Juliet was mesmerized as Ryder spoke. He was brilliant, she decided, listening to him pour out facts and numbers in a dramatic and emotionally engaging way. His eyes flashed, his cheeks flushed, and she could feel the electric attraction sparking between them.

The waiter approached to take their plates. They both declined dessert. If they were alone, Juliet thought she would climb right over the table and into Ryder's lap. He was everything, all of it, masculine and tender and gorgeous and smart.

"Have you ever been to China?" Ryder asked.

"I've never really been anywhere," Juliet told him. "Well, Boston, D.C., New York a few times." Memories of her mother talking about Florence or Paris and memories of Juliet's father leaving them somehow intertwined, leaving Juliet in a melancholy mood whenever she thought about Europe. "I think I'd like to see China, though. I know so little about it."

Ryder paid the bill. They walked out to his car and stood next to it in the shadowy light of the picture-perfect island street, so quiet on this summer night, so peaceful.

Ryder said, "I want to kiss you."

She took a deep breath. "I'd like that."

He leaned over, cupped her face in both hands, and brought his mouth to hers. It was as if she was weak with thirst and his mouth and breath were water.

Ryder said, *"You."*

To Juliet's surprise, Ryder pulled away. "You are a problem. No, *we* are a problem. We don't seem to have 'idle' in our relationship. It's either off or zero to sixty in two point five seconds. That's electric supercar acceleration, by the way." Before Juliet could reply, he continued, "I have to go to Miami tomorrow for a conference. You should know I'm always traveling, giving talks like the one I gave at the Nantucket Atheneum, or joining expeditions tagging great whites, or meeting with companies to discuss how they can change over from plastic to paper. All this before I go to China."

"What are you saying?" Juliet asked. "Or, what do you mean? That we can't . . . have a relationship because you're so busy?"

"No, I don't mean that. But I want to be honest. I'm a maniac about this cause. It's my first priority in life. I want to make a difference in the world, and I feel very strongly that never before has the world needed someone to make a difference. Right now, Ocean Matters is what I'm about, pretty much twenty-four-seven."

"So you don't have time for a little pleasure?"

His eyes burned into hers. "Do you think that's what we've got between us? *A little pleasure?*"

"I don't know," Juliet answered honestly. "You're the one who started this." She laughed at her own words. "Well, that sounded childish."

Ryder took her hand and walked with her along the sidewalk toward the 'Sconset chapel. The summer trees hung lush with leaves, and laughter drifted from nearby houses.

The heat of the day had diminished, and a slender breeze drifted past, cooling Juliet's neck.

"You see," Ryder began, "a girl like you—"

"A *woman* like me," Juliet said.

"Okay, a *woman* like you . . . well, I've never met a woman like you. You're beautiful and sexy. And you're smart and ambitious."

"I'm ambitious?"

"Oh, yes, I think you're deeply ambitious. You went to MIT, for God's sake. You're not satisfied working for Kazaam. You want something more important."

Ryder stopped walking and turned Juliet to face him.

"I think the two of us could do some amazing work for this old world of ours. Our knowledge and abilities weave together, and from the moment I saw you I knew I wanted to be with you. To touch you. To kiss you. To see you. To see you every day. To take you to bed every night."

Juliet put her hands on Ryder's face, lightly, and it was like making a discovery, like opening a door, or feeling warmth after cold, or seeing a new planet. "I'd like that, too."

Ryder gathered her close to him and kissed her deeply. They remained in each other's arms, breathing, learning this new sensation.

Juliet broke away. "You'd better take me home. I want to get back to work on the website."

Ryder grinned down at her. "You are perfect."

"Just wait until you see what I can do," Juliet told him.

twenty-one

Summer was officially here, with its heat and tourists and climbing dawn roses and convertibles bouncing over the cobblestones. Lisa lingered in bed for a moment, watching the play of sunlight through her curtains. She smiled, thinking of Mack. This summer was unlike any other.

Finally she rose, showered, and dressed. Theo was undoubtedly sleeping, and Juliet was either sleeping or tapping away as if possessed on the website she was building for Ocean Matters. Lisa wondered whether Juliet was working so hard to impress Ryder, who was away for a few days, but decided that for Juliet, working was her favorite kind of playing.

She left the house before Tom and Dave came, carrying her coffee as she hurried to her shop. She had two hours before she opened, but Gretchen, her summer help, had arrived last night and Lisa wanted some quiet time to discuss Gretchen's winter and organize themselves for the season.

She unlocked her front door and entered her shop. Everything looked tidy, enticing. She'd discovered a new fragrance by TokyoMilk called "Honey & the Moon," which had an original scent, spicy, not sweet, and she sprayed it around the shop lightly. It woke up her senses, and her customers noticed it, too. Later, when the shop opened, she'd play upbeat music, the kind that put people in a good mood, but for now, she wanted silence.

Someone tapped on the front door. Lisa went to open it and welcome Gretchen back. Gretchen was twenty-two, free-spirited, and energetic. She ran and did lots of yoga and she believed in living in the now. Gretchen hugged Lisa and immediately scanned the clothes on the racks.

"So!" Gretchen said. "What's going to be our big seller this summer?"

Lisa smiled. "You are a breath of fresh air!"

They set to work, unpacking new merchandise, arranging the jewelry in its glass case.

Lisa's phone buzzed. *Mack.* "I have to take this," she told Gretchen and went into the bathroom for privacy.

"Could you come home for lunch?" Mack asked. "Because we're working here and I've got something I want to talk to you about. We can sit out in the sun for a while."

"What do you want to talk about?" Lisa asked.

"I'd rather not say now," Mack answered.

"Oooh, a mystery," Lisa said.

"It's not that big a deal, it's just . . . I need your judgment on this."

"I'll be there at one," Lisa told him, and clicked

off. She felt unsettled and oddly annoyed. She had to brace herself emotionally. If Mack wanted to break off with her, it would be kinder to do it now, before it got serious, although Lisa had been serious from the moment she and Mack kissed.

It was fortunate that the shop was busy that morning. Lisa kept her attention back to the store, the clothes, the jewelry, the easy chatter about summer. At a quarter to one, Lisa left the shop to Gretchen's experienced care and walked home. Her heart was racing, and not because she was walking fast. She lifted her chin, preparing herself for a blow.

The house was quiet. Mack's truck was gone, and Tom and Dave with it. Theo and Juliet didn't seem to be around, although knowing Theo, he was still in bed, asleep.

"Hey." Mack was in paint-stained canvas pants and a white tee, and the cotton of his shirt was stuck to his back with sweat. Lisa's senses went bananas at the sight, at Mack, his big hands wiping a tool before setting it in his toolbox.

"Hey," Lisa replied with a forced smile.

"I picked up sandwiches at Fast Forward. Want a beer?"

"Um, no, I think I'll just get some ice water."

They took a tray of food out to Lisa's backyard. At the end of the garden, she had, over many years, trained a wisteria plant to grow over a wooden gazebo so that the long lavender clusters of flowers formed a shady canopy. A small table and two chairs sat waiting. Lisa and Mack settled themselves, and Lisa kept her hands in her lap, not touching her food, signaling to Mack she wanted the announcement *now.*

"So here's my question," Mack said. "What would you think if I asked Theo to work for me?"

"Theo?" It was taking a moment for Lisa's nerves to unscramble.

"Yes. He's damned strong, not surprising given how athletic he was in high school. He's adept with his hands. He's easygoing, pleasant to work with. The guys like him. And to tell the truth, now that summer's here, the work's piling up on me." Mack held up his hand. "Your house comes first, of course. Tom and Dave are the best men I've got and we'll stay here till the work is finished. But it would go faster if Theo joined us."

"But, he doesn't know how to do anything," Lisa said.

"Maybe not, but he's a fast learner. Plus, he could do a lot of the pickup and delivery service, driving out to the lumberyard, that sort of thing. It would be a great time saver for me."

"Does he want to work for you?"

"I think he does. He's been hanging around, helping Dave and Tom with basic stuff. I didn't want to ask him without talking to you first."

"Well, then, of course. I mean, why would I have any objection? Plus, he is an adult. I'm not in charge of him anymore."

"I wasn't thinking about him. I was thinking about you. You and me."

"Oh, right. Was Beth upset the other night when she came home?"

"Not upset. Curious. We talked about it, and I told her you and I are friends."

Lisa looked at Mack. His tanned arms bulged with muscles, and his nose was turning red from the sun. His hair, darkened by the winter, was developing white blond streaks, and his eyes were sea-green, clear and bright. She wanted to crawl over the table and sit in his lap and kiss him.

"Friends," she said softly.

"I want more than that, I think that's obvious. But it's complicated, with all our children cluttering up our lives."

Lisa laughed. "I should have called you about the ceiling when all three were living off-island."

Their eyes met and held.

"I should have called you years ago," Mack said and the hitch in his voice nearly melted Lisa into her chair. "But we got here and we've agreed we'll go slow, and I think we can do that."

"Yes, and summer goes fast," Lisa said. "I mean, I'm so busy all I want to do at the end of the day is flop on my bed."

"But maybe we can go to some of the galas," Mack said.

"As a couple?" Lisa asked.

"Yes. As a couple. Let the world get used to us. Let us get used to us."

Lisa nodded, thinking. "And at the summer galas, there will be so many off-island people that the year-rounders won't see us in the crowd."

"I want everyone to see us in a crowd," Mack told her.

Again, the eye lock, and Lisa saw the desire in Mack's eyes, and the affection. She was not ready to call it *love*.

"So," Mack continued, "it's okay if I ask Theo to join my crew?"

"It's fine. It's great."

Mack peeled back the wrapping of his sandwich and began to eat. Lisa pretended to eat, but could take only small bites, because whenever she was near Mack like this, she could hardly swallow, hardly breathe. *Maybe I'll lose some weight this summer,* she thought with a secret grin.

twenty-two

Marine Home Center was always crowded in the summer with plumbers, electricians, painters, and homeowners, so Beth felt slightly awkward as she zigzagged among them. Most of the workers wore coveralls or tees with sagging utility pants and work boots. Beth wore a pretty flowered sundress and wedged sandals. She felt like a ladybug creeping through a field of giant moles. All she wanted was Elmer's Poster Tack, and she couldn't find it among the nails, screwdrivers, duct tape, and batteries.

"Hey, Beth."

Startled, Beth froze. Looking up, she saw Theo's ridiculously gorgeous face. "Hi, Theo. What are you doing here?"

"Picking up some stuff for Mack. Your dad. What about you?"

"Oh, I'm an idiot. I want to put some posters up on the walls of our office, but I don't want to use tacks or nails and ruin the walls. It's a temporary loan and I don't know how long we'll be in there. So I'm looking for some Elmer's Poster Tack, but I can't find it, and I hate to bother a salesman when there are all these serious guys who need assistance, not that I'm even sure I could get a salesman's attention."

"You talk a lot," Theo said.

Beth blinked. "Well, that was blunt."

"Yes, and you're so mistaken. Any guy would be happy to help you just so he could look at you."

Beth was speechless.

"But you don't have to ask a salesman. I know where the tack is. Come on."

She followed him through the aisles until he stopped in front of a shelf of glues and tacks.

"Here," he said, handing her a blister pack of wall putty sticks. "I think this will work."

"My hero," she joked as she took it.

"I'd like that," Theo told her.

Beth was speechless again.

Theo grinned. He'd had this effect on girls many times in his life, but this time he wasn't messing around. "Need anything else? Let's go to the registers."

Beth went first, wondering whether she should leave or wait for him, wondering if she could suggest meeting him for lunch or something. But they'd only met by accident, he was only being kind.

"Do you need a bag?" the cashier asked, looking at Beth's one small item.

"No, thanks." Beth took the tack and hurried away, not wanting to hold up the line of looming serious workmen. She knew some of them because of her father, but many of them came over from the Cape to work and others were summer workers.

"Hey, Beth," Theo called. "Want me to come over and help you put up the posters?"

"Oh! Yes, that would be great." Beth paused, watching Theo at the checkout counter.

"See you there," Theo told her. He focused his charm at the cashier as she rang up his items. "Busy day, right?"

"Every day's a busy day," the woman in the green shirt told him. When she asked him if he wanted a bag, she gave him a smile.

Theo, Beth thought, with her own smile.

She had to drive around the block three times before she found a parking place close to the Ocean Matters office. As she walked along the brick sidewalk, she scanned Easy Street. Theo would have a hard time finding a parking place. She shouldn't expect him to show up right away.

Inside the space, she unrolled the posters and decided where each should hang. She'd taken her photo of the men removing the plastic collar from the seal out to Poets Corner, where she had it blown up to poster size to go in the window. That would catch people's attention.

She'd left the door open to the street, hoping people might come in and look around and ask about the organization. Theo arrived sooner than she'd expected.

"Did you find a parking space?" she asked.

"No. Just parked at home, gave Mack his stuff, and walked here. With all the traffic jams, walking's faster than driving. Now. Let's see what we've got."

Theo held the posters up against the wall while Beth stood back to look.

"I like this arrangement," she decided.

"Great. Do you have a bubble level?"

"A bubble level?"

Theo laughed. "How can you be your father's daughter if you don't know what a bubble level is?" Without waiting for a response, he said, "We can just eye it in."

"I have a ruler," Beth said meekly.

"That's good. That will help."

For the next hour, they moved around the room hanging the posters. Beth had ordered some generic but bright posters printed with whales or dolphins or fish and the words SAVE THE OCEANS. Once they were up, they hung the seal poster in the window and one of the bumper stickers she'd had made up saying OCEAN MATTERS. It was blue with brighter blue block print and a fish icon at the right end.

She had to stand almost in Theo's arms to help hold and tack the posters. She could hear his breathing and smell his male aroma and often they brushed arms. Once his arm brushed her breast, but she could tell it was accidental. The air conditioner kept the room cool enough, but she felt dizzy, as if she was climbing at a high altitude. She'd done that once when her summer camp hiked to the top of Mount Washington in New Hampshire. This was a different kind of dizzy. She flashed on a vision of Theo pressing her gently against the wall. She wished he would.

When they'd finished, Theo said, "Looks good."

"Do you think it's hot in here?" Beth asked.

"Yeah, probably because you're leaving the door open."

"Oh, right. Well, I want it to look . . . hospitable."

"But you don't want to look like a place that has money to burn."

"Good point." Beth walked across the room and pulled the door shut.

"So," Theo said, cocking his head. "Just think. Right now, your father is in my mother's house. Does that make us related?"

"Oh, I hope not!" Beth spoke before she thought.

Theo's smile vanished. "Right. See you later."

"Theo, that's not what I meant!" Beth ran to the door.

Theo was on the sidewalk. He looked back at her. "No problem," he said.

Beth felt sick. They'd been getting along so well, she'd felt the chemistry between them whirlpooling through her body. And she'd ruined it in one careless moment. Should she call him and explain?

A few minutes later, Juliet, cool as ice on this summer day, casually walked into the Ocean Matters office.

Beth tried to yank her thoughts into reality, at least a reality she could share with Juliet. Juliet was two years older, which had been a very big deal in high school, and Juliet was so innately *cool.* Theo was like an eager Lassie. Juliet was like a self-assured Siamese cat.

"Hey," Beth said as calmly as she could. "How's the website coming?"

"Almost done." Juliet dumped her backpack on a table, unpacked her laptop, and opened it. She twirled a chair around to face Beth, and said dramatically, "I've been working my digits to the nub. What are you up to?"

Beth glanced down at her list. "I've built a master list of possible board members and we're going to hold a gala fundraiser in early September. I've designed a logo to go on the website, our stationery, any publicity. I need to start an online appeal, but I'd like your input. I've friended nonprofits on the island that would be most like ours. Marine Mammal Alliance, the Shellfish Association, Nantucket Clean Team,

Nantucket Island Safe Harbor for Animals, and so on. I also made lists of names, email addresses, mission statements."

"You've done a lot."

"I'd like your opinion, and I'll need approval from Ryder for the mission statement."

"Have you heard from Ryder?" Juliet asked, her eyes set on the computer screen.

"No. I don't even know where he is."

Juliet grinned wickedly. "Let's google him."

Ryder Hastings had what looked like hundreds of hits on Google. Beth leaned over Juliet's shoulder while Juliet scrolled through the posts. Sometimes Ryder was at a fundraiser with a gorgeous woman at his side, but more often he was in the field—or in the water—in New Orleans or Miami or Venice, Italy, talking about rising seas.

"He's kind of a workaholic," Beth said.

"There are worse things," Juliet responded.

Beth returned to her chair, working on her laptop.

Juliet asked casually, "Would you ever date him?"

Beth almost laughed, but she remembered that Juliet was Theo's sister. She didn't know how close Juliet and Theo were but she didn't feel comfortable gushing about her feelings for Theo.

"I don't know," Beth answered vaguely. "He's kind of old."

Juliet stopped typing and swung around in her swivel chair to face Beth. "Do we have a hidden topic here?"

"What do you mean?"

"I mean," Juliet said with false patience, "you keep mentioning age. Like your father dating my mother. My mom's ten years older than your dad. Does it bother you?"

Yes, it does, because how can I see your brother if his mother is dating my dad? Beth thought it, but was afraid to say it. Afraid Juliet would tell her that Theo had never been and would never be interested in her. Or that Juliet would go home and tease her brother about Beth liking him.

"Does it bother *you?*" Beth countered.

"I don't know," Juliet replied, and all at once she seemed vulnerable. "My father left my mother when we were kids. She was so lonely for a while. I used to hear her crying after she thought we kids were asleep. I've heard her talk to Rachel, her best friend, saying she was perfectly happy without a man in her life, and for years she has seemed perfectly happy to me. And now, your father . . ."

Beth kind of wanted to hug Juliet, who looked so worried, but even open as she was now, Beth was afraid Juliet would snap back to her cool, superior self if Beth even patted her shoulder.

"My father's a good guy," Beth said quietly.

"Yeah, I think he is," Juliet said. "I like him a lot. I think it would be great if they were . . . a couple."

Again, Beth's mind cried out something she couldn't speak aloud: *But then what about me and Theo? Could we be a couple?*

Instead, Beth said, "But the age difference. That could be a problem."

Juliet rolled her eyes. "I know. Sometimes I think Mom's an idiot, dating your dad. Sometimes I want to *shake* her."

Beth said, "I don't think your mom is an idiot. I think she's beautiful and cool and smart. I just worry, for both of them."

"God," Juliet said. *"Love."* She turned back to the computer then had a thought. "Beth. If your father married my mother, you and I would be stepsisters."

"I've always wanted a sister," Beth said. "That would be cool!"

"That would be awesome," Juliet said. "I've always wanted a sister, too. I mean, Theo's great, but he's so male."

"Yeah, but at least he's a sibling." Beth opened a notebook and began a list. She hardly knew what words she was writing. Her head was spinning. Could she be with Theo if his mother married her father? She couldn't fit her mind around that. Plus, it was foolish of her even to imagine being with Theo. Well, maybe for one night or two, but no more. Theo was never a long-term relationship kind of guy. The attraction between them when they were hanging the posters was intense, but Theo was so sexy anyone would be attracted to him. Beth had to get real. She forced her mind to her work.

"I think what we're doing here is important," she said. She knew she sounded corny, but she'd gotten Juliet to stop talking about Theo.

"I agree," Juliet said. "Give me a few minutes, and I'll show you what our website looks like."

"Oh, really? You work fast."

"I probably belong on the far end of some personality spectrum," Juliet joked.

Beth sank deeper into her chair and brought up her mission statement on the screen. She emailed it to Ryder and to Juliet. Then she took a deep breath, told herself to shake it off, and brought up the ocean album she'd created for the website. It had pictures of sea creatures swimming in blissful innocence with their babes by their sides, interspersed with photos of whales, seals, and dolphins choked with plastic. With each photo she'd attached a quote by someone significant: Herman Melville, of course, and also Jacques Cousteau, JFK, Wendy Schmidt, Shakespeare, E. E. Cummings, and Rachel Carson. She reviewed it and emailed it to Juliet.

"Okay," Juliet said. "Here's what I've got so far. Subject to change."

Beth turned her chair around and scooted next to Juliet. "Oh, Juliet, this is gorgeous."

The home page of the website was a luminescent splash of azure. The words *Ocean Matters* were at the top, in a dark blue, slightly curly font that Beth didn't recognize but that fit the image perfectly.

"The mission statement," Juliet said, moving the cursor to an image of what had to be the absolutely cutest baby seal in the universe. Beneath the little creature were the words, in indigo, *Click here for mission statement.*

"I love that," Beth said, "but do we really need the words 'click here'?"

"What do you think?"

"I don't think we need them. People are fairly click-savvy now."

"Okay, we'll stick with 'mission statement.' Now let's go to the members of the board of directors." Juliet set the cursor over a glowing image of coral. "I wanted to use something native to Nantucket, so I tried a whale, then decided that someone was bound to be insulted by the very possibility that someone thought they were compared to a whale. Certainly couldn't use a shark."

"I like the coral. It's a living thing, and this is fabulous."

"Great. Now, your photo album. That's fabulous, Beth. Eye-catching, and words to think about."

Juliet moved the cursor to the words *Photo Album* over a pure white angel-wing shell, its raised radiating lines matching, the joined pair appearing delicate and almost unreal.

"This is to sign up for the newsletter," Juliet said, moving the cursor to a photo of seagulls flying over the water.

"That's funny," Beth said. "Seagulls are so insanely noisy."

Finally, Juliet showed an icon of a group of mussels, their inner shells beautifully iridescent, above the words: *Click here to become a member.*

"Let's leave 'click here' with this icon," Beth suggested.

"Done," Juliet said.

"This is amazing," Beth said. "How did you accomplish so much so fast?"

"Eh," Juliet joked, "I'm a genius. Also, I haven't had much sleep."

"Oh, you should go take a nap," Beth said. "I have to start calling the people I know about becoming board members."

"I don't need a nap," Juliet said. "Let me see your list of potential participants. I might be able to help."

"Thanks, Juliet!" Beth scooted to her computer, found the list of possible supporters, and emailed it to Juliet.

The two women sat side by side, discussing each name, omitting some, adding others.

"You should be the one to call them," Juliet said. "You're better with people than I am."

Beth started to disagree, to say she couldn't possibly be better at anything than Juliet, but she gave it a moment's thought and decided Juliet was right.

"If you think that's the way to go," Beth said, "that's fine with me. I suppose you are a bit more introverted than I am."

Juliet laughed. "That's an understatement. Give me a computer and a difficult task and I'm in blissful isolation for hours, days. Theo got all the personality in our family."

Beth smiled. "He is charismatic."

"Oh, my God," Juliet said. "You do like Theo!"

"I have always liked Theo."

"I guess I never noticed because you were two years behind me in school."

"You never noticed because Theo was always completely surrounded by a million other girls," Beth said.

"Well, there was that. But I'll tell you a secret, Beth. I think Theo likes you."

"Likes me?"

"More than that. But I'm his sister. He'll kill me if I say anything more."

"We wouldn't want that to happen." Beth's heart was a helium balloon floating to the sky. "Anyway," she said, bringing them back on task and feeling rather impressed with herself for doing it, “let’s go over the names again and decide who should be invited to join the board first.”

“Great,” Juliet said.

They worked together for another hour, talking easily, deciding with some discussion but no arguments, and Beth began to wonder if they could become friends.

And what would Theo think if they did?

twenty-three

The June day notched up the serious summer heat. Tom and Dave had installed the window in his mom's bathroom. Now they were tearing out the layers of old wallpaper so they could repair the plaster and hang new paper. Theo had a huge bulky bunch of old wallpaper in his arms and was carrying it down to dump into the trash barrels when Mack drove into the driveway.

"Hey!" Theo said, nodding a hello. He stuffed the load of paper into an already full barrel.

"Hi, Theo." Mack climbed out of his truck and walked over to him. "I need to talk to you a minute."

"Sure," Theo said, but his guts turned to ice.

"You've been helping out the guys almost every day, I hear," Mack said.

Theo couldn't speak. What could he say? *I'm a lazy useless bastard and don't have a job on this island where all the businesses are desperate to hire?*

"So here's what I'm thinking," Mack continued. "I'd like to put you on the payroll for the summer. I need a good worker and you could learn on the job. Is this a possibility?"

Theo stopped breathing. He wanted to hit the sides of his head as if he had water in his ears. Had he heard right? Mack wanted to put him on the payroll? Mack thought Theo was good enough to work for him?

"Yeah," Theo said. "I'd like that."

"Let's go up and tell the guys," Mack said. "Dave is the boss when I'm not here. You answer to him."

"Works for me," Theo said, adding, "I mean, great!"

Theo worked like Superman the rest of the day. While he drove a load of debris to the dump, he had time to think it through, why he was so exhilarated, so absolutely damn *proud* to be on Mack's crew. Theo had prided himself on his performance in sports, but he still had felt inferior to Juliet. She was older than he was, and way smarter, plus she was innately cool.

Now he thought maybe he wasn't inferior. Just different. He liked the clean, visible effects of his work. A shingle hammered, an old cracked baseboard pried loose and replaced with a nice, sweet-smelling piece of new board, the truck bed emptied at the end of the day. Helping transform a room from just okay to spectacular. He admired Mack for the kind of work he did, restoring and renovating houses rather than building ridiculously large vanity mansions.

He'd always known as a boy growing up that he could never model himself on his father. First of all, he never saw his father, but also, he knew he would go crazy trying to work in a bank. It might be a stretch to consider Mack as a father figure, but he could definitely qualify as a mentor. He was a man Theo would like to be. And while Theo learned, he'd be hammering, wrenching, carrying, painting, and his world would become just a little bit better, safer, lasting.

When he got home, Theo was still emotionally high, so he decided he'd make his one never-fail meal: meatloaf, baked potatoes, frozen peas. He understood that this was a meal enjoyed best in winter, but it was better than pizza or tacos. Also, he always enjoyed squishing the egg, crackers, onions, and grated cheese into the hamburger. He decorated the top of the loaf with a design of confetti made from ketchup. Disappointingly, once it had cooked, the ketchup had spread and didn't look like confetti, so he smeared it all around and it looked better that way.

"What smells so good?" his mom asked when she walked into the house.

"I made dinner," Theo announced, trying not to sound too pleased with himself. After work, he'd taken a quick shower and pulled on clean clothes, and while the meatloaf and potatoes were baking, he'd cleaned the kitchen and set the table.

"Why, Theo, this is wonderful!" His mom

hugged him. "It's so nice to have a hot, home-cooked meal for a change."

Juliet strolled into the kitchen. "Wow, Theo. Get you. Something must have happened. Tell us."

"Don't be so cynical," Lisa said. "I'm going to open a bottle of red wine. Anyone else?"

"I'm having beer," Theo said. "And Juliet's right. I've got an announcement. Mack has asked me to join his crew."

"Theo, how wonderful!" Lisa held up her glass. "Here's to you, Theo!"

Juliet said, "I wonder what Beth's going to think about this."

Theo knew he was turning red, partly from embarrassment at his cynical sister even knowing how he felt about Beth, partly in anger. He put on the damn oven mitts, took out the meatloaf, all shiny with ketchup, took out the four baked potatoes—he planned to eat two. His mother and Juliet bustled around filling glasses with water, putting the butter dish on the table, pouring the peas into a small serving bowl. Theo had already laid out the dishes and silverware and salt and pepper.

He swigged back a big gulp of beer, trying to think how to let Juliet know he was pissed off at her. He knew he wasn't as smart as she was. She was making a six-figure salary with her computer expertise. But she was always butting into his personal business, and he wanted her to step back.

"Juliet—"

"Theo," his mom said, "this meatloaf is delicious!"

"Theo," Juliet said, "I shouldn't say this, but Beth likes you."

His mom said, "Well, that's hardly a surprise."

Theo gave Juliet a wary look. "What do you mean, likes?"

"I guess you'll have to find that out for yourself," Juliet said with a wicked grin.

"I love the way you put shredded cheese in the potato," his mom said.

Theo sat there, confused and not even hungry.

"Oh, Theo," Juliet said. "Don't look so pathetic. I'm not trying to trick you. I was at the Ocean Matters office with Beth today, and she told me she likes you. A lot."

"Close your mouth, Theo," his mother said. "Now tell Juliet thank you."

"Thank you," Theo muttered to his sister. Then he ate both potatoes and at least half the meatloaf.

Theo wanted to ask Beth for a date, but he really wanted to do something different. Something special. Something that would set him apart from the other Nantucket guys. But he was committed to working all day, and so was Beth. The weather forecast was for rain, so a long walk on the beach was out. He flipped through the island weekly newspaper and came up with an idea. The Theatre Workshop of Nantucket was putting on *Grease*, which would be a lot of fun, and Laura McGinniss, one of their classmates, had the lead role.

He called Beth and asked her to go with him the following night.

"That would be so much fun!" Beth told him.

His spirits soared like an eagle toward the sky.

The next night, Theo showered and dressed in a decent-looking button-down shirt and board shorts. He thought he looked okay, and not like he was trying too hard.

Beth had asked him to pick her up at the Ocean Matters office. He walked down to Easy Street and found Beth inside, working at her computer.

"Hey." Beth gave him a great big smile when he entered the office. Theo wished he could freeze time right there.

"Hey," Theo replied. He ached to kiss her, but first of all, he wanted to treat her right and not act like his normal gorilla self. Second of all, Mack was her father, and he didn't want to make Mack mad.

"Sorry I had to work so late," Beth said. "We're really rushing to launch Ocean Matters."

"I wish I could take you out to dinner after the play, but I'm not sure how long it will be."

Beth busied around, hitching her shoulder bag over her arm, straightening a pile of papers. "Oh, don't worry about eating. Let's get ice cream cones and stroll the streets after the play. As if we're tourists."

"Good idea." Theo thought Beth was like Tinker Bell, light and glowing and brightening everything she touched. He didn't tell her that, though. She probably wouldn't appreciate the comparison.

They stepped outside. Beth locked the door and together they walked up the street to Bennett Hall. Dark clouds were rolling in from the north-east, and in the small harbor near the Steamship Authority, waves were beginning to dance in the wind. The wind whipped her skirt against her.

"Nor'easter on the way," Theo said.

"I know. I love it. The drama!"

They stepped off the curb and Beth slid her hand around Theo's arm. He almost fainted with happiness.

"So how's it going, working for Mack?" Beth asked.

"It's good. You know what, it's *really* good. Your father is so organized, and quick to respond if a problem comes up. I haven't seen him lose his temper yet."

"I have," Beth joked.

"How are you doing with your ocean group?"

"Okay, I think. Your sister got a fabulous

website set up. I've started a Facebook page and an Instagram account. Of course the other environmental groups have pages on Facebook, so we've liked each other and already a lot of people have become friends on our page."

"I hear Meghan Trainor's coming for the fundraiser."

Beth sighed. "Maybe. She's interested and she's going to get back to us, but we haven't pinned her down for sure. I've found a date in early September that isn't booked up for another event, so I've claimed it, but I can't send out invitations, put out publicity, all of that, until she's confirmed. Honestly, it's a lot of work."

"But you're enjoying it."

"I am enjoying it. A lot. Especially working with Juliet. Plus, it's the right thing to do."

Theo looked warmly at Beth. "You've always been the right thing girl."

She flinched. "Well, that sounds like an insult."

"God, no, Beth, I didn't mean it that way at all. I mean, like in high school you got all A's, and you chose Atticus over me because he was the better guy."

A long silence stretched between them.

"Chose Atticus?" Beth looked away. "That's not the way it felt. Besides, you went with so many girls."

"Yeah, I was kind of uncentered back them. But I *was* interested, Beth. I mean, if you and I had ever, well, if I'd ever had a chance with you, I'd have been so loyal."

Beth burst out laughing. "No, you wouldn't have," she shot back.

His mouth twisted in a smile. "Yeah, no, I probably wouldn't have." He looked into her eyes. "But I'd like to try, now. The moment I saw you in the café . . . well, couldn't we have a couple of dates and see where it goes?"

Beth stopped. "My father . . ."

"Beth, Mack *likes* me. He's *hired* me. I'm a good worker. I'm reliable, I'm strong. I'm learning a lot from him."

"What about surfing?" Beth asked. "Don't you want to go back to California?"

"No. I've had enough of that life. I'm glad I did it. It will be with me forever. But no, I'm not going back to California."

"Tell me about surfing, Theo. Surfing out in California."

Theo nodded. They started walking again toward the theater. "Wow. California surfing. Okay. Well, it's terrifying. Exhausting. Challenging. And a rush like no other. Beth, when you're really in the green tunnel, it sounds like thunder is chasing you, and it is. The whole orchestra. Kettle drums. There's a circle of light in front of you and the collapsing wave behind you and it's all about you and the wave, you and speed and control and this amazing connection with the wave." He almost stopped walking, caught in his memory. "It's *profound,* Beth."

"Won't you miss it?"

"Sure I'll miss it. But when that last wave slammed me into the ocean floor, okay, it hurt like a mother, but it also frightened me. Like it was *warning* me. Like it was personal. Like the ocean was saying, 'Don't mess with me, little man. Go away. You're nothing compared to me.' "

Beth said, "That's amazing."

Theo thought maybe for once he sounded like someone with a brain in his head. He continued, "Some people are saying that the ocean, the entire planet, is going to wipe human beings from the face of the earth because it, the planet, is so angry at us for our disrespect."

"I know," Beth agreed somberly. "I've read that, too."

They had arrived at the theater now. Theo put his hand on Beth's waist to guide her into the line for tickets. The buzz and chatter of other people was exhilarating.

Beth suddenly turned, stood on tiptoes, and quickly kissed Theo on his lips. "Thanks for this. Just what I need!"

"Yeah, me, too," Theo replied, reeling from her unexpected kiss.

They got their tickets and showed them to the usher, who led them to the middle row in the back. The theater was full, everyone expectant.

They flipped through their programs, pointing out people they knew from the island who were doing the lighting or the costumes. And of course Laura McGinniss, who had starred in high school plays. Then the house lights went down. Music filled the air. People settled back in their seats, watching the stage, and the show began.

The story of a good girl and a greaser in love was classic, and the songs had the audience cheering. The cast might not have been Broadway material, but it didn't matter, because the singing and dancing were so much fun. When it ended, there was a screaming standing ovation.

"Oh, my God," Beth yelled in Theo's ear, "would you please get a black leather jacket?"

"Anything for you," Theo told her, and it was easy to say this in the theater where the atmosphere was pure adrenaline and sugar. He wanted to pick her up and kiss her thoroughly, but he had to move so people could exit the row.

They laughed and talked as they headed for the lobby, and there they discovered that while they'd been completely immersed in the play, the weather had decided to become dramatic. Rain streamed down and wind shook the bushes and trees. Other people pulled their jackets over their heads and raced out into the storm.

Theo turned to Beth. "If you wait here, I'll run home and get my car and come back for you—"

"That's a very courteous offer, Theo, but let's

just walk to my house. It's not too far, and if we get wet, we won't melt."

"Well." Theo considered the rain, coming down so furiously the streets were running with water. "It's not cold out. So that's a good thing."

He opened the door. Rain blew against them, shocking them. Theo took Beth's hand and pulled her out onto the street. They ran, still caught in the mood of the music, and laughed. The raindrops were small, and the lights from the businesses along the streets turned the drops into thousands of sparkling sequins and suddenly running in the rain with Beth seemed like a glamorous, romantic thing to do. Theo's clothes quickly were soaked through, and a glance at Beth confirmed that hers were, too. They ran down Centre Street, zigzagged onto Main, and stopped beneath a shop's awning.

"I've got to catch my breath!" Beth cried.

"I've got to kiss you," Theo told her.

He put his hands on the sides of her face and lifted her mouth up to meet his. Her lips were wet and her skin was warm. Beth lifted up her arms around his neck and swayed against his body. Her clothes, his clothes, were only thin barriers between them, their bodies slid against each other as they kissed. A gust of rain splattered them. They drew apart.

"Oh, man," Theo said. "I want to make love to you right here on the street."

Beth laughed. “I think we’d get arrested.”

Theo glanced down Main Street. A few brave souls were on the brick sidewalks, fighting with their umbrellas, trying to wrest them from the force of the wind.

“I truly wouldn’t care,” Theo said. Even with the protection of the awning, water dripped down his face from his hair.

“I might,” Beth told him. “Plus, this pavement is hard.”

“Is your father home?”

“I don’t know. But my car is there. And the back seat is empty.”

Theo frowned. “Um, wouldn’t that lose some of the . . . romance?”

“We could lose some of the romance and have plenty to spare,” Beth assured him, tugging on the front of his shirt.

Theo gasped. “I’ve always wanted to see the back seat of your car, Beth.”

He took her hand, and they both ran toward Pine Street.

Their wet clothes showed their skin in many places. Their shoes were soggy, and their hair was plastered against their heads. Several times Theo stopped, pulled Beth against him, and kissed her, holding her close, and finally they stopped kissing but simply stood there in the rain, their arms around each other, catching their breath, feeling each other’s heartbeat, joining together in the rain as if they were taking part in a universal sacrament.

"Only a few more blocks," Beth said.

Holding hands, they walked fast, too winded to run. They turned the corner and went down Pine Street toward Beth's house. Her old trusty Volvo waited at the curb of her house. Lights shone from the living room window.

"Almost there," Beth said, smiling up at Theo.

Theo stared down the street, frozen. "Beth, look."

Coming toward them from the other direction were Beth's father and Theo's mother.

twenty-four

"Dad!" Beth cried.

"Mom?" Theo asked.

Mack and Lisa stopped dead in their tracks, like hunters suddenly faced with a grizzly bear. They were both thoroughly soaked, and Lisa's lipstick had smeared, and Beth was pretty sure it wasn't from the rain.

"Hi, kids," Lisa called, waving as if they were more than four feet away. "Isn't it fun to walk in the rain? I haven't done this since I was a child."

"Mom," Theo said. "Dude."

"Let's all go inside and get dry and have some hot chocolate!" Lisa chirped, as if unable to stop pretending they were all in fourth grade.

"I think," Beth began, her voice croaking, "I think I need a hot shower."

"Good idea!" Lisa was like a kindergarten teacher, determinedly cheerful. "Nothing like a hot shower and—"

Mack spoke up. "Why don't you go in, Beth. I'll drive Theo and Lisa home."

"Oh, we can walk, it's not that far," Lisa protested.

"Beth," Theo said, "I'll get my car and we can—"

"No, it's late," Beth said. "I have to work tomorrow." She ran toward her house.

"Come on, Mom," Theo said.

Beth turned in time to see Theo and his mother splashing down the street.

Beth kicked off her sandals and went up to her bedroom. She stripped off her wet clothes, pulled on a terrycloth robe, went into her bathroom, and wrapped a towel around her hair. She stared at her reflection in the mirror. How had this happened? In one moment she'd gone from ecstatic to miserable.

Her father knocked on her door. He entered, dressed in dry clothes but barefoot.

"So that was awkward, right?" His tone was light, friendly. He'd pulled on sweatpants and a tee, and his hair stood up all over from a speedy towel drying.

"It was." Beth bit off her words.

"Come downstairs. Let's talk."

Beth sniffed and nodded.

Mack led her into the large open room. Beth followed meekly.

Mack sat in an armchair. She sat at the other end of the coffee table, in another armchair. They looked at each other.

"Why don't you start?" Mack suggested.

"Fine." Beth tried not to sound angry, but her

throat was tight. "So what, Dad, you're in love with Lisa?"

Mack said gently, "I like her more than anyone I've met since your mother."

"So you're going to marry her?"

"It's far too early for me to be talking about that. And what about you and Theo?"

Beth folded her arms over her chest. "Well, obviously I can't be with Theo if you're with his mother. Plus, come on, Dad, you know she's ten years older than you are."

"That doesn't make any difference."

"Don't you think people will gossip?"

"Honey, it's a small town. Everyone gossips all the time."

Beth twisted uncomfortably in her chair. With a quavering voice, she asked, "And what were you two *doing?* Were you coming to the house to . . . to . . ." She couldn't finish her sentence.

"Beth, I don't think this is something you and I need to talk about."

"Isn't it?" This was more complicated than she could bear.

Her father bristled. "This is my house, too. I haven't brought anyone into it since your mother died. You're a grown woman now. If we lived in another town where real estate wasn't so expensive you wouldn't be living with me."

"So I'm in the way," Beth cried. "Why didn't you just tell me?"

"Oh, Beth, come on. I don't mean you're in the way. For God's sake, this is getting us nowhere."

"Actually," Beth said, lifting her chin, cooling her voice, "this is very helpful. Tomorrow I'll find another place to live."

"Don't be ridiculous." Her father ran his hands through his hair. "We can find a better way to resolve this."

"I don't think so. I think we've said everything we need to say." Beth stood up and walked across the room.

When she reached the doorway, her father called out, "You haven't told me about you and Theo."

She stiffened, but didn't turn her head. "I don't need to tell you anything. I'm an adult, not a child."

She went up the stairs, head held high, but in her room she threw herself on her bed and howled into her pillow. What was wrong with her? Why was she being so mean to her dad? She wanted him to be happy.

And she wanted to make love with Theo. *That* was the problem. She'd had such fun at the play with him, and it had been so romantic, walking home in the rain, holding hands, feeling the warm rain slide her clothes against her body . . . All her life she'd been dreaming of this moment with Theo, and it had been wrenched away from her by the sight of her father and Lisa. So Beth was acting like a spoiled child who dropped her ice cream cone.

She didn't want to be that spoiled child. She was an educated, enlightened, intelligent woman. She was much more herself when she was in school. It was living with her father that regressed her. If she'd been living somewhere else, tonight's situation wouldn't have happened. Her father and Lisa could have done, well, whatever they'd wanted to, but more important, she and Theo could have been together as adults, as two grown-ups who wanted to be with each other. In bed.

Tomorrow, Beth decided, she really would find another place to live.

"So that was weird, right?" Theo asked his mom as they walked in the rain to their house.

"It was," Lisa agreed.

"What were you doing?" Theo asked.

"What were *we* doing? The same thing you and Beth were doing. Walking in the rain."

"Mom."

"Theo."

"You know he's a lot younger than you."

"Really? Why didn't anyone tell me?"

Theo sighed. "Do you like him a lot?"

"I like him a lot."

"So what's going to happen?"

"Well, first of all, I'm going to keep seeing him. He makes me happy."

They were almost to their house. The rain was still racketing down so hard some of the drops bounced off the sidewalks. Lightning flashed in the distance and thunder rolled over their heads.

"I bet it's flooding down on Easy Street," Theo said.

Lisa smiled. "You're such a guy."

Theo was quiet for a while, then he said, casually, "I like Mack."

"I like Mack, too. And for what it's worth, he thinks you've got the makings of a fine carpenter."

Theo asked, "Is it too weird, me working for him, you, um, dating him?"

"I can handle it," Lisa replied. "Can you?"

After a beat, Theo answered, "Yeah."

"Is it nice, seeing Beth again? Do you talk about Atticus? You three were such a gang."

"Yeah, we were, but it's different now. Time has passed. We've changed. I like her, Mom." It was easy to say this in the darkness, while they walked side by side. "I like her a lot."

"I don't think she likes me."

"Really? She hasn't said anything. Give her time. She's kind of, well, I mean, she finds it hard to trust people, I think. Because of Atticus." After another long pause, Theo said, with a grin that carried into his voice, "She *really* likes me. So she's going to like you."

"Dear Lord," Lisa said. "You're as vain as you were as a teenager."

Theo woke to the irresistible aroma of bacon. He had such a good mom. As he quickly showered, shaved, and dressed, he replayed last evening. He'd experienced way more emotions than he was comfortable with. First, he was probably in love with Beth, which came along with a tangle of complications. Beth had changed so radically last night when she saw her father and his mother walking in the rain.

And it was odd, his mom and Mack. He couldn't wrap his mind around it. He wanted to talk with Juliet about this. When they were small, they used to hide behind the sofa and whisper with each other about whether or not they wanted a stepdad. Basically, they did not. They were a fine enough family as they were. Except sometimes Juliet cried because she wished she had a dad to see her in her ballet recitals, and Theo always got sick to his stomach because the school had father-son dinners once a year and Theo couldn't go with his grandfather because he wasn't in good health. They said he could come with a friend or his mother, but forget that. When they were younger, they hadn't considered that their mother might want a male . . . friend. Now they were older, and their mother seemed so happy when she was with Mack.

Theo didn't want to mess that up for her.

twenty-five

Beth unlocked the door and entered the Ocean Matters office. She was all discombobulated today, torn between sweet thoughts of Theo and hurt feelings because since their walk in the rain last night, he hadn't phoned or texted her. She could reach out to him, of course, but stubbornness stopped her. Call her old-fashioned, but she felt very deeply that *he* should call *her*. And there was the bonus misery of her father and Theo's mother. Did Theo want to drop her because he didn't want to get between his mother and Mack? Okay, he could at least man up and tell her that. And she wanted to move out of her house, but where could she go? It would be impossible to find a place to live on the island in the summer, even if she could afford a place the size of a closet.

She pulled out her chair and settled at her desk. She woke her computer. *Concentrate,* she told herself. *The ocean is more important than your little problems.*

The Ocean Matters inbox was full of emails, which was something positive. OM was getting noticed, people were responding. She scanned the emails before going back and answering them, one by one. It took all her willpower to stop thinking about Theo, and she still was sniffing back tears.

"Good morning, Beth."

Beth jumped in her chair.

"Oh, Ryder! I didn't know you were back."

"Sorry to startle you. I flew in just now and came right to the office. I should have texted you." Ryder frowned. "Beth, you're crying. Are you okay?"

Beth swiped at her face. "Sorry."

"Don't be sorry. Tell me what's going on. I hope it's not something about Ocean Matters that's upset you."

Ryder took hold of his desk chair and spun it over so that he was facing Beth. He sat there, with concern in his beautiful blue eyes.

"It's not Ocean Matters," Beth said, trying to smile.

"Can you tell me what it is?"

Beth dipped down to take a hanky out of her bag. "It's family stuff. I got into an argument with my father, and I can't live with him anymore."

"Why not?"

"Oh, it's so complicated and silly. I like this guy Theo, Theo Hawley. And he likes me. But my father is dating his mother. And my father's been widowed for most of my life and he deserves a chance at happiness."

"But why can't you live at home?"

"Because as long as I'm there, Lisa, Theo's mother, won't be comfortable at my dad's house. I mean, of course she can come over. I like her. We could talk and stuff. But later . . . and I think they might be serious and that's good for both of them." Beth looked up at Ryder. "I'm sorry. I'm babbling. None of this is your concern."

Ryder folded his arms over his chest and sat quiet for a moment. Then he said, "You know, my parents own a fairly sizable house on the island. I don't stay there very often because I'm seldom here. Anyway, it's got a caretaker's apartment over the garage. Small, but completely furnished. You're welcome to stay there."

"Oh. Oh, well, I don't know. I didn't mean to dump my troubles on you." Beth tried to smile.

"Look, this is completely no strings attached. I never go into that apartment. Mrs. Fletcher comes in twice a week to clean the big house, but she doesn't do the garage. You'd have complete privacy."

"This is so nice of you, but really, it's not necessary—"

Ryder leaned forward, planting his elbows on his knees. "Beth, it is necessary. I want Ocean Matters to be a success, and that depends on you and your work. If you're unhappy, you're not going to be as focused on our mission. But it's up to you. I'm just offering."

"Well," Beth said slowly, "it would solve a lot of problems for me. I'm sure I could concentrate on my work more. Not that I'm not working hard now—"

"Beth, it's obvious you're working hard," Ryder said.

Beth nodded. "Thank you, Ryder. I'm grateful for this offer, and actually, I'd love to stay in your apartment for a while. Maybe for the summer, until I get things sorted out."

Ryder rose, reached in his pocket, and pulled out a key attached to a miniature buoy. "Great. I like it when problems are solved. Now back to work." He headed to the door. "I've got a meeting."

"Aye, aye, commander," Beth said. "And thanks."

She focused on her computer, brought up the email, and ran her eyes down the new names in the inbox. One email caught her attention and she opened it.

Hi, Beth, hey, I'd love to meet with you and have a chat. Possible today? Tomorrow? XO Juliet

In a flash, Beth typed: *Sorry. No time.*

Immediately, Juliet answered: *This isn't about my idiot brother. It's about Ocean Matters.*

Beth hesitated. She didn't want Juliet, who was so infinitely superior tech-wise, to be more important to Ocean Matters than Beth.

Sorry, Beth emailed. *Maybe tomorrow.*

Oh! She wanted to scream! All the complications keeping her apart from Theo made Beth feel helpless and confused. She straightened her shoulders and told herself to pull up her big girl pants. There was one thing she *could* do. She left the office, locked the door, and hurried to her house.

Her father's house.

It was empty and quiet when she entered. Quickly she put together two duffel bags of necessities—clothes, toiletries, books, her laptop. She'd come back later when she'd figured out what else she needed.

She carried it all to her car—that car with its empty back seat—and drove to Ryder's family house and garage. They were on Hulbert Avenue, the long street that stretched right along Nantucket Harbor to the Coast Guard station and Brant Point lighthouse. She couldn't believe her luck. No cars were in the drive, but she parked her car on the street, not wanting to take someone else's place, and lugged her duffels to the garage door on the side of the house that opened to stairs leading up to the second floor.

It was *amazing.*

At the ocean side, sliding glass doors led to a small balcony with a small round table and two chairs. Just inside was the living room, with a sofa and two chairs placed to face the water. A low table between them held glossy books about the island.

The color scheme was pale gray, pale ivory, pale tan, merging with the world outside. The back half of the space was divided into a bedroom with a double bed and a long closet holding a clothing rack and shelves, a bath with a shower, and a galley kitchen. A small glass dining table stood between the living room and kitchen. Everything was simple and uncluttered. Beth sort of hated to clutter it with her bulging duffel bags.

Walking to the sliding glass doors, she opened them and stepped out on the narrow balcony. A short lawn led to a tumble of pebbles and then to a small private beach, and then to the harbor. It was a sweeping, breathtaking view. And for a while, it was her view.

Her cell rang.

"Where are you?" Ryder asked, his voice loud with excitement.

"Oh, I'm at your garage—"

"I'll pick you up. They've found a great white shark dead on Madaket Beach."

Before she could respond, Ryder cut off. She hurried down the steps and out to the driveway. In only seconds, Ryder was there.

Beth hopped in to the passenger seat. "Are you sure it's a great white?"

"They're unmistakable," Ryder said.

"What killed it?"

"We don't know yet. The great white's only enemy is humans. Maybe it was shot."

It didn't take long to get to Madaket Road, but once there, the narrow two-way road was packed bumper to bumper with cars. Ryder concentrated on driving, past the old pump, past the entrance to Sanford Farm and its walking paths, past the Eel Point turnoff leading to the 40th Pole Beach, past the dump, past the 1st Bridge off the Madaket Road where kids lay on the dock to catch crabs, past the sign for Madaket Marine.

Ryder groaned when he saw the line of cars U-turning and looking for parking spots. He found a place on a dirt road, parked, jumped out, and hurried toward the beach. Beth followed. At the far western tip of the island, this beach had the strongest waves and the worst undertow, but its long gleaming stretch of sand was unsurpassed in beauty. If you climbed the dune, you could see Madaket Harbor with its calmer waters and docks. The lure for most people was the brilliant sunsets, but swimming on the Atlantic side was also popular for everyone, especially strong swimmers.

And now a shark had washed up on the western shore, where families were swimming every day. This was a major event.

Beth saw photographers and journalists heading out to the site, among a crowd of people she recognized as conservationists and people she didn't know but guessed from their apparel were tourists: a father with a small child riding on his shoulders, a group of giggling girls, the town's local eccentric, covered with tattoos.

"Beth! Wait up!"

Beth looked over her shoulder. Alice Cameron, the head of the chamber of commerce, was striding toward her. Her salt and pepper hair, normally coiled into a neat bun on the top of her head, had come loose and flew around her face like loose strings.

"Isn't this terrible?" Alice cried when she reached Beth.

"It is," Beth agreed. "The poor shark—"

"The poor *shark? Are you kidding me?*" Alice's voice rose several octaves. "Do you understand what this means for tourism? A shark on a Nantucket beach? People will stop coming, our hotels and B&Bs will be empty, the restaurants will have no customers, and think of all the shopkeepers! The island will become a ghost town!"

"Alice, I don't think that will happen. I mean, the shark is dead. Maybe the currents brought it here from way out in the ocean."

"Oh, thank heavens, you are brilliant, yes, that's probably the reason it's here." Alice patted her chest to calm herself.

They finally reached the shore where the creature lay, at least fifteen feet long, showing its white underbelly. Its terrifying long mouth was open, exposing rows of triangular sharply serrated teeth.

Already a crowd had formed and Beth saw that the lifeguard and Ryder had drawn a circle in the sand around the shark and were standing sentry.

"Stand back!" Ryder yelled at the mass of people. "Scientists are on their way."

"You don't even live here!" a man shouted at Ryder.

The ring of watchers protested, pushing and shoving and cursing. They were an odd group, some dressed for swimming, some dressed for work, all of them enthralled to be so near this notorious creature.

Eddie Boyton, who owned an island outerwear shop, yelled, "This is OUR island, OUR property, and OUR shark!"

A little boy broke with the crowd and ran, zig-zagging past the crowd, to touch the shark. The mother screamed as if the shark was attacking her son.

"Stand back!" the lifeguard yelled, deftly and gently scooping the boy up in his arms. The boy burst into tears.

The crowd shouted and waved their arms in the air.

"This could get ugly," Alice said to Beth.

"Beth!" Ryder yelled. "Anyone who wants to help, come form a protective ring around the shark until Ocearch gets here."

"What the hell is Ocearch?" called a woman.

"A collaboration of scientists studying the great whites," the lifeguard told her.

"We don't need to study them, we need to kill them!" another woman yelled.

Bill Blount, a town resident and working fisherman, strode down between the shark and the crowd. "Leave this poor creature alone! Don't be so ignorant! Sharks are at the top of the food chain. If we didn't have sharks eating the seals, human beings would have no fish to eat. Give this animal some respect!"

Prudence Starbuck, her shining white hair piled so high she seemed taller than her true six feet, stomped through the crowd. "I'll help!"

This drew a number of people to stand guard around the shark. Beth was among them. She didn't see Theo or Juliet or Lisa although she continued to scan the crowd.

Ryder put his hand to his ear. Not until then did Beth realize he was wearing a Bluetooth device. "Everyone! Listen! Ocearch is coming with a boat. They've got a lift to take the shark from the water onto the boat. We need to get the shark out in the water. Who can help?"

"I will!" a man growled.

"Me, too!"

At least a dozen men came forward, and it took all of them to lift and pull the shark into the water.

“Beth,” Ryder said, tossing her his car keys. “Take my car back to the house. I’m going with the shark.”

“Sure,” Beth answered. She was secretly pleased to have the chance to drive a Range Rover SUV.

The crowd gradually broke up, trudging back up the beach to the road and their cars. A kind of fatigue came over them all, a letdown from the high of the shark finding. *A real great white shark.* They had been *this close* to a great white shark.

twenty-six

It was a good morning. Mack and his crew were pulling into the driveway when Lisa left for the shop. And miracle of miracles, Theo was already up, dressed, and out the door to help Dave and Tom unload Sheetrock. Lisa wanted to talk with Mack about the night before, but now was not the time. The summer day was hot and humid, and the streets were already busy with summer people doing errands. The Bartlett's Farm truck was parked on Main Street, and women were unloading baskets of just-picked tomatoes, strawberries, and lettuce. Men strolled past *Sail* on the way to buy a newspaper and a cup of coffee. They sat on the benches on Main Street, soaking in the sun and the pure clear sense of leisure, chatting with anyone passing by. For the summer, for the people from big cities, the small town was sweet with ordinary pleasures.

It was a quiet morning in Lisa's shop. She caught up on paperwork, put out new jewelry in the display case, and tried not to check her phone every five minutes. She'd caught only a quick glimpse of Mack as she walked away from her house earlier. He winked at her. She smiled back.

For a moment, Lisa allowed herself to lean on her counter, remembering last night, walking in the rain, with Mack. Before they saw his daughter and her son.

Moxie Breinberg, the unofficial town crier, burst through the door. "Did you hear about the shark?"

Lisa returned to reality. "No. Tell me."

Moxie couldn't speak fast enough, as if afraid someone else would steal the scoop. Moxie should have been a reporter, Lisa thought. She listened to Moxie prattle on about the shark for a solid five minutes without, it seemed, needing to breathe. Lisa was grateful when her best friend Rachel came in. Rachel was not only married to a lawyer, she was a lawyer herself, and she was six feet tall and willowy, with a self-assured demeanor. She rolled her eyes behind Moxie's back and pretended to check out the new dresses. Finally, Moxie left.

The moment the door closed behind Moxie, Rachel said with a mischievous grin, "So, what's new with you?"

"I suppose you heard about the great white out at Madaket," Lisa said.

"That's crazy, isn't it? But not what I want to know about. How are you and Mack?"

"We're wonderful," Lisa said. She lifted a scarf from the counter and folded it for a few minutes. "*He's* wonderful."

"But . . ."

"But first of all, *Theo* is working for him now. Really working, and happy. *But* Theo is seeing Beth. The four of us ran into each other last night when we were walking in the rain. It was awkward. I was holding hands with Mack and Beth shot daggers at me. Theo and I talked about it as we walked to our house, and he's okay with it, but you know Theo, he's the yellow Lab of men."

Rachel snorted. "I take it that Beth is a rottweiler?"

"I don't know if I'd call her that. She's too lovely and kind. Plus, Rachel, Beth's had a hard time, losing her mother at three, and then losing Atticus when she was a teenager. If she really cares for Theo as much as he seems to care for her, I don't want to get in the way of that. Not for her, not for Theo. I want them both to have love and romance."

"What about you?" Rachel put her hand on Lisa's. "And if you fold that scarf one more time, I'll strangle you with it."

Lisa sighed and left the scarf on top of the pile. "I've been thinking about that, Rachel. Especially after last night, after seeing how happy Theo was with Beth. And seeing him working for Mack. Theo really likes the work, and he's good at it. He's strong, and he likes being part of a team."

"Okay, but what about *you* and Mack?"

"We can slow down—"

"I didn't notice that you two were exactly speeding up."

"You mean we haven't slept together yet. No, we haven't, and it's not because I don't want to. I do. But I'm still . . . anxious."

"Lisa, you're gorgeous—"

"Let me finish. Erich and I married far too fast. I thought I loved him. I guess he thought he loved me. I wish we'd had more time to get to know each other. I wish I'd been able to get a job somewhere, find out what I could do—"

"Lisa, you worked for the National Museum of Women in the Arts!"

"I know. And I did an excellent job. But I was trying to conform to the role that Erich and his parents set for me. And if you'll remember, and you should remember because you were always championing Erich, I wasn't prepared for marriage when Erich proposed to me, in front of my parents and the entire restaurant. I wish we had waited, even for a summer, to get to know each other better, to find out what we really wanted."

"Because that's how life works," Rachel said. "We think about what we want and presto! Life gives it to us."

"The point is, Rachel, Erich and I made a mistake."

"Juliet and Theo aren't mistakes."

"Of course not. I wouldn't change anything in the past, because I have those two amazing children. But I *can* take a tiny bit of control over what happens to me next."

"You're going to be rational instead of romantic."

"If you put it that way, yes."

Rachel shook her head. "That sounds kind of sad, Lisa."

"I don't mean to be sad, Rachel. I mean to be . . . kind. Thoughtful. I want to let Theo discover if he can work for Mack, if that's the kind of life he'd like. I'd like to let him find out if he really cares for Beth. You know what he was like in high school, a new girl every week. Beth is wonderful, and Theo seems serious about her."

Rachel gave Lisa a warm smile that went all the way to her eyes. "You are one of a kind."

"I guess that's a compliment?"

"It is. Plus, I want to buy this scarf." She picked up the square of silk covered with flowers and tied it around her neck. "Elegant, no?"

"Anything you touch is elegant," Lisa told her friend. "And thank you for listening to me. I'll sell you that scarf at cost in exchange for the therapy sessions."

twenty-seven

Theo was carrying cans of paint up to the bathroom when Juliet came out of her room with her computer slung over her shoulder. "I've done my Kazaam work, so I'm going to the OM office now."

Theo put the cans down. "Hey, did you hear about the great white?"

"My Insta account exploded with photos. Poor Alice Cameron is losing her mind online. She's insisting the great whites are no danger to people."

"You're wearing a dress!" Theo blurted. Juliet was usually in black leggings and a T-shirt, but now she was all girly in a sundress with flowers on it.

Juliet shrugged. "So? It's summer."

Theo snorted a laugh. He never could resist taunting his older, totally cooler sister. "You like Ryder. You're showing it off for him."

"Don't be gross." Juliet rolled her eyes.

"You know Beth hangs out with Ryder."

"Beth *works* for Ryder." Juliet started to go down the stairs.

Theo reached out and took her wrist. "Hey,

wait. Seriously, Juliet, you don't . . . have a thing going with Ryder, do you?"

She wouldn't look at him. "Why do you care?"

"You may look sophisticated, but that man is leagues more experienced than you. I don't want you to get hurt."

Juliet jerked her wrist away from his grip. "You think I'm naïve? You think I'll fall for the old seduce and abandon trick *you*'ve pulled on every girl on this island?"

"Oh, come off it—"

"If you're so worried about someone getting hurt, why don't you stop seeing Beth? You know her father likes Mom."

Juliet could always hit above her weight. Theo felt like he'd been punched in the gut. "Yeah, I know that. But, Juliet, Mom and Mack are . . . old. They can take care of themselves."

"Theo?" Dave yelled up the stairs. "We've got another load."

"Be right there!" Theo yelled back. "Just think about it," he muttered to Juliet.

"You think about it, too," Juliet told him.

Juliet reviewed her conversation with Theo as she walked into town. It was true that Ryder was more sophisticated than she was. Could she trust him? Maybe he pulled the "we have such electricity" bit on every woman.

But what she'd experienced with him that

night after dinner at the Chanticleer had been powerful. She had been sure it was authentic. A bond existed between them.

She reached the Ocean Matters office. The lights were on but she couldn't see who was inside because of the posters, so when she pulled the door open, she was momentarily shocked to see Ryder and Beth side by side at the computer.

"Juliet!" Beth was flushed—with excitement or with hormones? "Did you hear about the shark?"

"Several times," Juliet said dryly. She stayed near the door, unsure what to do and hating herself for this. Her primitive alarm system was buzzing inside her at the sight of Beth and Ryder so close together. It took all her willpower not to turn and walk away. Run away.

Beth said, "Ryder just got back from Madaket. He's taken a great video. We're cleaning it up so we can put it on our social media."

Juliet looked at Ryder. "I didn't know you were back on-island."

"I just got in, and had to rush out to see the shark," Ryder told her. He pushed his chair back and stood up. "Beth was showing me the work you two have done. It's great. We're getting lots of attention."

"It's all because of Juliet," Beth said. "She's the expert. I'm learning a lot from her."

Surprised and grateful for Beth's praise, Juliet said, "Beth, you're a natural at this."

"You're both amazing," Ryder said, walking toward the door. "Juliet, could we take a break? I'd like to talk to you."

Juliet shrugged, as if this was of no importance to her. "Sure."

They left the office. Ryder took her arm and guided her to a small path between the office building and a shingled real estate office.

"Where—"

"Here," Ryder said brusquely. He pulled her against him and kissed her so long and hard her legs went weak.

When he finally released her enough for them both to catch their breaths, he said, "I missed you."

She couldn't help smiling. "I missed you, too."

"Want to get coffee?"

"No, thanks, Ryder."

"Want to see my etchings?"

Juliet laughed. "Okay, you could buy me coffee."

They walked up the street to a small café, ordered their drinks, and sat at a table in the corner.

"How was Miami?" Juliet asked.

"Lonely," Ryder said. "You weren't there."

"But seriously."

"Seriously?" He took a moment to gather his thoughts. "Miami has over eighty thousand people living below sea level. Now their 'King Tides,' unusually high tides because of the alignment of the sun and the moon, are rising even higher. Billions of dollars of real estate are going to be lost to rising seas." He paused. "Am I boring you?"

"Not at all. This is fascinating."

"I have to go to China next. You should go with me."

Juliet was stunned. Was he kidding? "Well, that would be cool, I guess."

"I'm not asking you to marry me. I'm suggesting that you work for me. I want to be with you, Juliet."

"You know I have a great job at Kazaam."

"Doing posts about cute dogs." His tone was completely neutral.

"Ryder, do you always make important decisions this fast? I mean, I consider myself an efficient decision maker, but you, well, you're way faster than I am. I really have to give some thought to this. I mean, I'm building up a pension at Kazaam and I've got health benefits, and a significant salary. I like my apartment, and I like coming back to the island whenever I want. To be honest, I need to be certain that I can trust you before I change my life so drastically. I want you," she whispered, looking him in the eye, "but I'm not sure I want to do anything long-term with you."

"Okay, then, let's just make love," Ryder said, smiling.

"What? Ryder, you're making my head spin."

"Sorry. I was only teasing. Kind of. Look, I've made you uncomfortable. Let's go back to the office and work on the fundraiser."

"Good idea," Juliet said.

They bought a mocha latte to take to Beth and went back to the office. For a while the three went over the figures, catalogued the members, brainstormed about the fundraiser. Ryder left for a meeting. Juliet and Beth sat back in their chairs, relaxing.

"He charges like a freight train coming through," Juliet said.

"I think he likes you," Beth told her, smiling shyly.

"Oh, really?" Juliet was amused—and pleased.

"Really. He keeps looking at you, and his eyes get all soft when you speak."

"Well, I have to admit, I kind of like him." Juliet started to say more, but Beth interrupted.

"I haven't had a chance to tell you or Theo, but I've moved into Ryder's garage."

"What?" Juliet's hands flew to her stomach. She was afraid she was going to throw up.

"He has an apartment over his garage. Next to his house. On Hulbert Avenue. Amazing views."

"Forget the views, Beth. Why did you move in with him?"

"I didn't move in *with him.* I need to get out of my father's house, and Ryder offered me the apartment. It's not permanent or anything."

Juliet's face had closed down. "And Theo doesn't know?"

"Not yet. I just moved today. I had a fight with my father—well, you should know why. I mean, he seems serious about your mother. I don't want to get in their way."

"But what about you and Theo?"

"To be honest, I don't know. Theo's working for my dad now. Dad says he's a good worker. I don't want to get in the way of that, either."

Juliet leaned toward Beth. "You are such an only child. Are you afraid that if Theo does something wrong, Mack will yell at him or fire him?"

"Well, that could happen."

"Realistically, it absolutely could. And you know what? Theo could go get a job doing something else. Maybe he's not cut out for the construction business, but maybe he is. Or he'll knuckle down and work harder. The point is, you can't be afraid of Theo and Mack arguing. You can't be afraid that your daddy will be mean to your boyfriend. Men argue all the time. And believe me, siblings argue all the time. We say terrible things to each other and slam out the door and fifteen minutes later we're sharing a bowl of popcorn in front of *Saturday Night Live*."

"I suppose you're right . . ." Beth fiddled with

a pen. Suddenly straightening, she said, "Okay, if we're being honest, let's talk about Ocean Matters. I could tell during the meeting today that you kept pushing Ryder's attention to what *I* have accomplished."

"Well, you have done all the organizational bit." Juliet shifted uncomfortably in her chair. "And I don't want to take your job."

"I don't think you need to replace me. I think Ocean Matters needs both of us, and I think you and I work well together."

"Do you have a contract?"

"No. It was Prudence Starbuck who contacted me about working here. I had barely landed back on-island when she sort of hijacked me into this. I'm getting an excellent salary but we haven't had time to do all the human resources groundwork."

Juliet folded her arms and settled back in her chair. "This is interesting, Beth. Very interesting."

"Does that mean you want to work with me?"

"I'm not sure." Juliet held up her hand. "Not being mean. Stating facts. Because, well, here, let me show you."

Juliet flicked open her phone and brought up her email. She scrolled down and handed it to Beth.

Beth read slowly, scrolling down. Sitting back, she stared at Juliet with admiration. "Juliet, all these groups want to hire you to do their social media."

Juliet smiled. "I know. Ever since we put up the OM website, I've had crazy mad offers from all sorts of places."

"But you're working for Kazaam, right?"

"Right. And I'm working for OM free of charge. Obviously I can't keep doing that forever—"

"But OM's budget is certainly large enough to pay you."

"I know. Plus, a lot of groups are offering a huge salary and great perks."

"But would you have to move to New York, or wherever?"

"No, that's the beauty of my job. I can work anywhere as long as I've got my laptop." Restless, Juliet rose and paced the office. "I like my job at Kazaam, but it's not very challenging. These other organizations, especially Ocean Matters, are important. Necessary. World-changing. I want to be part of that."

"But you couldn't work for two or three places at once . . ."

"Of course I could, if I had my own company," Juliet told Beth triumphantly. "I could pick and choose from these offers. So I could work and travel with Ryder at the same time."

"Travel with Ryder?"

"Yes." Juliet tilted her head and peered at Beth

from under her eyelashes. "Ryder asked me to travel with him. Well, to *be* with him."

"Oh, wow, Juliet. That's awesome." Beth hesitated. "Do you love him?"

"I don't know. And I don't want to rush into anything. I've done that and it doesn't always go well. But he's fascinating, Beth. I'm madly attracted to him. He's like work and romance rolled into one delicious Ferrero Rocher."

"Wow," Beth said. "This is huge."

"It is," Juliet agreed. "But I'm really excited about starting my own business, and Ryder is so passionate about Ocean Matters. I think we could both work and be together." Juliet paused. "I *think* we could. I'm not sure, and it's scary, but I want to try."

"You are amazing," Beth said.

"Thanks," Juliet said. She gave Beth a challenging look. "So you wouldn't mind working with me on OM, right?"

"Well, of course not," Beth said.

"Okay, then, how would you like to be my stepsister, too?" When Beth looked confused, Juliet said, "If your father marries my mother."

Beth said faintly, "Marriage? Are they talking about marriage?"

"I don't know, but wouldn't it be nice?"

"I'm not sure . . ." Beth studied her hands, as if the answer were there.

Juliet shrugged. "Well, your father could marry

a younger woman who could have a baby, and then you'd have a half-sibling."

Beth lifted her head and smiled at Juliet. "Oh, I think I'd much rather have you in my family."

"And my brother, too?" Juliet asked with a mischievous smile.

"I'd like to have your brother in my life," Beth answered honestly. "No, the truth is, I'd *love* to have him in my life. And, Juliet, don't tell him what I said."

"I won't. I promise. But I do think he's crazy about you."

Beth blushed. "I think we should get back to work."

"You're right," Juliet said. "Now where were we?"

"We've got to post about the shark," Beth reminded her.

They set their laptops together and worked side by side companionably, questioning, commenting, choosing, and both of them wondered secretly if this was what it felt like to have a sister, and both of them decided secretly that if so, it was extremely nice.

twenty-eight

Early in the morning, Lisa walked through her quiet house, a mug of coffee in her hands. Mack and his crew had done a great job of repairing the living room and dining room ceilings and renovating her bathroom. So they were finished here, and working hard on a summer house that needed to be done before the family arrived for Labor Day.

Everyone had been so busy the past few days. The autopsy had shown that the great white shark had had so much plastic in its stomach it couldn't digest food. Ryder went to an environmental meeting in Washington, and Beth and Juliet worked hard publicizing the shark's death. Theo came home at nine o'clock after working long hard hours for Mack's crew, and Juliet wandered into the house at all hours, always on her phone, talking to her Boston office.

Lisa liked having the kids home, and both Juliet and Theo were doing their share of the chores, laundry, grocery shopping, dishes, going to the dump. Lisa had no complaints there, but she did feel a low-grade irritation that she couldn't invite Mack to her house for dinner because . . . Why?

It was no secret that she was dating Mack. But it was also no secret that Theo cared about Beth, and Lisa didn't want to get in his way. She liked Beth, and she knew that Theo had crushed on her in high school, but the question remained: Could Lisa see Mack if her son was seeing his daughter? Or was she just being silly? After all, nothing had really happened between her and Mack yet.

But she missed him. It had been only a few evenings that she hadn't seen him, and their phone conversations had been short because they were both tired.

Still, they had to eat. And this was *her* house.

She pulled her phone from the pocket of her robe and called Mack. When he answered, she said, "Could you come to dinner tonight? I'll leave the store with Gretchen and get home early to make something delicious."

"That would be amazing, Lisa."

"Would seven work for you?"

"Absolutely."

They talked some more, about the ordinary events of the day, and she found herself leaning against a door, gazing out at her garden, which suddenly was full of flowers.

The hydrangea was blooming in that exquisite shade of turquoise blue. Her dahlias brightened the garden with every color, and daisies, daylilies, foxglove, and roses mixed together in complementary hues. Her everlasting flowers—Queen Anne's lace, strawflower, blue globe thistle, baby's breath—were flourishing, almost taking over her garden. The borders of her lawn looked wilder now, more colorful, and oddly pleased with themselves.

And so was Lisa, she realized.

Because Mack was in her life.

Standing in the open door, gazing at her flowers, Lisa felt a shiver of elation run through her. She hugged herself. This was her garden. This was her house. Mack was the man she loved. Her children were grown and healthy, and as always, they came bounding into the quiet shelter of her life, bringing color and noise and decisions and emotions. Her children were like gorgeous creatures escaped from a zoo, rampaging through the house, eating her food, complicating every hour of her day, and she wanted to be done with that. She loved them, but she loved Mack, too, not more, but in a different, intimate, and delicious way. And in a way she deserved. And would choose.

Lisa called Betsy and asked her to open the store. Lisa would come in later. In her knee-length night T-shirt and an apron, she moved around the kitchen, planning something Mack would like that was not a grilled steak. She settled on lasagna with lots of hamburger and cheese. She put it together and slipped it into the fridge to be baked that evening. She would pick up a bottle of red wine on her way home.

Dark clouds rolled over the sky as Lisa walked home that evening. She hadn't had a chance to check her weather app because the store had been so busy, but she ditched her plan to eat on the sunporch. They couldn't eat in the dining room. The ceiling still smelled slightly of paint, and they hadn't moved the furniture back in place. They would eat in the kitchen. That would feel cozy.

At home, Lisa changed into a summer dress and sandals. Pretty, but casual. She had an hour before Mack would arrive. She put her favorite cloth over the kitchen table, set out her daily china and silverware, put the lasagna in to bake. She worked at the sink washing lettuce, her thoughts all over the place. She was certain that Theo would bound in the door like an overgrown puppy, excited that she'd made lasagna, but she was equally certain she'd tell him it was for her and a guest. He could go eat pizza and drink with his friends at a bar. Juliet wouldn't want to eat with them. When Lisa told her daughter she was having Mack over for dinner, Juliet would make some sarcastic remark and leave the house. Which was fine. This *was* Lisa's house. It was her life.

As it turned out, Juliet texted Lisa that she

was going to be out for the evening. Theo didn't bother to text, but neither did he barge in after work. It was kind of a miracle.

Mack arrived a little after seven. Clearly he had showered and cleaned up.

"Wow, something smells delicious," he said when he followed her into the kitchen.

"That's lasagna," Lisa said, walking to the stove.

Mack came up behind her, put his hands on her waist, and pulled her against him. "That's you," he murmured into her hair.

A rush of desire swept through her. She leaned against him, closing her eyes, relishing the feel of his body against hers.

Mack kissed the top of her head and stepped back. "Where are Juliet and Theo?"

"I'm not sure. I think they're both out for the evening."

Lisa bent to take out the lasagna to let it set before cutting. She was aware of Mack behind her as she bent over, and she was glad she'd worn a dress with a full skirt. Would she ever stop worrying about the size of her bottom? Did *any* woman ever stop worrying about that?

She tossed a salad with wine vinegar and oil as Mack poured the wine.

"Good day?" she asked.

Mack talked about the summer house they were building and how glad he was that Theo had joined his crew. As they ate dinner, the conversation turned to the shark and all the concern its presence and its death caused.

"Beth talks about Ocean Matters all the time," Mack told Lisa. "Or she did, before she moved out to Ryder's place."

Lisa almost choked on her salad. "Beth is living with Ryder?"

"No, she's living in a garage on his property." Mack put down his fork. "Beth is . . . concerned about you and me."

"She doesn't like me," Lisa said.

"No. She doesn't like me with you. And it's not about our age difference. Beth is—" Mack cleared his throat. "Beth likes Theo a lot. She thinks she can't be with him if I'm with you."

Lisa also put down her fork and poured them each more wine. "It is an odd situation." Looking down into her glass, as if reading the future, she said, "I'm sure that Theo likes Beth a lot, too. No, more than that." Raising her head, Lisa took a deep breath and said, "I think Theo has been in love with Beth since high school. And the way the two of them looked together when they were holding hands, walking in the rain—they were glowing. They were so happy. Oh, Mack, I don't know what to do. I don't want to get in their way."

"But I don't want to lose the chance to be with you."

Lisa nodded. She felt her cheeks flame. "I want to be with you, Mack. But I don't really know what that means."

"It means we see each other exclusively and get to know one another better and maybe we'll get married someday."

Lisa was speechless.

"That's what I want," Mack said, "and I think that's what you want, too. I want us to live together for the rest of our lives."

"But, Mack," Lisa said, her face crimson, "we don't even know if we are compatible . . . in bed."

Mack smiled. "Yes, we do. I'm more aroused by you in the kitchen with a pan of lasagna than I have been in any other situation, with any other woman, for years. We're magnetic, you and I. And we'll do very nicely in bed."

Lisa flushed, her heart racing. After a minute, she asked, "Would you like more lasagna?"

"Yes, but not now," Mack said.

She looked at him, puzzled.

"Right now I'd like to drive you out to see a house we just signed on to renovate."

"Okay . . ."

"It's got a great view. No one is living there. I'm subcontracting it from the Redford Corporation. It has some furniture, and running water, but I think the electricity has been cut." He added softly, "It's an interesting house. An empty house, with no one coming or going."

"Oh," Lisa said, breathing out the word. Here it was, the decision, to be with Mack without interruptions by anyone. She met his eyes across the table and felt his desire as if it were a flame. "Yes, I'd like to . . . see that."

They stood up. She glanced around the kitchen. "I should put the lasagna away . . ."

"We can do it later," Mack told her, and held out his hand.

Lisa followed him to his truck and sat on the long bench seat in the cab. The air was sultry. A wind was beginning to rise. The sun hadn't set but the sky was dark with clouds.

Mack drove them out of town, onto the Madaket Road, and on out west before turning right on a narrow dirt road. An elegant modern house cast a low silhouette on the horizon. Bushes and scrub oak covered the surrounding land in green.

Mack handed Lisa down from the truck and led her to the front door.

"There's an alarm," he said. "I know the code."

Once they were inside the house with the door safely shut against intruders, Lisa felt herself relax. The house itself was spare and sparse, the interior minimalist, the floors and walls in shades of gray and taupe.

"Let me show you around," Mack said, taking Lisa's hand. He led her upstairs, to the empty bedrooms and baths. The master bedroom had a balcony overlooking the lawn and the swimming pool. Back downstairs, she saw the open plan living and dining room and the enormous kitchen.

"This is a marvelous house," Lisa said. "What could they possibly want renovated?"

"They want the living room turned into an entertainment room with a seventy-five-inch television and super speakers. They want the dining room extended to form an outdoor eating area near the pool. And other, smaller changes."

"Well, I wouldn't want to change a thing."

In a low voice, Mack said, "I'd like to change something."

Lisa faced him, trembling. "It's different, you know, simply to be in this neutral space with you. It seems we're always in my house or yours, always on guard for someone to barge in."

"I know. But here, we're alone, and safe." Mack ran his fingers just above her ear, smoothing her hair back, his touch light and gentle.

"Mack." She put her hands on his chest. She tilted her face up for a kiss.

Mack wrapped his arms around her, pulling her against him, kissing her for a long time. "Want to do this?" he asked.

"I do. Oh, I do. But, Mack, where? There are no beds . . ."

Mack grinned. Taking her hand, he led her to the back hallway. "Our suite tonight includes two grade-A swim floats of vinyl coated foam, complete with full circle pillow. In addition, we have a selection of super-size beach towels."

"Are you kidding?" Lisa asked.

"I'm not kidding," Mack said.

The floats had been stacked on their sides against the wall. Mack pulled them out into the dining room, laid them side by side, and covered them with the beach towels.

"But, Mack, this is something a teenager would do." Lisa was laughing and thrilled and terrified.

"Exactly," Mack said.

He approached her and pulled her down onto the twin-mattress-sized floats. They were surprisingly sturdy and comfortable. He eased her back so that her neck rested on the swim pillow, and he began kissing her on her ears, her cheeks, her neck. The light from outdoors was fading, and no shadows moved. It was like lying inside a rain cloud, dark and spangling with mysterious energy.

She felt his body press against hers. Oh, sweet lovely sensation, she'd forgotten this—had she ever known this? She helped him pull off his shirt, and in the dim light she noticed his muscular torso, scarred lightly here and there from, he told her, work accidents. He took off his shoes and socks and pants and his boxer shorts. Finally it was her turn, and she allowed him to tug her sundress up over her head. She quickly dealt with the business of removing her bra and panties, and then there she was naked before him.

She thought she would want to run away or hide her imperfect body with its extra cellulite and slight sags, but the touch of Mack's hand transformed all of her body that she'd disparaged into a creation she'd forgotten about. She was a magical vessel of sensations. Her heart raced, her breath shuddered, her limbs, smooth, round, and feminine, slid against Mack's rough, hairy, muscular limbs, and her body went right ahead without her conscious thought or worry, into a world of pleasure, and more pleasure, and then joy.

Afterward, lying there together, sweating and cooling, beach towels puddled around them, Lisa said, "Mack? I think I'd like to marry you. Someday."

"So you and I are secretly engaged to get married?"

Lisa took a deep breath. "Yes. Let's wait until the summer is over to tell the kids. That will give them some time to sort through their own relationships."

Mack laughed, a satisfied rumble in his chest. He reached over and took her hand. "And we can enjoy the summer with our secret and let the young ones chart their own course."

"Yes," Lisa said.

She stood up, and Mack rose, and they held each other for a long time, not only desiring each other, although there was always desire in their feelings for each other, but also in a companionable way. A comforting way. A promise.

They carried the beach towels with them as they went downstairs. Mack said he'd launder them at home and return them. They left the house and hurried to his truck. As they rode back to Lisa's house, she felt absolutely giddy. She giggled, and how long had it been since she'd done that?

"I feel light-headed," she told Mack. "I feel so *pleased* with myself. I'm a little bit crazy, I think."

"I'm crazy about you," Mack said.

"I must settle down before we get home," Lisa said, laughing. "I don't want Theo or Juliet to see me like this."

"It is going to happen again, you know," Mack told her.

"Oh," Lisa said. "I hope so."

Mack pulled into her driveway and they entered her house. No one else was there. Together they tidied the kitchen, enjoying each small moment when their arms touched, each easy normal task of covering the lasagna for Mack to take home, washing the salad bowl, putting plates in the dishwasher. It was as if they were already a couple living an ordinary life with its extraordinary joys.

Afterward, they sat on the sofa, watching the Red Sox beat the Yankees. A perfect evening.

twenty-nine

When Beth walked to work Thursday morning, she carried an umbrella and wore a light raincoat. For the past two days, the skies had been dark, muttering, and the mirroring seas had darkened, too. Something in the air was making everyone uncomfortable, restless. She wished the rain would go ahead and get it over with. As she reached Easy Street, the rain started full force, pelleting out of the sky in rapid hard drops.

At her office, Beth turned on all the lights, settled in at her computer, and tried to focus on Ocean Matters.

But her mind kept wandering. Theo hadn't called for three days, not since they walked in the rain and saw his mom with her dad. They needed to talk about it. Even if they broke up—although, were they even together?—they needed to talk. It had been great discussing it all with Juliet. Maybe Juliet had said something to Theo?

After a while, she realized the room had become cool, so she left her chair to find the thermostat on the opposite wall, and as she did, she glanced out the window.

Still raining. The sky was almost black, and

she could see the waves bouncing around in the harbor. In the distance, boats were rocking up and down and tugging at their moorings. The fast ferry *Iyanough* was still in its dock at the Steamship Authority, which meant the ferry hadn't made its eleven o'clock run to Hyannis.

Okay, so that wasn't good. That meant the seas were choppy and the wind near gale force, with powerful gusts. Beth wondered if she should close the office. Last year the town had added a foot of wood to the small Easy Street bulkhead where people sat on benches to watch the boats come and go. So far, no waves were breaching the wall, so all the water flooding the street was from the rain.

She returned to her desk. A note in the inbox from Ryder.

Beth, if you're in the office, go home. This storm is more serious than was predicted.

Well, Beth thought with a smile. That was nice of Ryder and funny, too. He wasn't from Nantucket, so he didn't know that the Weather Channel and all weather stations very seldom got Nantucket's predictions right. Something about being a small lump thirty miles from the continent seemed to amuse the weather gods, so gale force winds that were predicted often appeared as minor breezes and two inches of snow became twelve.

Still, she should close up and go home, or

maybe over to the library to check out a good book. She closed the files on her computer, and then, before she could shut it down, the power went out. The computer went blank. The ceiling lights died. The light coming from outside was gray and shadowy. It was spooky.

She stood up. Why did the gray light make her feel so lonely? Walking to the window, she could barely make out through the splatter of rain the way that waves were now surging over the bulkhead and onto the street.

Wow. But okay, don't panic, she told herself. Easy Street often flooded. No big deal. Returning to her desk, she picked up her cell and called her dad. He didn't answer.

She called Theo. He answered at once.

"Where are you?" he asked.

"In the office on Easy Street. Theo, it looks scary out there. I didn't realize the waves were coming in so fast. I don't know whether to stay or go."

"Stay there," Theo said. "I'll come get you."

"You can't drive on the street, it's flooded."

"Yeah, I'll drive as far as I can, then I'll walk down. Don't worry. I'll be there soon."

They disconnected. She'd been fortunate that her cell still worked. The last time her cell had quit was during the long winter blizzard that shut down the town's power and its cell towers. She hoped the cell towers didn't go down. She stationed herself at the window, watching the waves swell over the bulkhead and into the street, washing up against the building.

A powerful gust of wind hit the glass window fronting the office, causing her to instinctively jump backward. It was as if a superhero had slugged the glass with a giant fist. The glass didn't break, but it shivered. As she watched, heaving water rose in Easy Street, covering the sidewalk in front of her building. She'd have to wade through it to get to higher ground.

She shouldn't wait for Theo. She knew how the traffic into town could be on a day like this. People wanting to get home or to the grocery store for staples would have Orange, Union, and Washington backed up for blocks. This water was coming at the island like a machine. It wasn't going to stop soon.

She'd be lucky if she could even open the door against the weight of the water.

She shouldn't wait another minute. She'd call Theo when she got up to higher land.

Beth put her phone in her bag and looped the bag diagonally over her body so that her hands were free. She remembered all the times in high school when she and her friends drove out to Surfside to watch the waves swell and crash, giving off a crazy natural energy that made them dance on the beach.

Same kind of storm, she told herself. She

should enjoy it. She only had to go around the block and up one street to get to safety.

She opened the door, stepped outside, and turned to put her key in the lock. The lock clicked shut. At the same time, waves exploded against her, drenching her from head to toe, pushing her against the door. Water surged up past her ankles. Looking around, she saw the familiar landscape vanish. The bulkhead was merely an irritant for the harbor waves that swept up and over and onto the street, washing so high around the benches on the sidewalk that the water hid the legs and slapped against the seats.

It was still day, but the sky was an angry black, turning the heaving water gray. No lights shone, not from any of the other buildings around her, not from any of the boats bouncing in the harbor. The wind screamed like witches, high piercing wails that seemed supernatural and alive.

The OM office was in the middle of the block. It would be a short walk either right or left to one of the streets leading up to Water Street and dry land. But Oak Street and Cambridge Street were flooded, too, she was sure. They always flooded in storms like this. Which way should she go?

The wind screamed. Pieces of paper and fragments of plastic flew straight from the water to smash onto the OM office windows. Something feathery, a small bird, crashed into Beth's leg, making her jump and yell. It fell into the water and was pushed, relentlessly, into the glass window of the office. This was not a hurricane but it was much like the storms that came in the winter, and much more powerful than the ones she remembered as a child. This storm felt like the ocean was angry.

Glancing to her left, she saw that the flag for Kidding Around had been taken in, and no lights were on. No people walked or tried to drive through the river that had once been a street. She felt terribly alone. She knew enough about water and storms to know she could never trust them. They were powerful and they were uncaring.

The water was at her knees now, slapping against them, shoving her backward.

"Oh, don't be such a wuss," she told herself. Stepping away from the building, she walked toward Oak Street. Or tried to walk. It was like wading through molasses, as if the water were thick. Still, she was strong enough. She carried her purse tucked up high under her arm.

A new brick sidewalk had been laid on this section of the street. She knew it was there and tried to stay on it, although no cars were coming down the road that was now a river. It was eerie, the lack of cars or lights or people. She slogged on, almost to the corner, when something hard hit her in the backs of her knees and she fell over, sinking down into the heaving water. She struggled to get her face back into the air, to right herself, to stand, but the strength of the wind and the raging water forced her backward and down.

The waves slammed her against the white picket fence fronting a small lawn and an office. She clawed out for the fence, but she was heaved up by the water and smashed down toward the sidewalk. She screamed, but water filled her mouth.

Was she drowning? That would be ridiculous. A wave sucked her back toward the harbor, tossing her around like a doll. She managed to get her face above water and take a deep breath, and when she did, through her wet eyelashes, she thought she saw Theo.

thirty

Everything happened so quickly.

One moment, she was sitting at the kitchen table, working on her Kazaam website, and the next moment, her mother flew into the house.

Alarmed, Juliet cried, "What's going on?"

"Bad flooding. Bad storm. We've got to pile sandbags at the assisted living facility. The waves are crazy, Juliet, and headed right into the end of the harbor." As she talked, Lisa was pulling off her shoes and running up the stairs. "Put on sweats and sneakers," Lisa called. "Brownie Folger is picking us up in five minutes."

Juliet followed her mother up the stairs. In her bedroom, she pulled on a thick sweatshirt, jeans, and sneakers. She could tell from her window that this was a super storm, the kind that would make it ridiculous to wear the green rubber Wellington boots she usually wore when it rained. A surging wave would fill the boots in a flash, making it impossible to walk.

Downstairs, Juliet pulled on an old blue raincoat, put up the hood, and secured it with ties. Her mother had a plastic bonnet from the hairdresser's tied around her head, squashing her hair.

Juliet laughed. "Oh, Mom, you're such a fashion plate!"

"I've lost my rain hat . . . it doesn't matter. Brownie's here."

They ran through the rain to the Department of Public Works truck rumbling in front of the house. Brownie Folger, head of the DPW, was driving, his gnarled old hands clutching the steering wheel as if the wheel was pulling him. Harold McMaster, head of the Anglers' Club, sat in the passenger seat. Lisa climbed into the back, too, and Juliet squeezed up against her. A tower of sandbags took up most of the back seat and all of the truck's bed. Even with all the weight inside it, the truck rocked when a 60 mph gust of wind hit it hard.

"I haven't been this close to you since I gave birth to you," Lisa whispered, trying to lighten the atmosphere.

Up on the dashboard, the VHF marine radio was set to channel 16, the international calling and distress channel. A forty-foot sports fishing boat had headed off earlier today and was getting pushed out to sea and even with its powerful engines, it couldn't force its way back to the island. On the sound, several sailboats were getting spun around like a goldfish in a dishwasher. One had a cracked mast. One had a sailor who'd hit his head and was unconscious. The Coast Guard boats were out, fighting to rescue the people.

“I tell you, I’ve never seen anything quite like this,” Brownie said.

“None of the forecasters got it right,” Harold told him. “Not the Weather Underground, not the Marine Weather Forecast. This is a rogue storm.”

“Damn right it is. I’ve lived on this island eighty-six years and I’ve never seen anything like it. Closest I can remember is the No-Name Storm of ’91.”

Juliet’s cell beeped. With difficulty, she managed to slide it out of the pocket of her jeans.

“Juliet, are you all right?”

It was Ryder. She smiled. “I’m all right. How about you?”

As she spoke, a gust of wind hit the side of the truck like an enormous fist.

“I’m okay. Listen. I’ve got a jet on the tarmac to the right of the main airport terminal. Come here as soon as you can and we can get out of here, but you’ve got to hurry.”

“You’re kidding, right?”

“Don’t be afraid. These planes can cut through the wind like knives through butter, and my pilot was a military man. If you’re afraid to drive, I’ll send an Uber.”

“Ryder, we can’t leave Nantucket! At least, I can’t. I’m joining a bunch of people taking sandbags out to Our Island Home. The salt marsh is already swollen with all the water it can hold, and the waves are making inroads onto the lawn.”

"Can't they evacuate to the high school?"

"It's the nursing home, Ryder. Some of the people are ambulatory, but most aren't. Some of their relatives are coming to take them to safety, but many are bedridden and don't have relatives nearby. They're hooked up on IVs or can't walk without a walker. The best we can do is get the sandbags out there, and that should protect the building."

"Why not let other people do this, Juliet? There must be a lot of strong men who would be better than you at lifting sandbags, and I'm not being sexist, it's a fact about upper body strength."

"Ryder, you really don't understand. We've got a lot of people we love in that building. People who taught us in school or worked to raise money to build our skating rink or sold us tickets to the plays, or directed our school plays . . . these are our people. This is Our Island Home. No one who's grown up here is going to just fly off in a fancy plane to Boston and pretend everybody else will take care of the problem. We all have to take care of the problem." Juliet was crying from frustration and anger. What kind of guy was Ryder Hastings that he would run away at the first sign of trouble?

"Juliet—"

"Goodbye, Ryder." She clicked off and jammed her phone back in her pocket.

"Where is he?" Lisa asked.

"At the airport. With his very own private jet. What a douche." She was trying to sound tough, but her voice cracked when she spoke.

"It will be okay," Lisa said soothingly, like she used to say so often to her children. "It will be okay."

But as they headed to lower Orange, Juliet stared out the window and wondered if her mother was right. Small missiles—leaves, bits of paper, feathers, plastic bags—zipped through the air as if propelled by a slingshot. Brownie had to keep his windshield wipers on at full speed, and still the rain washed down the windshield as if they were driving inside a waterfall. Other cars on the two-lane road crept past, not wanting to stir up the deep puddles and spray their cars and everything else with muddy water.

They turned onto the Island Home road and sped down the street, right into the face of the storm. People were already there, some wearing high rubber boots and raincoats, others, mostly young guys, in jeans and sweatshirts and sneakers, everything thoroughly soaked. Juliet looked toward the harbor and saw waves someone could surf on rolling toward the building. Our Island Home was famous for having great views of the harbor that their residents enjoyed, and that was good, except now, when it was obvious that the building's length stretched almost the length of the salt marsh. More sandbags were needed if the waves kept coming.

"It's not going to stop for hours," Lisa yelled at Juliet.

"Okay!" Jim Snyder, one of the local firefighters, approached them. "Thanks for coming. Here's how we're doing it. We're making a bucket brigade. So there're four of you, good. Harry, you stand here and lift the sandbags off, and, Lisa, you stand here, take it and pass it on to this young woman here, and she'll pass it on . . ." He positioned the recent arrivals so they linked in with several others waiting to hand the sandbags to the battalion of firefighters, police officers, DPW workers, and twenty other people, their identities obscured by their rain hoods.

"Damn, these are heavy!" Juliet yelled at the man she passed a sandbag to.

He nodded but didn't reply. She realized he was out of breath, saving every breath for the job of passing along the sandbags.

In a few more minutes, she was out of breath, too. The sandbags were heavy, but the real problem was the force of the wind. She stood like the others, with her legs spread for stability, and she stopped talking. She stopped thinking really, as her arms received the weight of the sandbag and passed it along and the wind screamed and the rain soaked through her raincoat and down the back of her sweater. About thirty feet away, she saw guys stacking the sandbags against the side of the building. She saw three physical therapists from Jo Manning's office and grinned to think that after this, they'd need physical therapy, too. Her mother's best friend, Rachel, was there, and Juliet's high school math teacher.

And suddenly, Ryder was there, too.

"Let me take your place in line," he said.

For a moment, Juliet stalled, confused and amazed. Ryder was in jeans and a flannel shirt, with no rain gear except for rubber boots. He was already soaked through and water dripped off the bill of his scalloper's cap.

"You came," she said, smiling.

"Of course," he said. "Now, let me take your place in line."

"I'm staying right here," Juliet said. "But you can take my mother's place."

Ryder nodded. He spoke to Lisa, who let him in the line. Lisa joined the others who were taking a break inside the building as newcomers arrived to take their places. Ryder was tall and strong and long-limbed, and he passed along the sandbags as if they were filled with feathers.

No one was talking because they didn't have the breath in them, and besides, the wind whipped away their words. But Juliet was so happy she was crying, unabashedly, and her tears mingled with the rain.

thirty-one

He'd been an idiot to attempt to drive even part-way into town. The line of cars stretched from Main Street down to Flora, with more cars joining the line every minute.

"You idiots!" Theo yelled, even though the windows were rolled up and no one could hear him. "You should be driving up toward higher land!"

Possibly, he thought, they were all trying to get to someone they cared for, to take them to safety.

The line didn't move. Main Street was probably packed bumper to bumper, too.

Frustrated, he pounded his hands against the steering wheel. The wind shrieked as it forced itself between the houses on Union Street. Above him, trees bowed and shook with the wind. Something cracked, and a limb crashed down from a maple, barely missing the car in front of him.

Anger coiled with fear in his chest. The fear was because of the storm, this freak storm that no one had predicted, that was battering the island, *invading* the island like a battalion of crazed monsters with giant waves as shields. But he was sure they'd get through this. Of course there would be loss of property, but he was certain there'd be no loss of life. Lives were lost because of storms farther south, in Florida, in the Carolinas, even in Rhode Island, but not here on Nantucket.

Not yet.

A thought hit him in the gut so hard he gasped. Everyone was talking about the ocean these days, all the plastic in it, all the trawlers over-fishing, the disappearance of entire species of fish. A photo from Facebook haunted him: a polar bear, so starving its fur hung down around its empty belly, standing alone on an ice floe not much bigger than the bear. That animal, uncomprehending. Hungry.

And Theo thought that the ocean was angry. It was enraged at what humans were doing to it, and it was fighting back. People gave the ocean's actions the rather gentle phrase "rising seas," but the seas were not just rising, they were charging, they were destroying, they were at war. All the myths Theo learned in high school about Poseidon flooded back into his mind. Poseidon was the Greek god of the sea. When Odysseus blinded Cyclops, Poseidon's son, Poseidon took his revenge on Odysseus with such furious storms that Odysseus lost his ship and his companions.

Maybe Poseidon, or whatever god ruled the seas, was taking its revenge on them, at least all the people living on the coasts or making their living in the seas.

Theo didn't believe this, of course. But he didn't disbelieve it, either, not right now when the winds sent tempests of rain charging over the harbor and into the town.

Still the line of cars didn't move. Angry with himself for sitting there doing nothing, Theo suddenly jerked the steering wheel of his car and pulled into the driveway of a house belonging to no one he knew, but he didn't care. He slammed the car door shut behind him and began to run down the sidewalk toward town and Easy Street. Where Beth was, he hoped.

As he ran, he realized he had thought of the Greek gods because he wanted to be Beth's hero. He even wanted to be her husband, and that was a terrifying and challenging idea.

His legs were strong. His core was strong. He had surfing to thank for that. He passed the stalled line of cars on Union Street, turned right, slipped between the stalled line of cars on Main Street, and raced down Cambridge Street, which was already a river of water being driven by the crazed winds into town.

Easy Street was explosive as the narrow harbor funneled the powerful waves up and over the bulkhead, into the street, against the buildings, and up the side streets toward the library garden. Beth's office was only one building away from

Cambridge Street, and as Theo looked, he realized he was being lifted up by waves. Here, the water was almost four feet high. He half-slogged, half-swam toward the OM office. Already he could tell the lights were out, so maybe Beth had gone, or maybe all the power in town was out. He couldn't call her. His cell was in his jeans pocket, and his jeans were in four feet of water.

It was an eerie scene, this street where people usually sat on benches licking ice cream cones while watching the cute ducks waddle on the little beach and paddle in the calm waters of the harbor. Normally the parking spaces would be filled, parallel to the curb. Now, no cars. No people. Not even a duck, Theo thought, and wondered where they went just at the moment he saw Beth being lifted up by a wave and sucked backward over the bulkhead. She disappeared as the wave crashed down.

Theo dove. Walking was too slow. He was a strong swimmer. He headed for Beth—he was certain it was Beth—and his torso grazed the top of the wooden bulkhead as he swam over it. Water rushed over his eyes, water tugged him down and pushed him sideways, but he swam as hard as he ever had toward the form that he was sure was Beth. It was Beth. He grabbed hold of her with both arms, a stupid but instinctive action, and for a moment they both sank down, but then he held on to her with his right arm and swam with his left arm and kicked hard with his legs. He reached the surface and gasped for breath, and he looked at Beth, who was also gasping for breath but smiling, and he yelled, "I've got this."

And he watched for the next wave to gather itself and rise and rise, he pulled Beth with him into the channel of the wave and it carried them all the way over the bulkhead and onto the street. He swam to Cambridge Street, still clasping Beth with one hand. Water was already massing on North Beach Street, but he could stand. Beth could stand.

They stood on the brick sidewalk with waves slapping their ankles and Beth started to speak. Instead, she leaned forward and vomited out a stream of water. Her entire body shuddered. She stood up, wiping her mouth with the tail of her wet shirt.

"Theo!" she cried. "I love you!"

"I love you, too," Theo said.

He took her in his arms and held her tight as she broke down and sobbed with relief. His fractured humerus hurt like the devil but Theo held Beth tight and wouldn't let her go.

"I'm okay now," Beth said.

"Let's get out of here. I'll hold on to you. Tell me if I'm pulling you too fast."

Theo grasped Beth's hand and began slogging

through the high water. Beth kept up with him, but several times she was seized with a furious cough that shook her body.

They reached Union Street, where only an inch of water covered the bricks, and hurried to Theo's car. Once inside, Theo set the heat to high. A line of cars still clogged the street heading into town. They had to wait until ten cars passed before someone let them out onto the street.

Theo looked over at Beth. Her hair was plastered against her face. He gently removed a small leaf from her cheek.

"I need to go to Ryder's garage to get some dry clothes," Beth said.

"And there it is, my favorite sentence in the world," Theo muttered, not joking.

"Theo, Ryder doesn't ever come into the apartment. He's letting me use it so I don't have to make it impossible for my dad to have your mom over for . . . dinner."

"I still don't like it," Theo said, staring at the cars in front of him.

"Really?" Beth cocked her head and made her eyes wide and innocent. "I can't imagine why." Her hair was plastered against her face and she was shivering.

"Because, I told you, I love you," Theo said.

"Oh, Theo," Beth began, and then sneezed, a long, involved sneeze that made her shudder.

They parked in Ryder's drive, as close as

possible to the garage, and Theo followed Beth up the steps and into the apartment. Theo scanned the place for signs of male habitation, but the rooms, although attractive, were spare.

"I'll be right out," Beth called, shutting the bedroom door.

"You know that with your clothes sticking to your skin, I've got a fairly good idea of what you look like," Theo called. "Why don't I come in and help you change?"

Beth laughed from the other side of the door. "No, thanks. You're all wet yourself. Want to borrow a sweatshirt of mine?"

"Right," Theo said. "Because it would fit so well."

Beth came out of the bedroom wearing a baggy sweatshirt and jeans. "I should take a shower and wash my hair, but we need to get you to your house for dry clothes."

We, Theo thought. *She's thinking of us as a couple.* He touched her cheek affectionately.

Beth pushed him away lightly. "Dry clothes."

"Yeah," Theo said. "That would feel good." He glanced at Beth. "It won't take long. Will you come with me?"

Beth reached out and put her hand on his arm. "Of course I'll come with you."

Her touch, that gentle touch, broke something open inside him. He drove to his house very carefully, swallowing his emotions, working to keep his breathing light, but something mixed with fear and hope kept punching his heart.

He parked on the street so his mother could have the driveway. He left the engine running. He turned to Beth.

"Did you mean it when you said you love me?" he asked. Doing this took more courage than riding the fiercest wave.

"Of course I meant it. Don't you know? Haven't you always known?" Beth's eyes shone like jewels as she spoke. "I loved you in high school, but I was afraid of upsetting Atticus, and you were dating so many awesome girls."

Theo shook his head impatiently. "But now. Not love in a high-school-crush way, but in a grown-up way? Because, Beth, I love you. In a very grown-up way."

"I love you like that, too, Theo." Leaning forward, she kissed his lips solemnly.

Then she pulled away. "You know, you are still wet and you smell a bit from the water." Seeing his expression, she smiled. "But if you want to make out right now in the car, I don't mind getting damp."

"No," Theo said, "I've got to shower and change, but I don't want to leave you. I don't want not to be with you every second."

Beth touched his cheek. "Tell you what. I'll stand right outside your shower door."

Theo thought of his bedroom, which was,

as usual, a chaotic mess. His dirty laundry was flung in one corner of the room, his work pants tossed over a chair. "Maybe just wait in the living room?"

"Fine."

No one else was in the house when they entered.

"I'll make coffee," Beth said as Theo went up the stairs.

Theo quickly washed his hair, showered, and dressed, not in work clothes but in khakis and an old button-down blue cotton shirt.

He found Beth sitting at the kitchen table. She handed him a mug that was wonderfully warm on his hands, and the hot liquid slid down his throat, smoothly reviving him.

"I used your landline to reach Juliet and your mother," Beth told him. "They're safe. They were piling sandbags at the Island Home."

"Look, Beth," Theo said in a rush, "I'm glad they're safe, and I'm sure your father is, too, but can we not talk about anyone else right now? Because I have something to say and if I don't say it now, I might lose my nerve."

"Okay, Theo." Beth folded her hands in her lap and looked at him questioningly.

"Beth." Theo started to sit down, but stood up again. He was too nervous to sit. "I was thinking in the storm . . . I've been in love with you for years. And you have been in love with me, too, right? So, the thing is, I want to be with you." Pacing around the table, because his nerves wouldn't let him stand still, he said, "I want to be with you every day. I lost you when you went with Atticus, and I almost lost you again in the harbor, and I want to be with you all the time, and I don't want you living in another man's apartment, and I promise I'm capable of settling down—you should ask your dad! He'll tell you I'm a reliable worker."

"He already has told me that," Beth said softly. "He's said—I think these are his exact words—that you're a good, strong, congenial employee."

"He said that? Man, that's brilliant. You know, Beth, your father is the best. He's patient, and he's got a sense of humor, and he doesn't mind showing me what to do, and—"

Beth cocked her head. "I thought we were talking about you and me."

Theo stopped pacing. "We were. Well, I was. I wasn't very smooth about it, and I'm not really sure what I mean." He stopped talking fast and took a deep breath, gathering himself. "I love you. I've loved you for years. I want to live my life with you. I want you to be the last thing I see every night and the first thing I see every morning. I want to take care of you when you're sick. I want to stay in bed with you on Sunday afternoons in the winter and, well, you could read and I could watch football. What I mean is, could we . . . move in together? And maybe someday, if you don't think I'm a total slob, we could get married?"

Beth rose and faced Theo. "Wow. This is a lot. Living together . . ." Beth paused and studied Theo with an appraising look. "Theo, I like the thought of living with you. I can imagine coming home at the end of the day and telling you about the highs and lows, and hearing about your day, too. And sleeping with you all night would be heaven. But I don't want to get into the whole making a nest thing. I don't want to choose a china pattern and decide on the color of our sheets. I've worked hard getting my master's degree, and I want to start a career, accomplish something, do work I love—like working on Ocean Matters. Getting married, keeping a house, all of that homemaker stuff isn't what I'm interested in now."

"I totally get that, Beth. I've got to concentrate on work, too. Your dad knows so much I want to learn—"

Beth interrupted. "And living together is full of practical stuff, like buying toilet paper and taking out the trash."

"I can do that," Theo said.

"Can you cook? Can you agree to make dinner half the time?"

Theo frowned. "I've pretty much microwaved over the past few years." Seeing Beth's face, he added, “But I can learn. I will learn. And you know what? I’ll do half the cooking, and I’ll make you such fine dinners you’ll be glad to live with me.” His eyes lit up. “I made an amazing meatloaf for my mom the other day. Just ask her.”

Beth laughed. “I have a feeling it’s going to be an adventure, living with you.”

“So you want to do it? Move in together?”

Beth smiled. “Of course I do.”

Theo swept Beth up in his arms and swung her around in a circle. Beth folded her arms around his neck, leaned back her head, and laughed. Their eyes met, and they kissed for a very long time, then pulled apart, expecting the door to open any moment.

“We’ve got to get our own place,” Theo said.

“And soon,” Beth agreed. Softly, she added, “But let’s go to my place now. For a while.”

Theo looked puzzled.

“So we’ll be all alone.” Beth gave him a look.

“Yes,” Theo said, his voice husky. “Let’s go.”

thirty-two

After the sandbag brigade was dismissed, Ryder and Juliet went to Ryder's house on the harbor. He showered and changed clothes in his bedroom, and Juliet showered in the guest bedroom and wrapped herself up in the big white fluffy robe hanging on the shower door. The shawl collar of the robe warmed her neck, making her feel cozy and cared for.

She went down the stairs to the den where Ryder had started a fire. His family's summer home was a typical old Nantucket sprawl, large and drafty with old sofas, threadbare Persian carpets, sweet old appliances, and a sense of comfort and welcome.

"I love this house," Juliet said.

"So do I. The view is magic, not that I get to enjoy it often. But look how high the water is. We used to have a beach. Now the water is almost to the house. Someone two houses down has plans to raise his house on stilts like Florida houses. I don't have the time to focus on that. I don't want to sell the house, but I can't live here full-time, either."

"What about your sister?" Juliet settled into the corner of a sofa.

"She doesn't come down here. She is a dedicated farmer and doesn't like being away from home."

"Interesting," Juliet said. "You're always traveling and she won't leave her home."

Ryder was in the kitchen, and he returned with a glass of red wine and a board with cheese and crackers on it. "This is all I've got. I tossed your clothes in the dryer. When they're dry, I'd like to take you out to dinner."

"Maybe we can stop by my house first," Juliet said, accepting the wine with a smile. "Even if my clothes are dry, I won't want to wear them to a restaurant."

They clicked glasses and looked out the high sliding glass windows.

"The wind is dying down," Ryder said.

"And the tide is going out." Juliet looked up at him. "Ryder, thank you for coming to help with the sandbags."

"You're welcome. It was the right thing to do, but you must know I came because of you." He added, "Also, it was a great photo opportunity. I got some fabulous shots on my phone. I'll have Georgia in my Boston office add them to my other photos for my next slideshow and lecture."

"Where is your next lecture?" Juliet nibbled a bite of cheese. The physical work of hefting sandbags in the storm had exhausted her. She wanted more than a nibble. She wanted a five-course meal.

"I missed the one scheduled for tonight in Narragansett," Ryder said. "I don't have to leave the island for two more days."

Juliet smiled down into her glass, pleased that he had skipped a professional engagement to stay with her, helping during the storm, even if it had provided a great photo opportunity.

Watching the waves through the window, Ryder asked, "Have you thought any more about what we talked about? About you working for me, and traveling with me?"

"Yes, of course I have. It's complicated, and what you're suggesting isn't—clear."

"I see. Okay. I'll rephrase. I want you to travel with me and work for Ocean Matters but also sleep with me. Would you like me to propose marriage?"

Juliet tossed her head. "You do have a singular way of going about things."

"That's because I don't know you that well. I haven't been with you that long."

"You haven't *been with* me at all," Juliet reminded him.

"I'm here right now," Ryder said, meeting her eyes.

Juliet looked away. "Can we talk?"

"Of course."

Juliet perched on the end of the sofa. Ryder sat in a chair across from her.

"You look very businesslike," Ryder said.

"I'm trying to think how to say this. First of all, if you ever propose to me, please be a bit more elegant than you were a moment ago. But second, don't propose to me yet. I would say no."

"Juliet—"

"Listen, please. I've told you about my parents, the divorce, all that. It's made me afraid of marriage. At least getting married quickly. My mother and father knew each other for only a few months before they married."

"So," Ryder said, "a long engagement would work for you?"

"I don't know," Juliet said. "Ryder, I am so attracted to you. But that doesn't mean I could spend my life with you. And another thing, I'm not sure I want children. Maybe someday, but not soon. Not for years. And children often come with marriage."

"I'd like to have children someday," Ryder said softly. "I think you and I would have great children."

"Ryder, you would have great children with a lot of women." Juliet shifted away from his look. "It's difficult being rational when you're making me feel so . . . gooey."

"You prefer being rational to being romantic?" Ryder asked.

"I don't trust romance," Juliet said. *I haven't had very good luck with romance,* she thought quietly.

"You said you'd like to see China."

"Yes. Yes, I would. I'd like to travel, see the world, and now that Theo is back on-island, and now that my mother has Mack in her life, I feel free to travel. I've always stayed near Nantucket so that I can be here quickly if she needs me, and now she doesn't need me. I like this feeling of freedom. I'm not used to it yet."

"I have to go to China soon, you know." Ryder reached over and took Juliet's hand. "You could come with me. You could be my assistant. I need an assistant. You could have your own room in the hotel. I wouldn't press you. We could see how we work together, how we travel together." He leaned forward, his elbows on his knees, smiling at her. Seeing her, and wanting her so much it showed on his face.

"Not this time," Juliet said. She let her eyes rest on him, adoring the sight of him, his sexiness, and his intelligence.

"Ryder, listen. I'm going to start my own business. I've had a lot of really good offers from organizations that want me to build their websites. I want to catch my breath, find a good lawyer, and map out a business plan. I'll be able to work on the websites from anywhere, as long as I have my computer with me, but I think at this stage, in the beginning, I might need to hold some face meetings. I might have to travel to L.A. or Houston."

"Wow," Ryder said. "That's ambitious. And exciting."

She liked the admiration in his eyes.

"And terrifying," she added with a smile. "I'll have to organize my own pension, health benefits, all that. And I'll have to work hard and be as creative as I think I can be."

"But someday you might travel with me?" Ryder asked.

"Yes, someday."

"For now, you've got to focus on your own adventure."

She smiled. "Yes, that's absolutely right. You know, Ryder, I feel like I did years ago when our seventh grade class went on an educational tall ship cruise. I had to climb the rigging of the main mast while the ship was on open water. It was terrifying and exhilarating. I want that again."

"Then you should have it." Ryder sat next to her, watching her, not forcing her, not even charming her. "I'll be around whenever you want me. However you want me."

"Oh, magic words." Juliet set her wineglass on the coffee table. She stood up, took Ryder's hand, and pulled him up. "Want to have an adventure right now?" she asked.

"Absolutely," Ryder answered.

"I suppose the bedrooms are all on the second fl—" Juliet began.

Ryder interrupted her, kissing her, kissing her

passionately, and she matched his passion with her own, and they fell back onto the sofa. The house, as wide and spacious as the future, spread around them, clear and ready.

thirty-three

As Lisa entered her house, she didn't know if she was more tired or worried. She couldn't even decide whether to make herself some steaming hot tea or take a hot shower first. She decided on the hot shower.

She stripped off her sodden clothes in the hallway, not afraid that someone would see her in her undies, because she'd had a text from Theo saying he was fine, he was with Beth, and he was going to spend the night at her place, which was the apartment over Ryder Hastings's garage. Before they left the nursing home, Juliet told Lisa she was going to spend the evening with Ryder, in his family's house. That's going to be a busy block of territory tonight, Lisa thought.

The only person she hadn't heard from was Mack.

Of course, the cellphones had been out for over an hour, so he probably had tried to get through and failed. Or maybe he felt like she did, that he needed a hot shower before anything else.

She climbed the stairs to the second floor and entered her wonderful new bathroom. Mack and his crew had done a marvelous job. The floor was a glistening clean white ceramic tile, and all the fixtures were new. The walls had been painted a muted sea-green that she loved, and the trim was marshmallow white. She'd bought new towels and bath mats in a turquoise, so thick and fluffy she wanted to wear them.

Mack had found a way to install a shower next to her beloved claw-foot bathtub, and she peeled off her undies, stepped into the shower, and sighed with bliss as hot water rained down over her. She washed her hair and soaped her body, and finally, when her skin was almost red from the water, she turned off the faucets and stepped onto a bath mat. The room was filled with mist. Through the window, Lisa could see that night had fallen.

Because she would be alone tonight—unless Mack suddenly appeared—she slipped into her warm chenille robe with the thick collar and cuffs. She combed out her hair, creamed her face, and put on a touch of lipstick, just in case. Why hadn't she heard from Mack?

She stood in her bedroom, looking around. It was a nice room, airy and spacious. How many times had she cried in this room, or laughed, or cuddled a sick child, or read a book late into the night? Certainly she hadn't made love many times in this room, only a few times before Erich left her for his European mistress. So it was an attractive room, but now she thought it was a lonely room.

She stepped out into the hallway. Three more bedrooms and one more bath opened onto the hall, and as she stood at the head of the staircase, she wondered what on earth she was doing living in such a large house by herself. She'd been happy enough, but now, after weeks of Theo and Juliet coming and going and Mack and his men carrying tools and lumber in and out and Dave and Tom singing and laughing, now she thought she would be very lonely with the work done and the house empty.

She sat down on the top step and began to cry.

"Hello?"

The kitchen door opened and shut.

"Theo?" Lisa called.

"No, it's me, Mack. Your door's unlocked, you know."

For some reason, the tears came harder, faster. "I'm up here."

Mack climbed the stairs to her, large and comforting in his jeans and flannel shirt. His work boots made reassuring sounds against the steps. His hair was damp, and from where she sat, she could smell the light fragrance of Ivory soap. He sat down next to her, putting his hands on her shoulders and turning her toward him.

"Are you okay?" he asked.

"I didn't know where you were." She couldn't

stop crying. "Oh, Mack, look at your hands, they're all bruised and scratched! What happened?"

"I was out in Madaket when the storm hit. I was boarding up the homes of several families I caretake for. Then Millie Maxwell, you know Millie, her daughter Marianne was a couple of classes behind Theo and Beth, Millie ran over to get me because Marianne had gone into labor. The storm felled a large tree right across their driveway and Marianne's husband's in the Coast Guard and was out at sea. Fortunately, I had my chain saw in my truck, so I managed to cut the tree into thirds and move the middle third out of the way so Millie could drive her daughter to the hospital."

"Good Lord, Mack," Lisa cried. "What would they have done without you?"

"I tried to call you, but the cellphones were down. After they drove off, I finished boarding up the Stowes' cottage, then I went home for a shower. I wasn't so much wet as I was covered with twigs and leaves."

Mack smiled then, and she smiled, too. Her tears stopped. Her heart calmed.

"How's Juliet?" Mack asked.

"She's good. She helped with the sandbags, and then she went off with Ryder. She texted that she's having dinner with him. And I've spoken to Beth . . ."

"She just texted me. Theo saved her life, apparently. She was very dramatic about it. She's at Ryder's garage, preparing dinner for Theo, her hero."

"Really? So we'll be all alone here?"

"Looks that way."

Lisa grinned. "Would you like something to eat? Maybe some scrambled eggs or a brandy?"

"Both," Mack said. "Please."

Lisa stood up. "I'm in my robe. I'd better change."

Mack said softly, "Don't change. I like you in your robe."

Together they went down to the kitchen. Lisa scrambled eggs with cheddar cheese and chives from her garden while Mack poured them each a glass of wine. She toasted bread, spread it with butter, and set it on the table with an open jar of Nantucket blueberry jam. As they ate, they discussed the past few hours, the frightening flood that had shocked them all. What the flood forecast for the future of this island with the seas licking at the shores.

"Lisa." Mack left his chair and drew Lisa up out of hers. "Let's forget the floods for a while. Let's give ourselves a few moments to be happy. I found you. I love you. We're going into the future together. Right?"

"Right," Lisa agreed. She kissed him, then

stepped back. "Do you know what I'd like to do right now?"

"I know what I'd like to do right now," Mack said in a growl.

Lisa laughed. "I'd like for us to look at my photo album."

"What?"

"Well, I'm so very very old that I have actual photo albums, and I'd love for us to look at them together. I think maybe you'll have a better idea of who I was, who I've become, if you see them."

"Okay. I get that, kind of. But remember, you and I have lived on this island for decades."

"True. But we didn't hang out together. And I was different back then. You were, too." She pulled him by the hand into the living room, settled him on the sofa, and went to the bottom shelf of the bookcase to pull out three heavy leather-back albums. She put them on the table and sat next to Mack.

"What's this?" Mack asked when she opened the first album.

"This," Lisa said, "is my first wedding. Well, my only wedding so far."

"It doesn't look very . . . fancy. You guys must not have had much money."

Lisa laughed. "We had enough money for an extravagant wedding, believe me. But Erich was in a hurry, and his parents were in another country, and Erich thought that weddings were sort of provincial especially when we were going to change the world . . .”

Mack peered down at the photos, turning the pages. “You were beautiful.”

Lisa smiled.

“I mean, you still are, but, wow, Lisa. Where were you married?”

“In my parents’ house. With only my friend Rachel in attendance. I didn’t even have a special dress. That was my ‘dressy’ dress that I wore to church and certain events.”

Lisa leaned back against the sofa while Mack flipped through the pages. “Where did you marry Marla?”

“Here on the island, in the small chapel of the Congregational Church. It wasn’t elaborate, either. We didn’t have much money, and we needed it for rent. Marla’s mother made her wedding dress.” Mack chuckled. “Marla said she looked like a polar bear.” He chuckled again. “She kind of did.”

“It makes me sad thinking of my wedding,” Lisa told him.

Mack took Lisa’s hand in his own big hand. “Well, then, why don’t we have a spectacular wedding and a great big blowout party for the reception?”

“What a wonderful idea, Mack! Flowers, music, and we could fill the church. I’d love to wear a real wedding dress . . . but would you wear a tux?”

"For you, I'd wear almost anything. Please note the *almost.*"

"I promise, no blue velvet. We could have a band for the reception. A live band . . . do you dance?"

"I do. My own way. Please don't make me take cha-cha-cha lessons."

Lisa squealed with laughter at the thought. She drew her legs up, sat on her knees on the sofa, facing him. "We could have the full deal. A sit-down dinner! Champagne for everyone! Cool take-home gifts."

"No ice sculpture."

"No. No ice sculpture."

"Juliet and Beth could be my bridesmaids . . . if you think Beth would like to."

"And Theo could be my best man." Mack sobered. "Being realistic, Lisa, we're old enough to have the money for a party like this, but we certainly don't have the time to make all the arrangements this summer. Or even this fall. Or not until January, if we want to do it right."

Lisa slid off her knees and sat naturally. Actually, she realized, she couldn't sit on her knees comfortably anymore. When had that happened? "You're right, Mack. But really, January would be more fun. You and I are working straight-out in the summer and fall. Then Christmas makes us all crazy busy. So we can't plan an extravagant wedding for the summer even if we needed to, and we don't need to."

Mack wrapped an arm around her, pulling her against him. "So we'll plan for January. But I'll want to give you an engagement ring before then."

"Oh," Lisa sighed. "I would like to have an engagement ring I can keep."

Mack leaned toward Lisa, lifted her face toward his, and kissed her slowly and softly.

The back door opened and shut.

"Mom? You home?" Theo called.

"We're in the living room," Lisa called back. She whispered to Mack, "We need to visit that spec house again."

Theo came into the room and Beth was with him. They were holding hands and they were both *glowing*.

"Hi, Mom," Theo said.

"Hi, Dad," Beth said.

Their parents said hello, and for once Mack kept his arm around Lisa, holding her close to him.

thirty-four

Theo was glad to see his mom with Mack because she looked so happy. He hoped that would keep Mack calm when he and Beth broke the news to her father that they wanted to move in together.

Beth was her normal cheerful self. She went over and kissed Mack's cheek.

"Daddy, I'm sorry I was so cranky and unpleasant the other day."

"Don't worry," Mack said. "I'm just glad you're safe."

Theo kissed his mom's cheek. He and Beth sat in separate chairs facing the sofa.

"Was that storm crazy or what?" he asked.

"Theo rescued me!" Beth said. "Dad, he was amazing!" She launched into a dramatic description of the wave, her fall, her realization that she was going to drown, and Theo's sudden appearance, and his strength carrying her up and out of the water. It was all true, it had all happened, but Theo felt uncomfortable in the spotlight.

When Beth finally wound down, Theo's mom said, "Theo, how wonderful."

Theo nodded, waiting to hear Mack say something even slightly positive.

Instead, Mack stood up. "Son," he said. "Let me shake your hand. Words can't express how grateful I am that you saved my daughter's life."

Theo stood up. He took Mack's big calloused hand.

"Thank you," Mack said. He enclosed Theo in a quick gruff hug.

Theo's butt hadn't even touched his chair when Beth gleefully announced, "So we decided to move in together."

Theo choked. "Still got some water in my lungs," he muttered apologetically.

His mom sat there looking at him and Beth, and she was smiling radiantly.

Mack didn't look so radiant. "Well," he said, returning to the sofa, "I can see how, in the excitement of the storm and Theo saving you, you would feel that way. But, honey, you don't have to decide something so important so quickly."

Theo saw his mom glance at Mack.

Beth was exuberant. "But, Dad, we've been in love with each other forever. And we're not saying we're getting married. We both just got back to the island, and we both need to concentrate on our jobs. We want to be together, and live our lives day by day."

"But," Lisa said, "where would you both live?"

Theo and Beth had discussed this on their way

over. Now they gave each other an encouraging look.

Before Theo could speak, the back door slammed.

“Mom? I’m here with Ryder.”

Juliet came into the room. Her clothes were somehow dry, rumpled, and muddy, and her short hair stuck out all over the place.

“Dude,” Theo said. “You need some mousse.”

Ryder was with her. He looked more composed. Dry hair, clean shirt, pressed khakis.

“Ryder helped pass sandbags at the Island Home,” Juliet said, and she gazed up at Ryder as if she’d just seen him rescue a pack of puppies.

Everyone spoke at once. Theo relaxed because the talk was all about the storm and everyone’s experiences. Lisa slipped out of the room into the kitchen.

Theo followed. “Can I help?”

After a while, they returned with a pot of coffee, a bottle of wine, several bottles of beer, and a tray of cups and glasses.

Lisa returned to the kitchen and came back with a plate of cookies. “Wicked Island Bakery,” she said.

“I love their cookies,” Juliet said.

Theo, on his best behavior, stood up and offered his sister the comfortable wing-back chair. He pulled over a straight-back chair and sat next to Beth.

Ryder pulled over the other straight-back chair and sat next to Juliet.

The three men each reached for the beer. The women had glasses of wine. The conversation flowed easily, as they still spoke about the storm.

Then, suddenly, everyone was silent, like clocks that had run down.

Theo's mom spoke. "I think this is the first time we've all been in the same room together."

Mack leaned back and scanned the ceiling. "The ceiling looks perfect, doesn't it? You'd never know about the mess it was before."

"I know," Lisa said warmly. "And the bathroom is wonderful—"

Theo settled in his straight-back chair, even though it wasn't the kind of chair to settle in. It had a caned seat, and part of the caning had ripped and one small piece was poking into his thigh. He was aware of how Mack kept shooting looks at him, but the looks weren't like bullets, they were more like those little circles beside exam true-and-false questions. Or, maybe, those asterisks that could almost be stars. Mack knew by now that Theo was a good worker who always showed up on time, never backed down from a difficult job, and got on well with the crew. He didn't think Mack knew anything really bad about him, because Theo hadn't ever done anything bad unless he thought about how drunk he got in college. But Mack hadn't seen him then.

The fact was that Mack had been good to him these past few weeks. He'd trusted Theo to be a good worker, and he'd taught Theo about a hundred thousand things to do with carpentry. But that didn't mean Mack would want a guy like Theo, who didn't even have a profession, to move in with his only daughter. Also, his mom's question hung in the air: Where would they both live?

While Juliet paused to sip her wine, Ryder said, "Lisa, I'd like you to know that I've asked your daughter to marry me, but she has declined."

Lisa cocked her head. "Oh?"

"I did," Juliet declared. "But he didn't actually propose. And I didn't actually *decline.* I want to start a new website business of my own. That will take time and concentration. I have to wait to think about marriage."

"While you're thinking about it," Lisa said, "Mack and I have our own announcements to make." Lisa took Mack's hand. "We're going to get married."

"Oh, Mom," Juliet cried. "This is fabulous! Wonderful!" Jumping up, she threw herself on her mother and kissed her cheek. "Hooray! I want to be your bridesmaid."

"And I'll give you away," Theo told his mom.

"And I'll give *you* away," Beth told her dad.

Lisa said, "That sounds perfect. We're going to have a huge event. We're waiting until January so we can organize a proper ceremony and reception."

"So you'll live together?" Beth asked. "Where?"

"That depends," Mack said. "Where will you and Theo live together?"

"Wait," Juliet said. "What? Theo, you and Beth are moving in together?"

"Yeah," Theo told her, and he couldn't help grinning like he'd scored a major touchdown.

"Where are you going to live?" Mack asked.

Man up, Theo told himself. "What we thought . . . and we haven't had the chance to talk with Ryder about it yet, obviously . . . was that we would live in the apartment over Ryder's garage. Just for a while, until we sort out a better place to live."

Juliet snorted. "Yeah, because it's so easy to find a year-round place anyone can afford on this island."

Theo ignored his sister. He'd had years of practice. "What do you think about that, Ryder?" Theo asked. "We'd pay you rent, of course. Whatever you ask."

Ryder smiled. "Theo, it would be great with me if you both lived there. I travel so much, I'm seldom at home. My real home base is in Marblehead, about forty-five minutes from Boston. It would be helpful to have you two there keeping an eye on things. I certainly wouldn't charge you rent. I have a caretaker for the main house, but it would be good to have you two living there, too."

"Cool," Theo said. "Beth's committed to her job at Ocean Matters, and I—" Theo looked at Mack, handing the decision to him.

"I asked you to work for me this summer," Mack began, and stopped.

Theo's heart froze.

"And I've had it in the back of my mind to ask you to join my crew permanently. But you know, Theo, if you move in with Beth, I won't favor you over the others. I won't pay you more or give you the easy work."

"Well, that's too bad, Dad." Beth laced her words with sarcasm. "Because that is the only reason Theo has for wanting to marry me."

Mack cocked an eyebrow at his daughter. "I suppose that's true," he agreed in a terribly serious tone of voice.

"Oh, *Dad,*" Beth said, smiling back.

"Hang on a minute," Juliet said, in her most professional voice. "Let me get this straight, Mom. You are going to marry Mack in January. In the meantime, you'll live all alone in *this* house and Mack will live all alone in *his* house and Beth and Theo will live all squeezed up in a tiny little one-bedroom apartment."

"It's so not tiny," Theo said.

"It isn't," Beth agreed. "It's a beautiful space, with an incredible view of the water."

"Still," Juliet said.

Theo met his sister's challenge. "So where are *you* going to live while you start your new business? I mean, obviously, you've got your apartment in Cambridge. But also obviously, you're all charged up about Ocean Matters, so I assume you'll be coming down to Nantucket now and then. Where are *you* going to stay?"

Juliet, always one step ahead of Theo, ignored his question and threw her own at him. "What if you and Beth have a baby? Will the garage apartment be big enough then?"

"Oh, a baby!" Lisa cried. "How wonderful! We could—"

"Mom, chill! We're not pregnant," Theo said.

"And we won't be for a long time," Beth added.

Mack turned to Lisa. Somehow they communicated without words, because Mack turned to the others. "We all need to sit down and think about this. I have no problem moving into this house with Lisa, and then you and Theo could have our house, my house."

"Yeah," Theo said, "but hang on. If Beth and I get your house and you and Mom live in this house, what does Juliet get?"

"Theo, you sweet thing, looking out for me," Juliet said as tears sprung to her eyes.

Theo started to say *Don't get used to it,* which was the sort of thing he said to his sister, but Beth had made the slightest little kitten whimper of adoration at Theo's concern for his sister, and he could feel her eyes all warm and admiring on him.

Then Beth spoke up. "The crazy thing about life on Nantucket is that it's always about houses, finding a house you can afford to buy if you're only a normal person, or finding a year-round place to rent. I think we're going about this the wrong way. Somehow we have four places of residence on the island. Lisa's, my father's, Ryder's house, and Ryder's garage. We don't have to settle all the real estate talk now. Can't we just celebrate? I mean, look at us! We've got so many things going on!"

"And some of us are starting our own business," Juliet said.

"And some of us are making wedding plans," Lisa said.

"And some of us might get married someday, too," Ryder said.

"Let's go out to dinner," Mack said. "Let's go somewhere nice. The water didn't get as high at Le Languedoc or Dune or American Seasons."

"Right," Lisa seconded. "And let's drink champagne."

"But not too much," Juliet said. "Some of us have to work tomorrow."

"Stop it," Theo said to his sister.

In a small mob, they rose and the women went to various bathrooms to put on their lipstick, and the men stood in the front hall talking about the storm. When the women joined them, they had a slightly confusing discussion about which cars to take because no one had a car that would hold six people, so they decided that each couple would take a car. Then they decided they'd go to a restaurant in town, so no one needed to take a car. They could all walk.

So they walked, Lisa and Mack, Juliet and Ryder, Beth and Theo. The storm had blown itself out, leaving leaves and flowers torn from trees and bushes, and small pools of water everywhere. As they reached Main Street, they looked down toward the wharves. The water was receding, but puddles remained in low spots, reflecting the light of the early evening sun peeking out from the disappearing clouds.

thirty-five

The first Saturday after the Labor Day weekend, Ocean Matters threw a fundraising party at the yacht club. The theme was, of course, The Sea, and people were invited to come in underwater attire—a prize would be given for the best costume. The town's self-declared matriarch Prudence Starbuck appointed a decorations committee tasked with transforming the ballroom into an underwater palace. The committee went overboard.

All the overhead lights were veiled with blue, green streamers undulated from the ceiling like seaweed, and treasure chests spilling with glittering dime-store jewelry were the centerpieces of every table. A local band performed dance music interspersed with ocean-themed songs—"Beyond the Sea," "Octopus's Garden," "How Deep is the Ocean," "Under the Sea." The partygoers, celebrating the end of another prosperous and overwhelming summer, came in the dozens, their costumes more Vegas than starchy New England. Mermaids in a rainbow of colors danced with pirates and ship captains. The winner of the best costume was Prudence Starbuck, who came as

Queen of the Sea, complete with scepter and crown and necklaces of diamonds and other gems, some of them undoubtedly real. Her date for the evening was a handsome young man, Dylan Fernandes, congressman for Nantucket, Martha's Vineyard, and Cape Cod. There were several bars set around the room, as well as Spanky's Raw Bar in one corner, where people lined up to choose from mussels, clams, and oysters on the half-shell.

Because it was for Ocean Matters, Ryder insisted on buying a table for all six of them. No one argued with him. No one wanted to argue with anyone that night. The weather was perfect, warm but not humid, and the sky was clear and bright, freckled with stars. The doors were open to the porch, patio, and long green velvet lawn and people wandered outside to cool off after dancing or to fall back on the deep cushioned wicker chairs and stare up at the stars.

Lisa and Mack strolled along the boardwalk down to the dock, rubbing shoulders companionably as they walked. Mack had rented a large gold-trimmed swashbuckler's hat complete with purple plume. He'd found a large black morning coat at the thrift shop. For the final touch, he had fashioned a hook out of cardboard and aluminum foil, which he wore when he and Lisa weren't dancing. Lisa's costume was easier. She went as Tinker Bell, wearing a strapless green dress, a yellow wig, and lovely wide wings she fashioned from wire and iridescent chiffon.

"Let's sit," Mack suggested when they reached a bench overlooking the water.

"I can't cuddle up to you, Mack, my wings are getting in the way," Lisa said.

"I know. And I'm afraid if I try to kiss you, I'll take your eye out with my plume."

They laughed together, holding hands.

"This is a memorable night," Lisa said. "I'm delighted for Ryder and all the OM staff that it's going so well."

"Since it's such a memorable night," Mack said, "I think I'll do what I've been meaning to do for some time."

"Oh, yes?" Lisa turned toward Mack as far as she could in her restricting dress. She hadn't worn it for years, not since she was young and lithe, before she gave birth. She could stand and dance in it, but if she turned too quickly while sitting down, she worried that the seams might pop.

Mack reached into his pocket. He brought out a small black velvet box. In an easy movement, he knelt on the boardwalk. "Lisa Hawley, will you marry me?" He opened the box to display a small but fiery diamond solitaire ring.

"Oh," Lisa said. "That's beautiful, Mack. Of course I will."

Mack slid it onto the ring finger of her left hand

and leaned up to kiss her. "Good," he said. "Since we've booked the yacht club for the wedding reception in January, I thought you probably would say yes."

"It's beautiful," Lisa said. "Thank you, Mack." She turned her hand this way and that so the lights along the walk sparked fire in the stone. "I couldn't have dreamed up the chain of events that led from my dining room ceiling to this moment where we're sitting side by side as Captain Hook and Tinker Bell."

"I like you as Tinker Bell," Mack said. "Especially in that dress."

"It's old and too tight."

"I know. That's why you're bulging so satisfyingly over the top of the dress."

"Mack," Lisa chided, but she was pleased. A year ago she wouldn't have had the courage to dress like a petite green fairy. But knowing that Mack found her alluring no matter what she wore gave her a kind of freedom, a release from the restraints she'd imposed on herself because of her age. She never wanted to look like mutton dressed as lamb, or like the pathetic washed-up movie star Gloria Swanson played in *Sunset Boulevard*, but she found that Mack's love allowed her to dress more playfully. Not for him—but for herself.

"Let's go back to the ballroom and drink more champagne," Lisa suggested. "We should celebrate this ring."

So they rose, and Lisa tugged the dress into submission, and Mack put his hook back on, and hand in hook, they returned to the party.

Juliet, who in her lifetime had watched scores of old musicals, had found costumes from the play *South Pacific* on eBay. Ryder came as a naval lieutenant, looking magnificent in his dress whites. Juliet dressed as his doomed Polynesian lover, in a flower-printed sundress with blossoms around her ankles and a lei around her neck. She was letting her hair grow long, but it hadn't gone past her ears, so she rented a wig of long black hair. She was amazed and delighted at how the light sweep of hair over her bare shoulders lit up her senses.

"Let's walk down to the dock," Ryder told her when the band took an intermission.

"Sure," Juliet said. She was slightly tipsy, not from champagne, although she'd had plenty of that, but from the evening. A party. Costumes. Friends laughing. Music. Dancing more than she had for years. Catching a glimpse of her mother gazing up at Mack as he held her in his arms during a slow ballad. Spotting her brother laughing with friends while Beth leaned possessively against his arm. Tonight they were all happy. Bad times, sad times, would come, but so would more nights like this, when they were all happy.

"You seem pensive," Ryder said as they

walked over the soft green grass to the boardwalk.

"Mmm, I'm slightly and happily intoxicated," Juliet murmured.

They stood at the edge of the boardwalk, where wooden ramps led down to boat slips. Small sailboats and motorboats bobbed gently in the dark water, and a few burgees waved slightly in the breeze.

"I have something for you," Ryder said.

"Oh, yes?" Juliet stretched her arms out, yawning like a large, satisfied cat. The night could not be more beautiful, warm, and sweet.

Ryder reached into the pocket of his white uniform and took out a small box. He handed it to Juliet.

"Am I going to regret opening this?" Juliet asked suspiciously.

"I don't think so," Ryder told her. "And if you don't want it, you can just toss it into the harbor."

"Well, that's intriguing." Juliet opened the box. A key on a strip of black leather lay inside the box. "What's this?"

"It's the key to my house in Marblehead," Ryder told her.

"Ryder, I'm not moving in with—"

Ryder interrupted. "Hear me out. If you didn't pay rent on your Cambridge apartment, how much money would you save to put toward building your computer company? You would have your own space. I've shown you the suite

I think you'd like, with the private bathroom and office. Greta, our housekeeper, could keep the kitchen stocked with the coffee and bagels you like so much. You could come and go as you please. We probably wouldn't spend much time together at the house since we'll both be traveling a lot, but now and then we can enjoy dinner together. And so on."

"Ryder—"

"And if you wanted a break from me, you could always come down to Nantucket."

Juliet picked up the key and dangled it from her fingers. Such an ordinary object, small and brass and notched and safely attached to the long leather strip that would fit easily in her pocket. The outdoor light struck it, sparking gold, and she smiled. She still didn't trust Ryder's feelings for her. They'd only known each other for three months. But to be merely practical, it would be very helpful not to have to pay rent. She needed a virtual assistant, and this would free up funds to pay for one.

And to be merely romantic, it would be absolutely lovely to arrive home from a long business trip, take a cab to Ryder's house, and find him waiting there. This had happened twice now, and both times her whole heart brightened with joy to see him. They'd opened a bottle of good wine, microwaved Greta's sensational meals, and eaten in the kitchen, Juliet with her shoes off, both of them talking nonstop about their days. Other days she had spent in "her" office at his house, tapping away at her computer, forgetting to brush her teeth or dress until her stomach growled for lunch. And those days had ended in Ryder's great big bed, so comfortable, so easeful, so welcoming. She had never known the pleasure of falling asleep in someone's arms until she slept with Ryder. Being next to him, warm and safe, allowed her to sink into such deep restorative sleeps that she woke feeling as energetic and optimistic as a child.

If this man broke her heart, she'd kill him.

"Thank you," Juliet said to Ryder. "I'm glad to have this. A little terrified, but mostly glad. I love you, Ryder."

"I love you, too," he told her, and pulled her away from the dock, into the shadow of the pro shop, where no one could see them kiss.

Theo had, of course, opted to come to the gala as a surfer, because really? He wore his board shorts, his inflation vest, a rope bracelet, and flip-flops. Beth had planned to come as a surfer, too, but Theo had freaked out at the thought of her showing up in front of everyone in her bikini and insisted she wear her chiffon cover-up. Even so, Theo thought she looked way too sexy to be seen. She'd woven blue and green ribbons in her hair, clipped on glittering starfish and seashells, and added a speck of

Coppertone on her wrists so she'd smell like summer.

During the band's intermission, they'd talked with friends, and Theo had a couple of beers, but not so many he'd feel legless. One thing he'd learned in his life was how to handle quite a few brews without getting wobbly.

Besides, he wanted to show Beth something tonight. It was the perfect night to do it, with the air so sweet and warm and the harbor full of lighted boats and laughter everywhere.

"Beth," he said. "Walk down to the dock with me."

"Sure," she replied easily, and slipped her hand into his.

"You know, your cover-up doesn't really do a great job of covering you up," Theo said.

Beth grinned. "It's not supposed to."

"I wish you'd wear a one-piece. Maybe a Speedo."

"Or maybe one of those bathing suits with a skirt?" Beth teased.

"Or maybe just never go swimming," Theo told her.

Taking her hand, he led her to a bench on the boardwalk. "I want to give you something."

Beth arched an eyebrow. "Should I be excited?"

"It's not what you think. But it is a surprise."

"Well, stop teasing me! Show me!"

Theo reached into his pocket and solemnly

brought out a small pebble. Beth held out her hand, and he gently placed it in her palm.

"A pebble," Beth said. "How unique. I don't think I've seen pebbles anywhere on the island."

"It's not just *a* pebble," Theo said. "It's *our* pebble."

"I don't understand."

When Beth leaned toward him, her cover-up clung to her body, making it hard for Theo to concentrate. But this was important.

"I bought a piece of land. Off Polpis Road. I'm going to build us a house there."

Beth gasped. "How could you afford land on this island?"

"Well, it's not big. No ocean view. But it's got beach plum bushes."

"But, Theo—"

"Sawyer Daly was my running back in high school. He's in real estate now. I told him what I wanted, and he gave me a deal. My mom had to co-sign the mortgage on the land, and your father advanced me some money on my wages. I'll drive you out there tomorrow to see it." He expected Beth to throw her arms around him and kiss him.

"How could you do this without me?" Beth demanded.

"Beth, it's a sweet piece of land—"

"I'm sure it is, but if we're going to live there, then I'm going to pay for half of it."

"But—"

"Theo, please. We've talked about this before. I love that you rescued me the day of the storm, but I'm a perfectly capable human being and I do not want to be dependent on you."

"I thought this would make you happy," Theo said, puzzled.

"In a way, it does, Theo, of course. But what would really make me happy would be for us to go to the real estate office tomorrow, and have someone show me the financials, and allow me to put in exactly as much money as you've put toward the mortgage. And put my name on the deed."

"I already put your name on the deed," Theo said. "Of course."

"Oh, Theo." Beth leaned forward and hugged him. "You are so romantic. And I'm glad. I'm sorry if I hurt your feelings somehow, but can you understand why I'm saying this?"

"I can," Theo admitted. "Now that I think about it, I can understand what you're saying. So of course we'll go to the bank and you can withdraw your money and put it toward the mortgage. Then we can give your dad and my mom some of the money back."

"Thank you. I'm glad you can see my point of view."

"Actually," Theo teased, "I can't see anything but you in that cover-up."

"I'll take it off when we get home," Beth told him. "But first, let's go back to the party and dance."

They held hands as they walked back into the ballroom. The band was playing again, a nice slow sixties' medley, and Beth slid into Theo's arms as if she belonged there.

They saw Theo's mom dancing with Beth's dad, and Juliet dancing with Ryder. In the room full of mermaids and Neptunes, pirates and naval officers, they danced together through rippling green ribbons of silky seaweed, holding each other tight, knowing that tonight was only the beginning.

about the author

NANCY THAYER is the *New York Times* bestselling author of more than thirty novels, including *Surfside Sisters*, *A Nantucket Wedding*, *Secrets in Summer*, *The Island House*, *The Guest Cottage*, *An Island Christmas*, *Nantucket Sisters*, and *Island Girls*. Born in Kansas, Thayer has been a resident of Nantucket for thirty-five years, where she currently lives with her husband, Charley, and a precocious rescue cat named Callie.

nancythayer.com
Facebook.com/NancyThayerBooks

Books are produced in the United States using U.S.-based materials

Books are printed using a revolutionary new process called THINKtech™ that lowers energy usage by 70% and increases overall quality

Books are durable and flexible because of Smyth-sewing

Paper is sourced using environmentally responsible foresting methods and the paper is acid-free

Center Point Large Print
600 Brooks Road / PO Box 1
Thorndike, ME 04986-0001 USA

(207) 568-3717

US & Canada:
1 800 929-9108
www.centerpointlargeprint.com